THIS DAY AND TIME

Dust jacket from the 1930 edition of *This Day and Time*, published by Alfred A. Knopf.

THIS DAY AND TIME

A Critical Edition

ANNE W. ARMSTRONG

Edited by Linda Behrend

APPALACHIAN ECHOES

The University of Tennessee Press

Knoxville

Copyright © 2025 by The University of Tennessee Press / Knoxville.
All Rights Reserved.
FIRST EDITION.

Library of Congress Cataloging-in-Publication Data

Names: Armstrong, Anne W. (Anne Wetzell), 1872–1958 author. | Behrend, Linda, editor.

Title: This day and time : a critical edition / Anne W. Armstrong ; edited by Linda Behrend.

Description: First edition. | Knoxville : The University of Tennessee Press, 2025. | Series: Appalachian echoes | Includes bibliographical references. | Summary: "Anne Armstrong moved to Knoxville as a teenager in 1885 and spent her formative years in the city, growing up in west Knoxville (Cumberland Avenue and Kingston Pike, in particular), and other notable areas in what we now know as the university and downtown districts. Her first novel, This Day and Time, was published by Alfred A. Knopf in 1930. It is credited by scholars as the first realistic fictional account of the Appalachian region-in stark contrast to, for instance, Mary Noailles Murfree's In the Tennessee Mountains published in 1886. Behrend has written a critical introduction to the work and provides a bibliography as well as appendices of reviews and materials from the stage play that was produced from the novel"—Provided by publisher.

Identifiers: LCCN 2024056384 (print) | LCCN 2024056385 (ebook) | ISBN 9781621909835 (paperback) | ISBN 9781621909859 (adobe pdf) | ISBN 9781621909842 (kindle edition)

Subjects: LCSH: Armstrong, Anne W. (Anne Wetzell), 1872–1958. This day and time. | Armstrong, Anne W. (Anne Wetzell), 1872–1958—Criticism and interpretation. | LCGFT: Literary criticism.

Classification: LCC PS3501.R5654 T483 2025 (print) | LCC PS3501.R5654 (ebook) | DDC 813/.52—dc23/eng/20250214

LC record available at https://lccn.loc.gov/2024056384
LC ebook record available at https://lccn.loc.gov/2024056385

In Memoriam

Dr. Allison Ensor (1935–2024)
Dr. Thomas Haddox (1972–2024)
English teachers extraordinaire

Contents

ILLUSTRATIONS

ᴀᴄᴋɴᴏᴡʟᴇᴅɢᴍᴇɴᴛꜱ

I especially thank Thomas Wells, my editor at UT Press, for inviting me to be involved in this project and to write the introduction for this critical edition of Armstrong's Appalachian novel.

My thanks to David Madden, who read the initial draft of my introduction and offered numerous suggestions which resulted in a greatly improved manuscript.

The late Tom Haddox, professor of English at the University of Tennessee before his untimely death, also read a draft of my introduction, including my proposed changes to improve it. I appreciated his positive feedback at the time and am most grateful now to have had his comments on my work.

I would be remiss if I did not acknowledge the teaching and scholarship that the late Dr. Robert "Jack" Higgs and the late Dr. Allison Ensor contributed to the study of Anne Armstrong during their academic careers.

Once again, I wish to thank archivist Joanna Bouldin and other members of the staff at McClung Historical Collection of the Knox County Public Library for their assistance, especially with photographs from the Anne Wetzell Armstrong Papers (MSC 0930).

Although no longer associated with Barter Theatre, Ross Egan was most helpful when I visited the Barter Archives in 2023, and he provided me with valuable new information concerning Anne Armstrong and her association with Barter.

I will always be in debt to Ed and Roger Naylor, great-grandsons of Anne Armstrong, who graciously accepted me in my pursuit of her life story and have enthusiastically supported me as I continue to tell her story.

Introduction

This Day and Time, Anne Wetzell Armstrong's Appalachian novel, is set in the mountainous knobs of the Big Creek community of southeastern Sullivan County, Tennessee—near its border with Virginia—where Armstrong and her husband lived for many years. Originally published in 1930, the book has long been considered the first novel to portray the region's mountain people in a realistic way, though it was considered scandalous at that time. Armstrong had written one other novel, *The Seas of God*, published in 1915, which was partially set in a thinly disguised Knoxville, called "Kingsville."

THE AUTHOR

Anne Wetzell Armstrong knew the Southern mountaineers intimately, because she lived among them for twenty-six years. Born in Michigan, she was thirteen in 1885 when her family moved to Knoxville, Tennessee, where she grew up. She married Robert Franklin Armstrong, son of a prominent Knoxville family, in 1905, and, after moving around for several years, the Armstrongs settled in Bristol, Tennessee, in 1911. They lived in Bristol until 1916 when they built their home, "Knobside," in a mountainous area near the South Fork of the Holston River. In her memoir, *Of Time and Knoxville*, Armstrong relates:

> . . . more or less by accident we found an excellent site in the mountains
> of upper East Tennessee. On the side of a wooded knob, virgin forest all

around, facing the mountains (a spur of the Blue Ridge), only two miles away, not a human habitation, not even a cabin, in sight, and below a river (that "river which goes with heaven"),[1] not the broad Tennessee on which Bob had grown up, but one of its rushing roaring tributaries, visible for miles and miles from this height—here we built a home.[2]

Anne Wetzell Armstrong had lived among the southern mountaineers twenty-six years before she was forced to move in 1942 when the Tennessee Valley Authority (TVA) began construction on South Holston Dam, which created a lake that flooded her home. Armstrong, whose husband had died in 1931, at first lived in Bristol, Tennessee. In 1951, an Asheville, North Carolina, newspaper reported that she had been a resident of that city for the past two and a half years. She was living at 296 Montford Avenue (called the Montford Inn boarding house at that time) in what is today the Montford Historic District of Asheville.[3] During the spring of 1951, she moved to Abingdon, Virginia, and took up residence at the Barter Inn, where she lived until her death March 17, 1958.

SETTING

Armstrong used the mountainous knobs in the Big Creek area, along with the river which ran below, as the setting for *This Day and Time*. The south fork of the Holston River, fed by the many mountain streams and branches which were its tributaries, ran through the area. At that time, "town folk" from nearby Bristol and the surrounding area had built summer cottages at Big Creek where they came to escape the summer heat. Local journalist Robert Loving and Bristol historian V. N. "Bud" Phillips both wrote about Big Creek, as well as some of its residents, in books and newspaper articles.[4]

Besides the Big Creek settlement, Armstrong mentions other actual places in upper East Tennessee—Piney Flats, Shady Valley, and Josiah Creek—in her story.

CHARACTERS

Because of the multitude of characters in *This Day and Time*, a list (arranged by family) has been inserted after the introduction. Armstrong undoubtedly had specific people in mind for some of the characters in her story. Rosy Duncan, her longtime housekeeper and cook, was the model for the novel's heroine, Ivy Ingoldsby. Rosy also shows up in Armstrong's article "As I Saw Thomas Wolfe" (*Arizona Quarterly*, Spring 1946), which describes the time when Wolfe visited Armstrong in September 1937 and spent several days in a cabin on her property.[5] Why Armstrong chose to call Ivy's husband "Jim Ingoldsby" is not known, but there *was* a James Ingoldsby in Bristol around that time. In fact, he was chief of police in Bristol, Virginia, in 1935.[6] And an "Enoch Duncan" is named in Robert Loving's book chapter "Going to Big Creek." So it is possible that "Enoch" in Armstrong's novel was Rosy/Ivy's own son or close relative.[7]

Armstrong may have been thinking of Colonel John Pemberton and Sullivan County's historic Pemberton Oak when she gave Shirley Pemberton and her father their surname. In September 1780, Col. Pemberton mustered Revolutionary War soldiers under the giant oak and, after joining other troops at Sycamore Shoals of the Watauga, marched "over the mountain" to defeat the British at the Battle of King's Mountain, a turning point in the war. The Pemberton Oak and historic Pemberton Mansion house, located on "Royal Oak Farm" in the Emmett community, near where Armstrong lived and is buried, were placed on the National Register of Historic Places in 1973. The tree, estimated to be nearly 100 feet tall with a 125-foot branch spread, was believed to be 700 or 800 years old before it fell during a storm in 2004.[8] The storekeeper in the novel is undoubtedly based on Dave Bolling, who kept the general store at Big Creek and was "one of the section's most colorful figures."[9] Some local people recognized themselves as characters in the story and took offense, because they were portrayed unfavorably. When asked how he knew a certain villainous character was modeled after him, one local man (who had to have the novel read to him) replied: "Because, by damn, it's just like me."[10]

THEMES

Prominent among the themes woven throughout the novel are a sense of place and the mountain people's love for the land, contrasted with the coming industrialization and the negative effect it will have on their lives. Although people from outside the mountains see industrialization and moving to town as an improvement in the lives of the mountaineers, Ivy tells Old Mag: "I 'ud as soon to be a-layin' up in Bane's Buryin' Ground, as to think I had obliged to live out my time in town" (52). Mr. Pemberton, who had grown up in the mountains, says to her: "Folks like you and me, Ivy, don't belong to towns and factories. We belong to the mountains" (98).[11]

Related to this love of the land is the mountaineers' fear of the damming of the waters. Dr. Robert J. Higgs of East Tennessee State University said that Armstrong may have been the first writer to deal with this theme.[12] The writing and publication of *This Day and Time* preceded the building of the Tennessee Valley Authority (TVA) dams. This is in stark contrast to, for example, novels by Borden Deal and James Dickey, as pointed out by Dwight Rodgers in a thesis on Armstrong, Deal, and Dickey.[13] Armstrong saw the damming of the waters as key to the demise of a culture that she loved. In his doctoral dissertation, H. R. Stoneback also mentions *This Day and Time* as "one of the first works of hill fiction to use the 'TVA motif.'" He points out that Armstrong gave the visiting senator—who thinks industrialization and dams will give the mountain people a better life—the name "Timberlake," which "suggests the senator's calculating interest in the dam which will give him shoreline property as well as a simple method of selling off the timber on his property."[14] Armstrong herself lost her home in 1942 when TVA took her land to build South Holston Dam and flooded her property.

Another theme is the victimization of women, exemplified by Jim Ingoldsby's desertion of his wife and son, and later the horror of Shirley (a town woman) upon hearing that the mountain men hit their wives and the women accept it as normal. Violence—feuding, killing, incest, infanticide—seems to be just a part of life for the mountain people. The merciless beating of tubercular Bertha Jane Dillard by her father, which no one in the story attempts to stop, caught the eye of a social worker who cited this incident and others from the novel in an article published in a scholarly journal.[15] In a book chapter on Lee Smith's Appalachian novel *Fair and Tender Ladies*, Michel Bandry discussed other 20th-century works of fiction about Southern women saying: ". . . the Appalachian woman has been mostly portrayed as a victim of dire social and economic conditions, a woman old before her age." Bandry included Armstrong's *This Day and Time* among "other works of fiction by female authors giving a realistic picture of the difficult living conditions of women living in the mountains." Also mentioned were novels by Edith Summers Kelley, Elizabeth Madox Roberts, Grace Lumpkin, and Harriette Arnow.[16]

Over and above the struggle of Ivy and the mountain people to endure, the overarching theme throughout the story is Ivy's longing—and hopeful expectation—that her husband will eventually return to her. Over and over she thinks perhaps he will come back when spring arrives, or, if not then, at harvest. Throughout the story, various men attempt to entice Ivy into marriage or an extramarital affair. Among these are Andy Weaver, the storekeeper, who, although married, tells Ivy in the first chapter that he won't charge her anything for hauling her belongings back from town "if you won't deny me." (6). We later learn that he has supposedly fathered daughters by two women who are Ivy's neighbors (144). Other men who come courting Ivy—even offering to pay for a divorce from her husband—are Jack Yancy, who calls himself a "grass-widdy" man (115–17) and Hop Harlow (a widower with three children), who writes her a letter saying that he is lonely and tired of being single (137). Doke Odum flirts with Ivy throughout the novel, and numerous neighbors tease her about Uncle Abel Dillard, even though it has not been long since the death of his wife.

In her foolish pride and the shame of having been deserted by her husband, Ivy tells Doke Odum, "I don't never want to lay eyes on Jim Ingoldsby agin long as blood warms my body"(81), and this careless remark leads to her downfall. When Jim finally returns (at Christmastime), Doke informs him of what she said—and Doke makes it worse by adding the lie that all the local men had been "enjoying" her (196). Jim leaves, again, without even seeing Ivy or his son.

Anne Armstrong's other novel, *The Seas of God* (1915), is quite different from *This Day and Time*, but the two books tell basically the same story. The protagonist in both novels is a single mother who must raise a young son after having been deserted by the boy's father. In *This Day and Time*, the father is her husband, and she remains true to him despite the numerous propositions from other men. In *The Seas of God*, the father is not the protagonist's husband but an older family friend who seduces her. Ostensibly unaware of the child he has fathered, he returns to his wife in another city, and the deserted mother becomes a courtesan in order to support herself and her son. Throughout the story in both books, the heroine continues to long for the return of her son's father. However, although the absent man returns toward the end in both books, in neither does he remain to assume his responsibilities as a father.

Another similarity between the books is Anne Armstrong's account of a father's death. In *The Seas of God*, Armstrong's detailed description of the death of Lydia's father[17] is very like the account of her own father's death as she tells it in her memoir, *Of Time and Knoxville*,[18] which she wrote long after publication of the novel. *This Day and Time* also includes an account of a father's death, but, in this case, it is the father of Shirley

Pemberton, for whom Ivy works in the second part of the novel. Shirley is somewhat reminiscent of Anne Armstrong herself, since Rosy Duncan worked for Mrs. Armstrong, an "outsider" who came to live in the mountains, just like the "town people" who came to stay at Big Creek during the summer. Armstrong's father, like Mr. Pemberton, traveled to the mountains in search of good timber, and Armstrong sometimes accompanied him on these trips. Her description of Mr. Pemberton's death is echoed in her later description of her own father's death. Shirley's father's faults, however, (his separation from his wife and his paramour, Mrs. Buskill) certainly do not seem to have been part of the life of Armstrong's father as he is portrayed in her memoir.

STYLE AND TECHNIQUES

Anne Armstrong relied heavily on descriptive language and narrative techniques to tell her story. Her use of dialect was chief among the techniques she used to create a realistic depiction of the mountain people. "Eye dialect" (the use of nonstandard spelling to reflect the pronunciation of words), although no longer in use, was a major feature of southern writing from the stories of George Washington Harris, in the nineteenth century, up until the 1940s. Armstrong used "eye dialect" not only to show the mountaineers as uneducated and perhaps stuck in the past but also to portray illiteracy as another aspect of Appalachia. Ivy is keenly aware of her lack of education. She cannot make out more than a few words in a letter she receives from a suitor, and, later in the story, she even asks her son to "learn me to speak proper" (140).

Armstrong's use of dialect has long been recognized as one of the main features that made her book realistic. In 1971, Earl Schrock Jr. published a study, "An Examination of the Dialect in *This Day and Time*," in the *Tennessee Folklore Society Bulletin*. It was later included in the Appalachian anthology *Voices from the Hills* (1975) and has been widely cited.[19] Some readers may be put off by the dialectal spellings; others may not be familiar with the expressions and colloquialisms that Armstrong's characters use or may not be able to decipher the mountaineers' speech. For that reason, a list of books containing dialectal words, phrases, expressions, mountain speech, etc. is provided.

In contrast to the spoken dialect, many lyrical passages are interspersed among "hillbilly" talk. Armstrong's descriptions of nature are full of imagery: bloodroot holding up a "snowy chalice," the "purple-rose cloud" of a flowering redbud, the weeping willow "a cascade of foaming green," "fragments of pearly cloud" clinging to the summit of the mountains (52). The river figures prominently in the story and is personified near the very beginning when Enoch says to his mother: "Sounds like it's a-rainin', . . . but it's jest the old river a-talkin' to hisself" (8).

Armstrong employs the activities of daily living in telling her story: rituals of death and burial, birthings, courting, hog killing, molasses making, apple peeling, and going to church. She also uses cooking a special meal, such as the birthday party Ivy organizes for Ol' Mag, or after a death, as in the case of Mrs. Dillard, to show local customs. At times there are flashbacks, such as when Ivy thinks back about her childhood, courtship and marriage, and coming to live in the cabin of her husband's parents, who represent the old mountain values (17–22). The cycle of life is always present in the struggles of Ivy and the mountain people to endure—getting through a hard winter, spring planting, the joys of summer, harvest time, and then the approach of another winter. Life for the mountain people goes on: Leola goes into labor not long after the death of Mrs. Dillard; Molly Diggs and Alf Bunts get married soon after the lovers Buck and Nova are killed.

Cratis Williams, in his doctoral dissertation on southern Appalachian literature, called *This Day and Time* "a study in contrasts."[20] Armstrong contrasts the old and the new, the young and the old, life in town and mountain as she portrays the culture and customs of the people. Novy remarks, "Ain't it a sight? Me a-usin' a lipstick, an' Mammy—her a-usin' a snuff-stick!" Ivy, on the other hand, feels a little resentful about the way that "times is changin'" (61). She seeks to be self-reliant while other families are buying furniture and Victrolas "on time"; her neighbors go to church on Sunday but accept promiscuity and physical brutality; a granny woman still delivers babies, but the young women and girls are reading "confession" magazines cast off by town folks; Buck comes home with a new Ford car, but the men are still making their own moonshine to drink. While living in town and working at a poultry-house, Ivy remarks, "I reckon I've died an' went to torment" (25). She longs for "the boundless sky above, the clean sweet air, the mountains walling her in protectingly, the river below with its soothing, never ceasing murmur" (30). Back in the mountains, climbing a ridge among banks of laurel and rhododendron, she exclaims: "I don't reckon heaven could be no prettier" (57–58).

RELATED WORKS AND STAGE ADAPTATIONS

This Day and Time was published in August 1930 by Alfred A. Knopf. Anne Armstrong had spent three years working on the novel, but even after its publication she continued working with the same characters and themes. In August 1934, "Mountain Ivy," a folk play adapted from the novel, was presented by a group of actors from Barter Theatre in Abingdon, Virginia,[21] in conjunction with the nearby White Top Folk Festival. The town of Abingdon, although in Virginia, is not far from where Big Creek was in Sullivan County, Tennessee. Barter Theatre founder and managing director Robert "Bob" Porterfield wrote in his unpublished memoirs:

> I also made it a point, at least once a season, to do an original folk or mountain play, preferably by a regional writer. . . . [I]n 1934, it made me proud to present the premiere of Anne Armstrong's "Mountain Ivy," dramatized from her best-selling novel, *This Day and Time*. "Mountain Ivy" was honest and authentic, presenting a picture unromanticized and unglamorized, drawn from the experiences she had observed and told with an uncanny ear for the colorful mountain vernacular.[22]

In 1951, "Mountain Ivy" won Anne Armstrong first place for best original play in the Raleigh (North Carolina) Little Theatre's playwriting contest, and "Mountain Ivy" was performed there on May 24, 25, and 26.[23] Armstrong kept working with the stage adaptation of her novel, eventually writing five versions, and on August 6, 1951, the world premiere of "Some Sweet Day," the latest version of the play, was presented at the Barter Theatre in Abingdon.[24]

In March 1935, five years after the release of *This Day and Time*, Armstrong published an article, "The Southern Mountaineers," in *Yale Review*, America's oldest literary magazine. That essay, condensed in *Reader's Digest* (May 1935) and later anthologized in *American Points of View, 1934-35* (1936), dealt with many of the same themes and issues as the novel, but in a factual way. In it she blamed prohibition for the mountaineers' reliance on making moonshine as a means of earning money. She denounced industrialization and the industrialists who were luring the mountaineers away from their native environment and drastically changing their way of life. Other subjects from the novel that she discussed in "The Southern Mountaineers" include feuding and killings, incest, promiscuity, and the introduction to the mountain people of "the Gospel of Things" through mail-order catalogs, "which in almost every cabin have superseded the Bible."[25]

CRITICISM

On August 3, 1930, Vanderbilt professor, poet, and social/literary critic Donald Davidson announced the forthcoming publication of *This Day and Time* in his weekly book page in Nashville's *Tennessean* newspaper. Under "Forecast of Fall Books by Tennessee Authors," Davidson listed Armstrong's book immediately following the forthcoming southern Agrarian publication *I'll Take My Stand*, a manifesto to which he himself, as one of Vanderbilt's Agrarians, was a contributor. Commenting on the forthcoming publication of *This Day and Time*, Davidson called the book: "among the few authentic pictures of Southern mountaineer life."[26] Just as Armstrong's book attempted to portray Appalachian life and to protest changes that were coming to it, *I'll Take My Stand* praised the agrarian way of life and revolted against changes that industrial capitalism was bringing to the south. Other prominent Agrarians were John Crowe Ransom, Allen Tate, Robert Penn Warren, and Andrew Lytle.

Davidson's book page, which included his own column of literary commentary and book reviews, had originally been published only in *The Tennessean*, but was syndicated to *The* (Memphis) *Commercial Appeal* and *The Knoxville Journal* beginning in 1928, which meant that publication of Armstrong's book was announced across the state. On September 7, Davidson himself reviewed *This Day and Time* in his book column, saying that the book is probably "as true a novel of the mountains as has been written" and "[t]he dialogue is especially well done." He concludes: "We should welcome it and give it the serious attention that it deserves. . . ."[27]

Although *This Day and Time* was reviewed widely, not all reviews and opinions were favorable. David McClellan, who wrote a personal reminiscence of Armstrong for the 1970 reprint edition, said that his grandmother burned their family's copy of the book when it first came out, because she thought its realism "amounted to obscenity."[28] Ten years after its publication in 1930, Edd Winfield Parks discussed *This Day and Time* in his biography of Mary Noailles Murfree calling Armstrong's book "a grimly realistic novel of the present-day Tennessee mountaineers."[29] Incidentally, Armstrong reviewed Parks's book for *The Yale Review*.[30]

Armstrong's book continues to be cited for its realism and portrayal of Appalachian life. The late Allison Ensor, professor emeritus of English at the University of Tennessee Knoxville, said: "I believe that in Ivy Ingoldsby we have one of the earliest realistic portraits of an Appalachian woman."[31] Dr. Ensor, who taught English (including Appalachian literature) at UTK from 1965 until his retirement in 2007, died August 10, 2024, while this book was in process. He reviewed the 1970 reprint edition for the *Knoxville News-Sentinel*. Jack Reese, another English professor (and later chancellor) of the University of Tennessee Knoxville, also reviewed the 1970 reprint edition, calling the novel "a valuable repository of information about a fascinating subculture of American society" and "a document of special interest to the study of the Southern Appalachian region," although he declined to call it a "satisfactory" novel.[32] Herschel Gower, professor emeritus of English and American literature at Vanderbilt University (as well as editor and literary executor of Mildred Haun, another Appalachian author), called Armstrong's book "still timely in 1970" when he reviewed it.[33]

Cratis Williams, considered the father of Appalachian literature, included Armstrong's *This Day and Time* among the ten books of fiction that he felt would give any reader a representative overview of mountain life and culture.[34] Also on his list were works by Mary Noailles Murfree, Sarah Barnwell Elliott, John Fox Jr., Grace Lumpkin, James Still, Jesse Stuart, and Harriette Arnow. Williams had discussed works by all of these authors in his 1961 doctoral dissertation, "The Southern Mountaineer in Fact and Fiction," along with *This Day and Time*, which he called "an honest tale of lechery, fornication, incest, murder, and betrayal." He then went on to say: "Armstrong's book . . . possesses stretches of genuine power. It is a more significant novel than any of the better known Glen Hazard books . . ." by Mary and Stanley Chapman (husband and wife), who wrote under the name Maristan Chapman.[35] Among other notable Southern Appalachian authors that Williams discussed are Elizabeth Madox Roberts, Grace Lumpkin, Olive Tilford Dargan, and Mildred Haun. Since Williams's groundbreaking work, many other theses and dissertations have dealt with *This Day and Time*. All the theses and dissertations listed in the bibliography cover *This Day and Time* in some way, sometimes in conjunction with other Appalachian authors and novels.

CONCLUSION

Anne Armstrong defended her portrayal of mountain people in a 1951 Sunday feature article, saying: "I do not desire to depreciate these people. . . . I want to record their triumphant survival through near-insurmountable difficulties, their preservation of a remarkable humor, and the beautiful qualities that most of us, who have felt the pressure of time in the outside world, have lost."[36] Another newspaper reported her statement that she and her husband "came to know the mountain people intimately" after having lived among them for twenty-six years. "When I realized that they were gradually leaving the hills for the factories, not through desire but sad necessity, I was impelled to put down my first-hand impressions of them. The thing that impressed me was that through all their poverty and degradation their heroic virtues somehow managed to survive."[37]

Even if *This Day and Time* is basically a regional novel, and may not be a great novel, it is still historically significant because Anne Armstrong was able to capture a picture of life among the mountain people during a time that has now disappeared.

Notes

1. Allusion to Howell Vines' novel: *A River Goes with Heaven* (Boston: Little, Brown, 1930).

2. Anne W. Armstrong, *Of Time and Knoxville: Fragment of an Autobiography*, ed. Linda Behrend (Knoxville: University of Tennessee Press, 2022), 478.

3. "Mrs. Anne Armstrong's Play Wins Contest at Raleigh," *Asheville Citizen-Times*, April 8, 1951, 17.

4. Robert S. Loving, "Going to Big Creek," in *Double Destiny: The Story of Bristol, Tennessee-Virginia* (Bristol, Tenn.: King Printing, 1955), 151–166; V. N. (Victor N.) "Bud" Phillips, "Secrets of Big Creek Revealed," *Bristol Herald Courier*; Phillips, "Big Creek Summer Resort Scheme Quickly Dried Up," *Bristol Herald Courier*, April 12, 2009 www.heraldcourier.com.

5. Armstrong, "As I Saw Thomas Wolfe," *Arizona Quarterly* 2 (Spring 1946): 5–15.

6. "27 Homeless Kiddies Find Shelter at Hammitt Home," *Bristol* (TN) *Herald-Courier*, Oct. 13, 1950, 5.

7. Loving, "Going to Big Creek," 152.

8. Carolyn Sakowski, *Touring the East Tennessee Backroads* (Winston-Salem, N.C.: John F. Blair, c1993), pp. 28–29; National Register of Historic Places.

9. Loving, "Going to Big Creek," 155.

10. Loving, "Novelist of Big Creek, Her Colorful Life Story," *Bristol* (TN) *Herald-Courier*, March 15, 1951, 8.

11. Armstrong, *This Day and Time*. References to this work are given parenthetically throughout this introduction.

12. Robert J. Higgs, "Anne W. Armstrong," in *An Encyclopedia of East Tennessee*, ed. Jim Stokely and Jeff D. Johnson (Oak Ridge, TN: Children's Museum of Oak Ridge, 1981), 36.

13. Dwight C. Rodgers, "Dams and the Concept of Melioration in the Works of Anne Armstrong, Borden Deal, and James Dickey" (MA thesis, East Tennessee State University, 1976), 32.

14. Harry Robert Stoneback, "The Hillfolk Tradition and Images of the Hillfolk in American Fiction Since 1926" (PhD dissertation, Vanderbilt University, 1970), 420, 160(note 47).

15. Grace A. Browning, "The Application of the Basic Concepts of Case Work to Rural Social Work," *The Family* 19, no.1 (1938): 14.

16. Michel Bandry, "Lee Smith's Appalachian *Fair and Tender Ladies*," in *L'espace du Sud au Féminin*, ed. Brigitte Zaugg, Gérald Préher (Metz: Université Paul Verlaine-Metz, Centre de Recherche "Écritures," 2011), 215–216.

17. Armstrong, *Seas of God*, 48–50.

18. Armstrong, *Of Time and Knoxville*, 332–34.

19. Earl F. Schrock Jr., "An Examination of the Dialect in *This Day and Time*," in *Voices from the Hills: Selected Readings of Southern Appalachia*, ed. Robert J. Higgs, Ambrose Manning (New York: Ungar, 1975), 460–73.

20. Cratis Williams, "The Southern Mountaineer in Fact and Fiction," 3 vols., PhD dissertation (New York University, 1961), pt. 3, 1323.

21. "Armstrong's Book Made into a Play," *Bristol News Bulletin* (Bristol, Tennessee), August 14, 1934, 5.

22. Unpublished memoir, Robert Porterfield Papers, Barter Theatre Archives.

23. Jane Hall, "Asheville Woman Receives Little Theater Award," *News and Observer* (Raleigh, NC), May 25, 1951.

24. "Some Sweet Day Barter Offering This Week," *Bristol Herald-Courier* (Bristol, Tennessee), August 5, 1951, 2-D.

25. Armstrong, "The Southern Mountaineers," *Yale Review* 24 (March 1935): 539–54.

26. "Forecast of Fall Books by Tennessee Authors" (The Weekly Review—A Page About Books, ed. Donald Davidson), *Nashville Tennessean*, Aug. 3, 1930, 28.

27. D[onald] D[avidson], "Anne Armstrong's Novel Deals with Mountain Life" (The Weekly Review—A Page About Books, ed. Donald Davidson), *Nashville Tennessean*, Sept. 7, 1930, 19.

28. David McClellan, "A Personal Reminiscence," in Anne W. Armstrong, *This Day and Time* (Johnson City: Research Advisory Council, East Tennessee State University, 1970), xvi.

29. Edd Winfield Parks, *Charles Egbert Craddock (Mary Noailles Murfree)*, (Chapel Hill: University of North Carolina Press, 1941), 203.

30. Armstrong, "Miss Murfree's Novels," *Yale Review* 31 (Sept. 1941): 211–13.

31. Allison Ensor, "American Realism and the Case for Appalachian Literature," in *Appalachia Inside Out*, ed. Robert J. Higgs, Ambrose N. Manning, Jim Wayne Miller, vol. 2: Culture and Custom (Knoxville: University of Tennessee Press, 1995), 636.

32. Jack E. Reese, rev. of *This Day and Time* by Anne W. Armstrong (1970 reprint), in *Arizona Quarterly* 27, no. 2 (1971): 178–180.

33. Herschel Gower, "Mountaineer Novel Still Timely in 1970," *Nashville Tennessean*, July 12, 1970, 6-C.

34. Cratis Williams, "Appalachia in Fiction," *Appalachian Heritage* 4, no. 4 (Fall 1976): 53.

35. Williams, "The Southern Mountaineer in Fact and Fiction," pt. 3, 1325 (349 in edited version).

36. "'Some Sweet Day' Barter Offering This Week," *Bristol Herald Courier*, Aug. 5, 1951, 2D.

37. Jane Hall, "Asheville Woman Receives Little Theater Award," *News and Observer* (Raleigh, NC), May 25, 1951.

Expanded Bibliography

ARCHIVES AND MANUSCRIPT COLLECTIONS

Anne Wetzell Armstrong Papers, MSC 0930. Calvin M. McClung Historical Collection.

Barter Theatre Archives Collection. Southwest Virginia Digital Archive. https://di.lib.vt.edu/.

Historical Society of Washington County, Virginia (HSWCV).

Performing Arts Research Collection. New York Public Library. Some Sweet Day: typescript. RM 542. https://legacycatalog.nypl.org/record=b16591942~S1.

Robert Porterfield Papers. Barter Theatre Archives.

Primary Sources

Armstrong, Anne W. *The Seas of God*. New York: Hearst's International Library, 1915; London: Mills & Boon, 1916.

———. *This Day and Time*. New York: Knopf, 1930. Reprinted, with a personal reminiscence by David McClellan. Johnson City: Research Advisory Council, East Tennessee State University, 1970.

———. "Mountain Ivy" [play]. Adapted from *This Day and Time*, 1934.

———. "The Southern Mountaineers," *Yale Review* 24 (March 1935): 539–54. Condensed in *Reader's Digest* (May 1935): 67–70. Reprinted in *American Points of View, 1934–1935*. Ed. William H. Cordell and Kathryn Coe Cordell. Garden City, N.Y.: Doubleday, Doran & Co., 1936.

———. "As I Saw Thomas Wolfe," *Arizona Quarterly* 2 (Spring 1946): 5–15.

———. "Some Sweet Day" [play]. Adapted from *This Day and Time*, 1951.

———. *Of Time and Knoxville: Fragment of an Autobiography*. Ed. Linda Behrend. Knoxville: University of Tennessee Press, 2022.

Secondary Sources

BOOKS, JOURNAL ARTICLES, AND ESSAYS

Bandry, Michel. "Lee Smith's Appalachian *Fair and Tender Ladies*." In *L'espace du Sud au Féminin*. Ed. Brigitte Zaugg, Gérald Préher. Series: Collection Littératures des mondes contemporains / Série Amériques, no. 7. Metz: Université Paul Verlaine-Metz, Centre de Recherche "Écritures," 2011. 215–227.

Browning, Grace A. "The Application of the Basic Concepts of Case Work to Rural Social Work." *The Family* 19, no.1 (1938): 8–14.

Ensor, Allison. "American Realism and the Case for Appalachian Literature." In *Appalachia Inside Out*. Ed. Robert J. Higgs, Ambrose N. Manning, Jim Wayne Miller. Vol. 2: *Culture and Custom*. Knoxville: University of Tennessee Press, 1995. 630–41.

Higgs, Robert J. "Anne W. Armstrong." In *An Encyclopedia of East Tennessee.* Ed. Jim Stokely and Jeff D. Johnson. Oak Ridge, TN: Children's Museum of Oak Ridge, 1981. 36.

Loving, Robert S. "Going to Big Creek." In *Double Destiny: The Story of Bristol, Tennessee-Virginia.* Bristol, Tenn.: King Printing, 1955. 151–166.

McClellan, David. "A Personal Reminiscence." In: Armstrong, Anne W. *This Day and Time.* Johnson City: Research Advisory Council, East Tennessee State University, 1970. xi–xvii.

Miller, Danny L. *Wingless Flights: Appalachian Women in Fiction.* Bowling Green, OH: Bowling Green State University Popular Press, 1996. N.B. Introduction, and Chapter 3, "Mountain Gloom in the Works of Edith Summers Kelley and Anne W. Armstrong."

Mitchell, Tanya. "Beyond Regional Borders: The Emergence of a New Sense of Place, from Mary Murfree to Lee Smith." *Journal of Appalachian Studies* 8, no. 2 (2002): 407–420.

Parks, Edd Winfield. *Charles Egbert Craddock (Mary Noailles Murfree).* Chapel Hill: University of North Carolina Press, 1941.

Roy, Roberta Teague. "Land and the Southern Appalachian Woman: Sensual or Poetic?" *Kentucky Folklore Record: A Regional Journal of Folklore and Folklife* 25, nos. 3–4 (July-Dec. 1979): 68–74.

Sakowski, Carolyn. *Touring the East Tennessee Backroads.* Winston-Salem, N.C.: John F. Blair, c1993.

Schrock, Earl F., Jr. "An Examination of the Dialect in *This Day and Time.*" *Tennessee Folklore Society Bulletin* 37 (June 1971): 31–39. Reprinted in *Voices from the Hills: Selected Readings of Southern Appalachia.* Ed. Robert J. Higgs, Ambrose Manning. New York: Ungar, 1975.

Williams, Cratis. "Appalachia in Fiction." *Appalachian Heritage* 4, no. 4 (Fall 1976): 44–56.

Lists *This Day and Time* among the ten books of fiction about Appalachia "for a representative overview of the Southern Mountaineer in fiction ... recommended, not always on the basis of their literary quality but, rather, on the basis of their adequacy in the presentation of mountain life and character."

NEWSPAPER ARTICLES

"Author Interested in VFW's Big Creek Plans." *Bristol Herald-Courier,* 5 Aug. 1951, 6A.

"Forecast of Fall Books by Tennessee Authors" (The Weekly Review—A Page About Books). Ed. Donald Davidson. *Nashville Tennessean,* Aug. 3, 1930, 40. Syndicated to *Commercial Appeal* (Memphis) and *Knoxville News-Sentinel.*

Loving, Robert. "Novelist of Big Creek, Her Colorful Life Story." *Bristol Herald Courier,* March 15, 1951, 8.

Matheny, Ralston. "Granny's Millions: Former Knoxvillian Writes Play Based on Memories of Life Here." *Knoxville News-Sentinel*, Sept. 22, 1954, 15.

Owen, Craige. "Knoxvillian Heads State Women Writers." *Knoxville News-Sentinel*, 20 Oct. 1957, A-13.

> Dr. David Harkness, speaker, mentioned Anne Armstrong as a Tennessee woman writer who had used dramatic material about East Tennessee in her book *This Day and Time*.

Phillips, [V. N.] Bud. "Big Creek Summer Resort Scheme Quickly Dried Up." *Bristol Herald Courier*, April 12, 2009. http://www.heraldcourier.com/news/big-creek-summer-resort-scheme-quickly-dried-up/article.

Phillips, V. N. (Victor N.) "Secrets of Big Creek Revealed," *Bristol Herald Courier*. Updated by Joe Tennis, April 17, 2019. https://heraldcourier.com/lifestyles/secrets-of-big-creek-revealed/article_4cb48899-b468-52e9-8dd0-4e562b02c9cb.html.

"VFW Post Plans Museum and Big Creek Memorial." *Bristol Herald-Courier*, July 29, 1951, 2B.

Yoe, Della. "Summer Colony Is in Dam Area: More Than 30 Cottages Are Located at Big Creek." *Knoxville News-Sentinel*, Jan. 19, 1942, 10.

THESES AND DISSERTATIONS

Banner, Laura Leslie. "The North Carolina Mountaineer in Native Fiction." PhD dissertation, University of North Carolina-Chapel Hill, 1984.

Doman, Katherine Hoffman. "Setting the Record Straight: Anne W. Armstrong, Regionalism, and the Social Efficacy of Fiction." PhD dissertation, University of Tennessee, 2008. https://trace.tennessee.edu/utk_graddiss/428.

Haslet, Susan Litton. "Assimilation or Acceptance: The Effects of Industrialization on Appalachians in Anne W. Armstrong's *This Day and Time* and Harriette Arnow's *The Dollmaker*." MA thesis, Longwood University, 1999. *Theses & Honors Papers*. 185. https://digitalcommons.longwood.edu/etd/185.

Kirkpatrick, Barbara Saunders. " 'Their Names Are Myth, Legend, Dust': The Southern Mountaineer in Twentieth-Century Novels." PhD dissertation, University of Maryland-College Park, 1974.

Miller, Danny L. "Images of Women in Southern Appalachian Mountain Literature." PhD dissertation, U of Cincinnati, 1985. <http://uclid.uc.edu/record=b3925131~S39>

Rodgers, Dwight C. "Dams and the Concept of Melioration in the Works of Anne Armstrong, Borden Deal, and James Dickey." MA thesis, East Tennessee State University, 1976.

Shelby, Anne Gabbard. "Appalachian Literature and American Myth: A Study of Fiction from the Southern Mountains." MA thesis, University of Kentucky, 1981. Reprinted in: *Appalachian Heritage* 13, no. 3 (Summer 1985):29–36; 13, no.4 (Fall 1985):50–63; and 14, no. 1 (Winter 1986):42–55.

Stoneback, Harry Robert. "The Hillfolk Tradition and Images of the Hillfolk in American Fiction Since 1926." PhD dissertation, Vanderbilt University, 1970.

Williams, Anne St. Clair. "Robert Porterfield's Barter Theatre of Abingdon, Virginia: The State Theatre of Virginia." PhD dissertation, University of Illinois, 1970.

Williams, Cratis. "The Southern Mountaineer in Fact and Fiction." 3 pts. PhD dissertation, New York University, 1961. Edited version (Martha H. Pipes, ed.) published in *Appalachian Journal* 3, no. 1–4 (1975–76).

BOOK REVIEWS: *THIS DAY AND TIME* (1930)

Advertisement for *This Day and Time* by Anne W. Armstrong, with citations to Philadelphia *Public Ledger*, *Book-of-the-Month Club News*, and *New York Herald Tribune Books*. In *Saturday Review of Literature*, (Aug. 30, 1930), 89.

Alexander, T. H. Under: "I Reckon So" (syndicated column). *Nashville Tennessean*, Aug. 28, 1930, 4.

"Bible, Banking, Literature, on Ossoli Program Tomorrow" (under Club Activities). *Knoxville News-Sentinel*, Sunday, Nov. 9, 1930, D-3.

> Mrs. L. A. Haun will review Mrs. Anne W. Armstrong's book, *This Day and Time*.

Booklist 27 (Nov. 1930): 103.

D[avidson], D[onald]. "Anne Armstrong's Novel Deals with Mountain Life" (The Weekly Review: A Page About Books, ed. Donald Davidson). *Nashville Tennessean*, Sept. 7, 1930, 19. Syndicated to *The Commercial Appeal* (Memphis) and *Knoxville News-Sentinel*.

Dawson, Margaret Cheney. Review of *This Day and Time* by Anne W. Armstrong. *New York Herald Tribune*, Aug. 10, 1930, XI: 3.

"Forecast of Fall Books by Tennessee Authors" (The Weekly Review: A Page About Books). Ed. Donald Davidson, *Commercial Appeal* (Memphis), Aug. 3, 1930, p. 40.

> *This Day and Time*, by Anne W. Armstrong ". . . considered to be among the few authentic pictures of Southern mountaineer life. . . . To be published in August."

I. G. G. Review of *This Day and Time* by Anne W. Armstrong (under: "How to Be Happy Though Married"). *Woman's Leader and The Common Cause* (London, England) 22, no. 50 (Jan. 16, 1931): 383+

Jocher, Katharine. "Folk Life in Fiction." Review of *Long Hunt* by James Boyd, *The Great Meadow* by Elizabeth Madox Roberts, *This Day and Time* by Anne W. Armstrong, *Thursday April* by Alberta Pierson Hannum, *A Buried Treasure* by Elizabeth Madox Roberts, *Cimarron* by Edna Ferber, and *The Tides of Malvern* by Francis Griswold. *Social Forces* 10, no. 3 (1932): 453–55. https://doi.org/10.2307/2569693 (viewed March 29, 2023).

Literary Editor. "Among the New Books." *Chicago Daily Tribune*, Aug. 9, 1930: 10.

Loveman, Amy. "Making Hit." Review of *This Day and Time* by Anne W. Armstrong. *Saturday Review of Literature* 7 (Aug. 23, 1930): 69–70. Correction, Oct. 11, 1930: 218.

McHugh, Vincent. "Rich Novel Built of Substance of Tennessee Hills." Review of *This Day and Time* by Anne W. Armstrong. *New York Evening Post*, Aug. 9, 1930: 5s.

Review. *Monthly Bulletin of the Carnegie Library of Pittsburgh*. 35 (Nov. 1930): 79.

Review. *Times* (London) *Literary Supplement*, Nov. 13, 1930: 945.

Templeton, Lucy. "Books—Old and New." *Knoxville News-Sentinel*, Aug. 17, 1930, p. C-5.

Review of *This Day and Time*: "Mrs. Armstrong has shown herself absolute master of the mountain dialect." ". . . thru the cycle of the year Ivy moved brave and cheerful but with the thought always in her heart that Jim would return. . . ." In Ivy's immediate circle of neighbors—4 murders, infanticide, incest, stark brutality. ". . . the reader wonders a little."

Templeton, Lucy. "Books—Old and New," *Knoxville News-Sentinel*, Aug. 23, 1931, C-3.

Reviewer Goldsby Swan compares *The Great Meadow* by Elizabeth Madox Roberts and Anne Wetzell Armstrong's *This Day and Time* with John Fort's *God in the Straw Pen* (New York: Dodd, Mead, 1931).

Templeton, Lucy. "Books—Old and New," *Knoxville News-Sentinel*, Oct. 9, 1932, C-3.

In her review of *Mountain Born* by Emmett Gowen (Indianapolis: Bobbs-Merrill, 1932), Templeton compares and contrasts Gowen's book with *This Day and Time* and other such "Appalachian" books of that time. In Templeton's opinion, Armstrong stresses too much the "lawless and criminal strain of the mountaineer." However, Templeton goes on to say: "In spite of this flaw, her book *This Day and Time* comes more nearly to recapturing the spirit of the mountains than any other book that I have ever read about them."

"Tennessee Hill Billies." Review of *This Day and Time* by Anne W. Armstrong. *New York Times Book Review Digest*, Aug. 10, 1930: 30.

"Tennessee Hill Billies." Review of *This Day and Time* by Anne W. Armstrong (under: "'The Family' and Some Other Recent Works of Fiction"). *New York Times Book Review*, Aug. 10, 1930, BR4.

"*This Day and Time*. By Anne W. Armstrong." *London Quarterly Review*, vol. 155 (1931): 137.

V. N. L. Review of *This Day and Time* by Anne W. Armstrong. *G.K.'s Weekly* (United Kingdom) 12 (Nov. 29, 1930): 188.

West, Douglas. "Books of Today: A Country-Life Novel that is out of the Rut."

Daily Mail (London, England), Dec. 9, 1930, 17. *Daily Mail Historical Archive* (accessed August 24, 2023).

One paragraph about Armstrong's *This Day and Time* (under subheading: "Hard Lives").

THIS DAY AND TIME (1970 REPRINT)

Ensor, Allison. "ETSU Reprints Book by Knoxville Author." *Knoxville News-Sentinel*, Nov. 8, 1970, F-7.

Gower, Herschel. "Mountaineer Novel Still Timely in 1970." *Nashville Tennessean*, July 12, 1970, 6-C.

"This is a very much neglected piece of Tennessee fiction. There is nothing dated or embarrassing or parochial in what it says and the way it says it."

Reese, Jack E. Review of *This Day and Time* by Anne W. Armstrong (1970 reprint). In *Arizona Quarterly* 27, no. 2 (1971): 178–180.

STAGE ADAPTATIONS: REVIEWS AND NEWSPAPER ARTICLES

MOUNTAIN IVY (1934 ADAPTATION)

"Anne W. Armstrong's New Play ..." *Asheville Citizen-Times* (Asheville, North Carolina), April 5, 1951, 17.

"Armstrong's Book Made into a Play." *Bristol News Bulletin* (Bristol, Tennessee), August 14, 1934, 5.

"Mountain Ivy" . . . depicts with authenticity

Hall, Jane. "Asheville Woman Receives Little Theater Award." *News and Observer* (Raleigh, NC), May 25, 1951.

"Mrs. Anne Armstrong's Play Wins Contest at Raleigh." *Asheville Citizen-Times* (Asheville, North Carolina), April 8, 1951, 17.

"Summer Theatres List 21 New Plays." *New York Times*, August 13, 1934, 9.

"SOME SWEET DAY" (1951 ADAPTATION)

Anderson, Eleanor Crist. "Authentic Mountain Lore in 'Some Sweet Day' at Barter." Review of "Some Sweet Day." *Washington County News* (Abingdon, Va.) Sept. 9, 1951, 1–2.

"Barter Theater to Give New Plays at Festival." *Knoxville News-Sentinel*, July 15, 1951, 15.

Childress, Lilian. "Town Chatter." *Bristol Herald Courier* (Bristol, TN), August 8, 1951, 1-D.

Childress, Lilian. "[Town] Chatter." *Bristol Herald Courier* (Bristol, TN), August 15, 1951, 6.

Lindeman, Edith. "Barter Company Will Premiere 20 New Scripts August 6."
    Richmond (Va.) *Times-Dispatch*, Aug. 1, 1951.
Schroetter, Hilda Noel. "'Some Sweet Day' Draws Ovation from Bartergoers,"
    Bristol Herald Courier (Bristol, TN), August 8, 1951, 10.

Comment: "There has already been a great deal of controversy about the novel
from which this play was adapted, and there will be more controversy about the
play. . . . Whether you like 'Some Sweet Day' or not, it is well worth seeing."

"See How They Run by Philip King, [Some Sweet Day [by] Anne W. Arm-
    strong]" *Southwest Virginia Digital Archive*, (accessed November 15,
    2023, https://di.lib.vt.edu/items/show/395).
"'See How They Run' Plays Monday at Barter Theatre." *Bristol Herald Courier*
    (Bristol, TN), August 12, 1951, 2-D.

Calls "Some Sweet Day" "the most controversial new theatre piece that Barter has
ever presented."

"'Some Sweet Day' Barter Offering This Week." *Bristol Herald Courier* (Bristol,
    TN), August 5, 1951, 2-D.

Dateline: Abingdon, Virginia. Includes pictures of Mrs. Armstrong and principal
characters John Faulk and Ann Buckles.

"Some Sweet Day." Under: Strawhat Reviews. *Variety*, Aug. 15, 1951: 58.
Virginia State Chamber of Commerce. *The Commonwealth*. Richmond, Va.:
    Virginia State Chamber of Commerce, 1951. 38.

CHRONOLOGY

1970   reprint of *This Day and Time* (Johnson City: Research Advisory
        Committee, East Tennessee State University)
2022   publication of Armstrong's memoir *Of Time and Knoxville* (Knoxville:
        University of Tennessee Press)
2025   reprint of *This Day and Time* (Knoxville: University of Tennessee Press)

List of Characters

Because of the large number of people and multiple family members named in Armstrong's story, I have provided a list of characters arranged by families.

Ivy Ingoldsby—a mountain woman
Jim Ingoldsby—her husband
Enoch—their son
Aunt Jane and Uncle Jake—Jim Ingoldsby's parents
Andy Weaver—the storekeeper
Mrs. Philips—a 'granny-woman'
'One-Arm' Press Philips—her husband
Nova (Novy)—their daughter
Other children: Bruce, Dave, Adam, Simon Peter
'Old Mag' Rider—mother of 9 illegitimate children
Children: Gid, Martha, Odie (married to Rat Bunts), Belle
Mrs. Betty Byrd—12 children
'Big Bill' Byrd—her husband
Children: 'One-Eye' Buck, Wash, Linsey, Essie, Woodrow Wilson
Doke Odum—a moonshiner
Leola (Leoly)—his wife
Children: Guy, Ibbie, Ruby, Opal, Noah (Noey)
Uncle Abel Dillard
(Mrs. Dillard—dies early in the story)
Children: Short, Roosevelt (deceased), Wesley, Matthew, Isaac, Bertha Jane
Godfrey Tipton

Theta—his half-witted daughter
Luke Diggs (lives with his widowed mother)
Molly Diggs (his sister, marries Alf Bunts)
Alf Bunts—marries Molly Diggs

Ivy's Suitors

Jack Yancy ("widdy" man)—from Shady Valley
Hop Harlow—from Piney Flats

Town People

Shirley Pemberton
Her father, Mr. Jesse Pemberton
Mrs. Nan Buskill (Mr. Pemberton's former girlfriend)
Senator Timberlake

$\mathcal{S}$OURCES FOR $\mathcal{D}$IALECT

Words, Phrases, Expressions, Mountain Speech, etc. In *This Day and Time*

Cavender, Anthony, ed. *A Folk Medical Lexicon of South Central Appalachia.* Miscellaneous Paper No. 1. Johnson City, TN: History of Medicine Society of Appalachia, East Tennessee State University, 1990.

Dictionary of Southern Appalachian English. Comp., Michael Montgomery, Jennifer K. N. Heinmiller. Chapel Hill: University of North Carolina Press, 2021. Rev. and expanded ed. of: *Dictionary of Smoky Mountain English*, Michael B. Montgomery, Joseph S. Hall, eds. Knoxville: University of Tennessee Press, 2004.

Farwell, Harold F. Jr., and J. Karl Nicholas, eds. *Smoky Mountain Voices: A Lexicon of Southern Appalachian Speech Based on the Research of Horace Kephart.* Lexington, KY: University Press of Kentucky, 1993.

Fink, Paul M. *Bits of Mountain Speech Gathered Between 1910 and 1965 Along the Mountains Bordering North Carolina and Tennessee.* Boone, NC: Appalachian Consortium Press, 1974.

Green, Paul. *Paul Green's Wordbook: An Alphabet of Reminiscence.* Ed. Rhoda H. Wynn. 2 vols. Boone, NC: Appalachian Consortium Press, in association with: Chapel Hill, NC: Paul Green Foundation, inc., 1990.

Hall, Joseph Sargent, ed. *Sayings from Old Smoky: Some Traditional Phrases, Expressions, and Sentences Heard in the Great Smoky Mountains and Nearby Areas: An Introduction to a Southern Mountain Dialect.* Asheville, NC: Cataloochee Press, 1972.

Still, James. *The Wolfpen Notebooks: A Record of Appalachian Life.* Foreword by Eliot Wigginton. Lexington, KY: University Press of Kentucky, 1991. See: "Sayings," p. 43ff; Glossary: pp. 161–163.

Williams, Cratis D. *Southern Mountain Speech*. Edited with an introduction and glossary by Jim Wayne Miller and Loyal Jones. Berea, KY: Berea College Press, 1992.

Wolfram, Walt. *Appalachian Speech*. Arlington, Va.: Center for Applied Linguistics, 1976.

Illustrations

Landscape of the Holston

Edgar Bingham

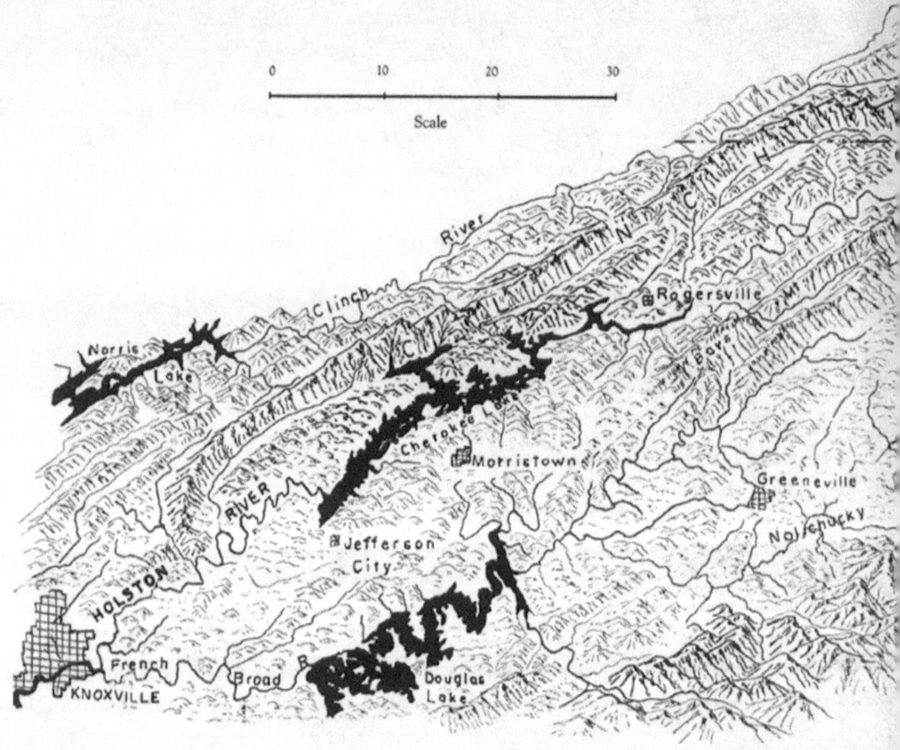

Published as a supplement to The Iron Mountain Review, Volume 1, No. 2.

Copyright © by Edgar Bingham 1983.

Holston River—from its headwaters in the foothills of the Blue Ridge Mountains in Southwest Virginia to its confluence with the French Broad River just above Knoxville, Tennessee (and showing TVA lakes that were built after the time of Armstrong's book). South Holston Lake, at the border of Tennessee and Virginia near Bristol, is where the story of *This Day and Time* takes place. Downstream, in Knoxville, after the Holston joins the French Broad to form the Tennessee River, is where Robert F. and Anne Armstrong grew up. Map by Edgar Bingham, originally published in the Holston River issue of *The Iron Mountain Review* 1, no. 2 (Winter 1984). Courtesy of Emory and Henry College.

Picture postcards of cottages at Big Creek where "town people" stayed during the summer. Courtesy of the Historical Society of Washington County, Virginia.

The mountains—what Ivy longed for while working in town: "the boundless sky above, the clean sweet air, the mountains walling her in protectingly, the river below. . . ." Anne Wetzell Armstrong Papers, McClung Historical Collection.

Rosy Duncan worked for Anne Armstrong as cook and housekeeper just as Ivy Ingoldsby worked for Shirley Pemberton in the novel. Anne Wetzell Armstrong Papers, McClung Historical Collection.

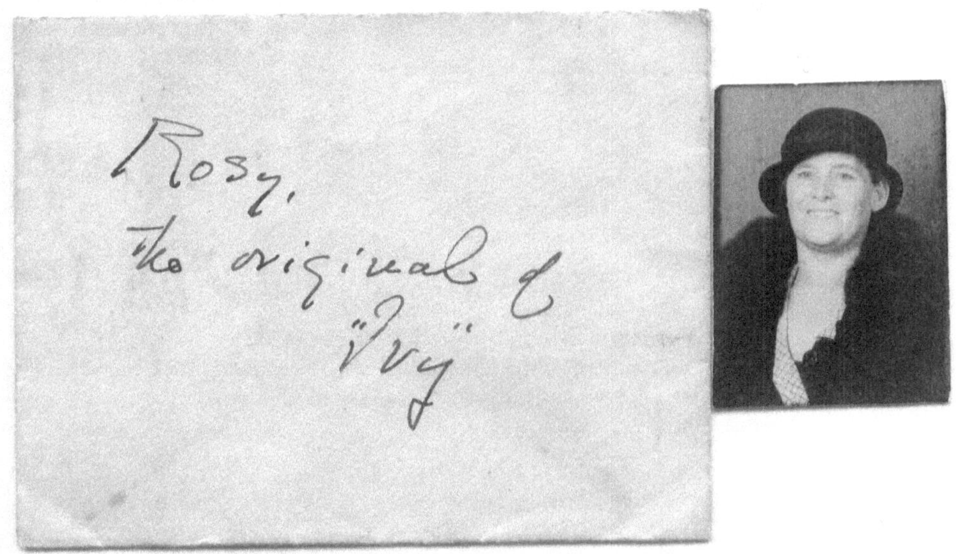

Photograph of Rosy Duncan and envelop with note in Anne Armstrong's handwriting identifying Rosy as the model for Ivy, heroine of *This Day and Time*. Anne Wetzell Armstrong Papers, McClung Historical Collection.

Robert Porterfield, founder and managing director of Barter
Theatre, and Anne Armstrong (at left, back row). Playwright
Clare Boothe Luce (seated, lower right), and others, in Abingdon,
Virginia (1942).

Picture published in the *Barter Theatre Review* showing a scene
from "Mountain Ivy." Checkmarks added by Anne Armstrong.
Anne Wetzell Armstrong Papers, McClung Historical Collection.

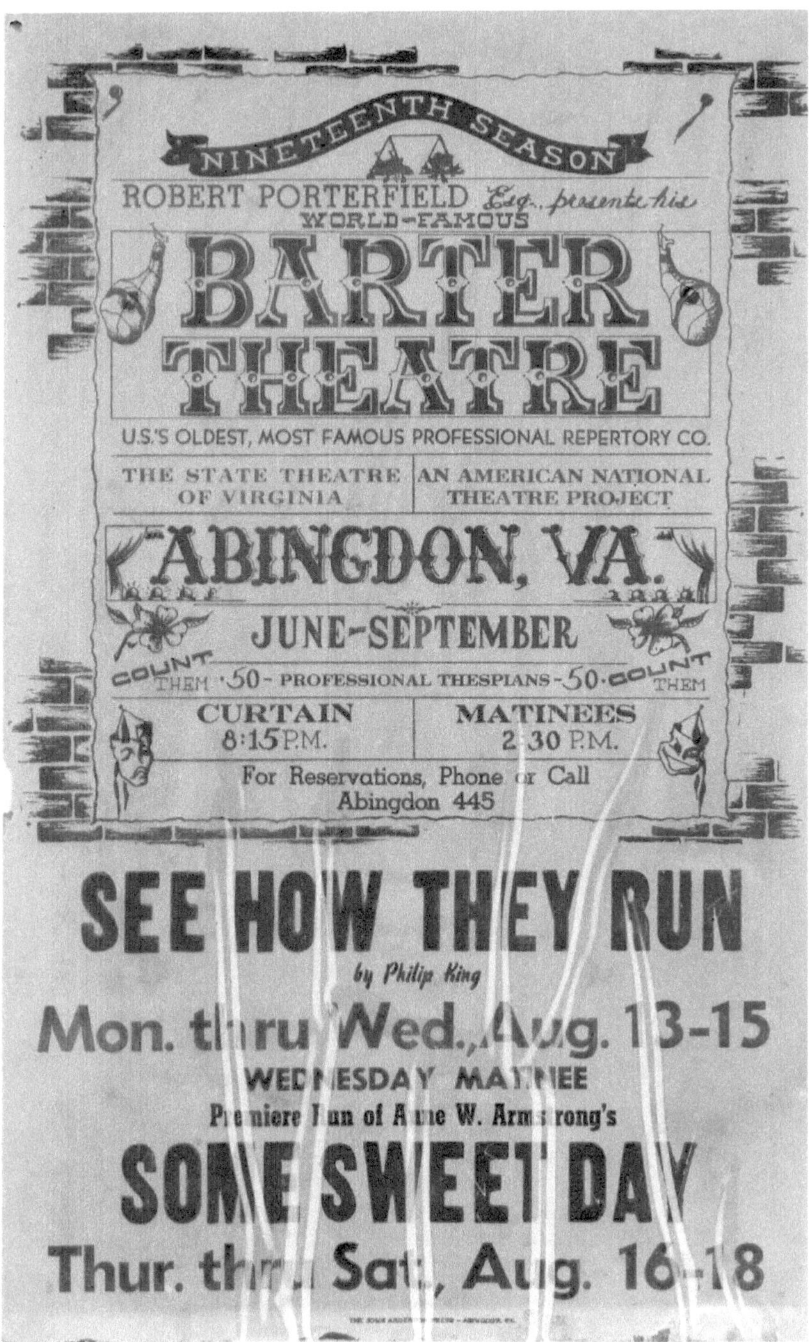

Barter Theatre playbill for the premiere of Anne W. Armstrong's "Some Sweet Day." Barter Theatre Archives, Southwest Virginia Digital Archive.

"The River" (as referred to in *This Day and Time*, likely the south fork of the Holston River). Anne Wetzell Armstrong Papers, McClung Historical Collection (MSC 0930), folder 14.

HOME TO THE MOUNTAINS

Chapter One

A HEAVILY LOADED farm-wagon wound in and out among the knobs, creaking and clattering over the frozen ground as the road climbed higher and higher. At short intervals the driver pulled up to rest his team. He was a lean man approaching fifty, with a red face, carefully shaven, an ink-black mustache showing a grizzled line next the skin, and keen dark eyes that kept blinking continually, darting from side to side. His black suit, his broad-brimmed black hat, his white shirt and black tie, marked him as a man of some importance in a region where men habitually wore overalls, work-shirts or jumpers, and no ties at all. Beside him on the wagon-seat a young woman with a knitted scarf wound around her head sat bolt upright, the lines of her sturdy figure only partly concealed by a faded threadbare coat. Her regular features indicated that she had once been pleasing to look at, perhaps pretty, but her face was thin and worn at present, deep lines, already almost furrows, replacing what a few years before had been dimples. Behind, in the wagon-box, a little boy of nine in blue overalls and with a cap pulled down around his plump but pasty cheeks was curled up trying to get some warmth from the straw tick on which he was perched, part of a load of household effects exposed to the gaze of whoever should care to observe them—a flimsy iron bedstead, a battered chest of drawers, slick from use, a thumb-marked safe with perforated tin doors, a couple of splint-bottomed chairs, some crocks, an iron kettle, and a big bundle tied in a clean sheet.

"Mammy, I'm cold," whimpered the boy, raising his head and addressing the young woman on the front seat.

"Hesh, Enoch!" she answered in a positive voice. "We're mighty nigh there. Cain't you see?"

The sun all at once burst from the clouds as they reached the top of a zigzag climb, and before them stretched a range of snow-covered mountains, not far distant now and shining like silver, with a grey-green river winding its way below, through a long, glittering snow-covered valley in which, to a casual observer, there seemed to be not a single human habitation. To a more searching scrutiny cabins with small log barns were revealed here and there, long distances apart.

"Hain't everything pretty!" exclaimed the young woman, gazing at the sparkling trees, pines and giant hemlocks whose branches, under their weight of snow, bent over the road. It was one of the few remarks she had made since leaving town, hours before.

"Pretty!" the driver sniffed. "Pretty, shucks! Never seed such weather for March. When's a feller to git his plowin' done?" And a moment later: "I don't reckon you'd a-fixed to come back in today, Ivy, if you'd a-knowed it was goin' to be like it is."

"Law, yes, I'd a-come the same," her voice rang out. She kept blowing on her purple fingers and stamping her aching feet in their low-cut town shoes up and down on the wagon-floor. "Ever since I heerd you was a-comin' to town fer chop, an' to git you some things fer your store, I've been a-lookin' fer ye, a-aimin' to git you to haul me an' Enoch back in, ef you would, an' our things—the little we got."

"Had enough of town, did ye, Ivy?" he asked slyly, suddenly bringing his head close to hers.

"A plenty!" she answered, and offered nothing further. She had gone out of the mountains with little or nothing and was coming back with less. But she wasn't going to let old Andy Weaver gloat over her return.

"I told 'em you'd be comin' back in, soon as spring come," Andy resumed, as they jolted along over the rough road, strewn with boulders. "But, Ivy, looks to me," he said, a faint tinge of sympathy in his voice, "like you'd do better for yourself in town. Looks like there ain't much for you to do here, with your few miserable little acres but starve."

"As well fer a body to starve as to grieve hisself to death!" Ivy returned. The moment the words were out of her mouth she realized they would be repeated next morning to the throng of idle men circling the stove in Andy's store, spitting tobacco juice into the sawdust boxes, swapping gossip. "Reckon Ivy's made her fortune in town an' hain't got to chop corn an' pull fodder fer a livin' no more, an' drap taters an' like o' that," this one or that would say, and be met with snickers. She started as Andy's high-pitched voice reached her again, this time from what seemed some distance away: "Reckon you don't never hear nothin' from Jim, do ye?"

"I don't know nothin' more about Jim Ingoldsby 'an you do, Mr. Weaver," she answered with dignity. "I don't know whurr he's dead or alive."

"You don't reckon he's got him another woman, do ye?"

"I hain't a-carin'!" Ivy tossed her head. "Jim Ingoldsby hain't no more to me 'an the dirt under my feet."

"I rickolict the day you-all married in the sugar grove," Andy persisted. "Boy, you was somethin' to look at in them days! I'll say you was!"

"A heap o' good hit done me!" an angry murmur from Ivy.

"Your cheeks was pink as pineys, and your little old eyes bright as a bead. . . . You was pretty as a chiny doll!"

There were no sounds for a while, save the rumbling and creaking of the wagon and Andy's occasional cluck to the horses, till they jolted around a curve, and at the top of a long steep hill Ivy called out: "Look, Enoch! Don't hit look natural?"

The wagon descended to the deafening scrape of the brake. At the foot of the hill, around another turn, but plainly in sight, a cabin stood out against a steep snowy knobside that was bare of trees except for some scattered blackjacks, a thin spiral of blue smoke curling up from the cabin chimney. "Reckon," Ivy thought to herself, "Mis' Philips is a-fixin' to git her supper. No, hit's too soon. The sun hain't drapped yit." Enoch pointed over her shoulder towards two boys in overalls about his own size. "Yon's Adam and Simon Peter, 'tother side the corn crib."

The wagon lumbered past, Enoch exchanging a shy "Howdy" with his old playmates, while Ivy waved to Mrs. Philips and Nova, two dark heads at the cabin window, discerned across a square of fenced garden that lay between the cabin and the road.

"There's a gal," Andy nodded backwards, "Novy Philips—I swan if she ain't gittin' to be the prettiest gal anywheres around."

"Hit's a sight on earth," Ivy thought, "how that old Andy Weaver is al-lays a-studyin' about pretty gals!"

"Novy looks well enough," she said, "ef she hadn't a-gone an' bobbed her hairs, an' ef 'ud quit off usin' them face-powders, an' that 'ere paint she—"

"Lord, Ivy," Andy broke in, "where you been? Don't you know, gal, that that there is all the style this day an' time—paint an' face-powders? You orter git ye some," he added with a wink.

Ivy laughed in spite of herself. "Oh, go 'long!" showing her teeth, shell-like and broken.

The road, hardly wider than the wagon-tracks, descending gradually, curve upon curve, clung to the partly cleared, partly wooded ridge that rose above it. The river was always in sight now, winding below, and a short distance ahead appeared an old cabin huddled among some snowy apple-trees in a slight depression beneath the road. Above and below the cabin, separated by the road, were the few miserable little acres to which Andy had referred.

Ivy's breathing suddenly became oppressive. To that cabin Jim Ingoldsby had brought her, a bride at sixteen, home to his old folks, to Uncle Jake and Aunt Jane. There Jim had left her one fine spring day, nobody knew why, least of all herself, but never to return. There Enoch had been born a few weeks later. From that cabin Aunt Jane first, then Uncle Jake—the thought filled her eyes—had been borne up the long trail to the burying-ground. From that cabin she and Enoch had departed on their own brief adventure into the world.

A long-drawn-out quavering "Whoa!" put an end to her reverie. She began to unload her belongings, with Andy's help carrying the safe and the chest of drawers down a steep path, through the gate, lifting them on to the narrow porch that ran across the front of the cabin, a step or so above the ground.

"I shore am obliged to ye, Mr. Weaver," Ivy said, "fer fetchin' us in." Enoch had disappeared and she stood in rather disturbing proximity to Andy on the narrow porch. After a silence, her heart beginning to pound, "How much do I owe ye?"

Andy, fidgeting a little, had taken his hat off. His hair, ink-black, like his mustache, showed the same grizzled line next the skin.

"His hairs is gray as a badger's," Ivy thought, as she waited for him to speak, "but he's gone an' painted 'em till they're black as a crow."

Andy cleared his throat several times. "Ivy, I'll be plagued—" He flung his head back, as if to take her in better—her straight well-knit figure, her flushed finely-cut face, with its square but delicate chin, her crackling gray-blue eyes. "Ivy, you wouldn't need to take a back seat fer Novy Philips or none of 'em, if you'd jest fix yourself up a little!"

"I hain't no call to fix myself up. How much do I owe ye, Mr. Weaver?"

Glancing around him, he thrust his face into hers. "Not a God-blessed cent, Ivy, if you won't be so everlasting prickly!" In a whisper: "If you won't deny me!"

Ivy pushed back against the door-jamb. "I'll give ye to understand I don't kiss men;" and, as he came a step nearer: "I thank ye, Mr. Weaver, I don't kiss men."

"Lord 'a mercy!" Andy threw back his head with a guffaw. "Who said anything about kissin'?" He put on his hat, settling it with both hands. "Well, I reckon I ought to have three dollars. It 'ud be more 'an that, of course, for anybody but you, Ivy, the roads what they are, but I know you ain't got much."

"Oh, that's all right!" Ivy walked into the cabin and, turning her back, drew a wadded-up handkerchief from her bosom. The familiar smell of the old dusky room, so different from any town smell, struck her with curiously mingled emotions. Suddenly, almost anguishingly, it brought to her the conviction that she was home. She counted out the money. "Glad I've got hit to give ye," she said, as she reappeared on the porch, adding civilly: "Tell Mistress Weaver to come to see me."

"Yes, you come. You-uns come to see us," Andy called back, as he scrambled up the path, turning as he climbed over the brake to call down cheerfully: "Look's like the cold spell's broke. Reckon we'll have a pretty day tomorrow."

Enoch came running up from around the corner of the cabin. "What did he charge ye, Mammy?" and then, seeing the furrow in her brow: "Did he taken all you got?" The child's pale, rather sickly face suddenly took on a vindictive look. He shook his fist after the wagon disappearing down the hollow. "He's mean as a snake, that man! He don't need that there money nary mite, him and Mis' Weaver without ary young un to their name, an' three cows, an' more chickens 'an a body kin count, an' a hog they ain't kilt yet, an' it a-comin' spring. He's mean as a snake, that man!"

Ivy bent down to the little boy where he stood looking up at her from the porch step. "Enoch, we've got a place that's ourn, hain't we? An' hit free of mortgage—that's more 'an some folks kin say. An' I hain't never failed to git us somethin' to eat, have I? I was in hopes he'd a brung us in fer nothin', bein' he's rich. But, honey, don't you weary yourself a-studyin' about hit. An' don't never agin," she warned, "blackguard Mr. Weaver that-a-way. Them's the independentest-soundin' words ever I heerd outen your mouth. An' ef you go a-sayin' 'em around, somebody 'ull tell him, shore as jedgment day. Don't never forgit, Enoch, that me an' you's alone in this world, an' hit hain't a-goin' to help us to git folks' ill will. Now, Enoch," and she shouldered the straw tick to carry it into the cabin, "me an' you's got to hustle or we'll be in the night."

A few minutes later, the little boy at her heels, she was climbing the almost perpendicular slope across from the cabin. The sound of her ax rang out on the clear air. "Law, Enoch, don't hit seem nice," she panted between strokes that were bringing the color to her cheeks, "to be a-gittin' firewood, place o' that old dirty coal in town!"

The strong aromatic perfume of the pines stung her nostrils. She felt a sudden return of her old strength, a comforting sense that things were beginning to be better for her than they had been for some time past. Dragging the hickory saplings and the young pines she had felled down to the road, she split them there. "A many an' a many's the time," she thought, "we hain't had us ary copper to our names, an' I allays made hit somehow or 'tother. . . . The old fool, a-stickin' his face up in mine! He knows good an' well I've allays kep' to myself. I hain't never trafficked with men. But I wisht he hadn't 'a saw fit to name Jim to me. Hit's a right smart spell sence I studied much about Jim. Enoch," she said aloud, "afore long you 'ull be plenty big to bust firewood fer me. Then I kin see a heap easier time."

Squatting on the sunken hearthstones, she laid the green sticks across the broken and rusty andirons, thrusting some knots of fat pine underneath and, calling to Enoch: "Fetch me the lamp oil," poured kerosene over it all to start a quick blaze. "I'm glad I cooked my beans afore I left town," she said, as she hung a kettle from the crane. "They on'y need to be het up. But I'm parched fer a drink—"

Enoch ran to the spring some distance below the cabin. Staggering back up the steep slope, he deposited his bucket on the shelf that ran across one side of a small back porch that adjoined the lean-to.

"Law, hain't hit the best?" Ivy exclaimed, draining the last drop from the gourd.

"Seems like that old water where comes out of a fasset in town never did taste no good," Enoch echoed. "'Tain't sweet, like this here water, is it, Mammy?"

They sat down to their supper of boiled beans and cold corn-bread set out on a table covered with red oilcloth in front of the fire. Outside, it was black, but the fire threw a ruddy glow over the smoke-darkened rafters and the walls of wide boards, dark and glossy from age. A dull murmur reached them. "Sounds like it's a-rainin'," Enoch remarked, "but it's jest the old river a-talkin' to hisself." He was gazing dreamily at his plate, sopping his bread in the soup from the beans. "Mammy, seems like I ain't never in my hull life tasted nothin' as good as these here beans an' this here corn-bread. I never did like that old steak an' light-bread an' stuff they hev in town."

But all at once he realized his mother had dropped her head beside her plate, flinging an arm around it, and that her back under her faded gingham dress was heaving. He got up and awkwardly touched her hair, clay-brown and brushed back plainly, revealing her small shapely ears. Enoch smoothed her hair. "Mammy, you're a-cryin'!" The little boy bent over her helplessly. "What are ye a-cryin' about, Mammy? Is it 'cause Mr. Weaver taken all your money fer fetchin' us in?"

Ivy sat up and blew her nose. She hugged the little boy close to her. "Don't you be afeared, honey. Hit hain't nothin'. Hit's jest 'cause I'm so glad to be back, an' me an' you to ourselves agin."

Chapter Two

A LOUD "HELLO!" warned them from the road above that someone was approaching.

Hurriedly drying her eyes, Ivy flung the door open. "Well, forevermore, ef hit hain't Mag an' Gid!" she called out as a gaunt elderly woman, emerging from the darkness, stepped up on the porch, a youth's dark handsome face peering smilingly over her shoulder.

The women embraced, the older one inquiring: "How air ye?" while Ivy's "Well as common" was lost in noisy confusion. She moved the table back from the fire. "Have ye a cheer, Mag. Git ye a cheer, Gid."

"Hain't no use lightin' no lamp fer jest me an' Gid," the older woman protested, lurching from side to side. "We hain't no company, mercy me, I hope not!" With her powerful raw-boned frame, her awkward unpremeditated movements, Old Mag seemed to fill the cabin, almost to imperil it. "You kin save your lamp oil, Ivy. Hit's plenty light with the fire. I hain't so pretty, nohow, me—" and she broke off with a boisterous laugh that disclosed two or three discolored snaggle-teeth with yawning spaces between. Seating herself in one of the splint-bottom chairs close to the hearth, she threw her hat—a shabby, rowdy-looking man's hat—on the floor, smoothed her apron, and ran her big-knuckled hand over a few broken strands of hair that were skinned back to a knot no larger than a walnut.

Opposite her on the hearth Gid, the youngest of nine, all born out of wedlock, and the only one of Old Mag's brood left at home, stretched out his long legs in khaki breeches and puttees, which Enoch, on a stool beside him, studied admiringly.

Ivy put another stick on the fire, stirring it into a blaze. "Them there electric lights," she remarked half apologetically, "like to put my eyes out what time I were in town."

Old Mag spat in the fire. "How did you like in town?"

"I didn't like," Ivy said. "Seems like," she added, after a pause, "there hain't nothin' to see in town, like here."

"Town hain't no place to live at," Old Mag agreed. "I hain't never seed nothin' to town, me. Seems like there's so much dust on the air in town."

"Law, I reckon."

"A body cain't breathe to do no good in town."

"Law, no, the houses is so clost togither hit shets off the breeze."

Huddled over the fire, no one spoke for a while.

"Did you think strange on hit," Ivy asked at length, "when you heerd I were a-comin' back in?"

Old Mag shook her head. "I knowed in reason you'd be back."

There was another long silence, broken at last by Gid, who had been looking at Ivy intently. "What you been doin' to yourself, Ivy?"

Old Mag brought her chair down with a bang now, whirling the younger woman around with a rough but playful movement. "Well, I do know, Ivy, you're pore as a weasel!"

"There hain't nobody," Ivy said, "got no health in town."

"Well, you look plumb puny is all I got to say." Old Mag spat again.

"How *you* been, Mag?" Ivy asked.

Old Mag's voice suddenly became a wail: "I hain't seed a well day sence you left. I hain't been peert the endurin' winter. I cain't eat, what's to say eat. Seems like I cain't keep more 'an a mouthful o' victuals on my stomick."

Gid got up and stretched himself. He had traded with a returned soldier for the khaki breeches. The sweater and puttees had been given him for securing a gallon of apple brandy for their former owner, one of the "summer people" who came each year to a row of rough cottages along the river. But he wore cast-off clothing, his rags and patches, with an air, and his hair no longer hung over his collar in straggling untidy locks, as it had a year or so before; it was cut close and slicked back, town-fashion.

"Gid, you're fine as a lawyer," Ivy commented teasingly. "You must be courtin.'"

Old Mag sniffed, her cavernous eyes suddenly lighted with a fire that was not all fun.

Lighting a cigarette with the nonchalant grace of the town sports he had observed around the summer cottages, Gid paused in the doorway, his towering head almost grazing the low lintel. "I'll be back afore long, Ivy," he announced, lazily emitting a stream of smoke, and adding with a mischievous glance at his mother: "an' take my old woman home."

"Gid's goin' back to the Philips'." Old Mag nodded in the direction whence they had come. "He were there when you-uns come down apast with Andy. He never come over the ridge till his supper were plumb cold, an' now he's a-goin' back agin. Him an' Novy's a-talkin'."

"Well, forevermore, Gid an' Novy!"

"An' hain't no more need, Gid hain't, fer a wife," Old Mag tossed her head, "'an I've got fer—fer nothin'!" she ended impatiently.

The women bent over the fire, Enoch nodding on the stool. The fire snapped and crackled faintly.

"What's been a-happenin', Mag?"

"Not a blessed thing I knows on." But after a pause: "Mis' Dillard is bad. She's down in the bed."

"Well, I do know!"

"Hit's the tubercles, I reckon."

"Law, I reckon. She's had 'em a time."

"They're a-lookin' fer her to die."

"Well, forevermore, an' all them young uns!"

"Seems like trouble don't never come single. Short Dillard, he had his leg took off—"

"The Lord help my time, Short!"

"He won't be no manner of help to his pappy now. He were hurt in the mines. Somewhars up in West Virginy. Hain't you heerd no tell?"

"I hain't heerd nothin' about hit afore, nothin' in any shape, form, or fashion—nary word. Short!"

"They's done writ him his mammy's bad off, but I don't reckon he'll git to come. He's in the hospital yit."

"I do know, Short!"

Again the two women sat for a while without speaking, only the distant purring of the river and the near-by purring of the fire to break the silence. Ivy felt herself growing drowsy. She jumped as Enoch toppled off the stool. "I'll fix him a pallet. I didn't aim to put up no bedstid tonight, nohow." Pulling off the little boy's worn and clumsy shoes, she covered him with quilts. She wished Gid would return, so she could pull off her own shoes and drop down on the floor beside Enoch. But as she mended the fire again, spreading above it her long, slender fingers, red and rough with cold— "The wind chaffs a body's hands so"—she was startled by Old Mag's asking:

"Reckon, Ivy, you don't never hear nothin' from Jim?"

From Jim! Oh, God! Just what Andy had asked!

"Why, no, I hain't heerd nothin'. Not a God-blessed word sence the day he left. What's more, I hain't a-rarin' an' a-chargin' to hear," she added grimly, her drowsiness gone now, "from nobody where's treated me like Jim done. The jail-house is too good fer Jim Ingoldsby."

Old Mag continued to gaze at the low licking flames. After some time, musingly: "Jim had a turn, seems like a body couldn't holp a-likin' him. He useter run with my boys where's dead, what time they was all little fellers togither. Many's the night Jim Ingoldsby's slept aside Floyd and Trigg in my loft. Many's the time Jim's et at my table. Jim useter brag on my pumpkin custard an' huckleberry dumplings." Old Mag spat in the fire, her eyes still fixed on it. "Jim allays thought a heap o' me." Old Mag was fumbling with something in her apron pocket, and Ivy's heart gave a wild leap as she held out to her a crumpled postcard. "Hit's from Jim. He writ me. Hit come awhile back."

All at once Ivy felt faint. She took the card, holding it close to the fire, and heard Old Mag saying: "I've studied on hit a heap, Ivy, whurr I orter name hit to you or no."

Ivy turned the postcard from side to side, her hands shaking. Underneath a picture of some soldiers drilling was printed *Parade Ground, Fort Omaha*. She read only with some difficulty, but on the address side made out, word by word:

How are you, Mag? Say howdy to Ivy for me. I don't guess the little fellow would know his daddy if he was to meet him, but tell him I'm coming to see him some sweet day. Jim Ingoldsby.

"I allays 'lowed," Ivy said quietly, at last, "Jim 'ud go back inter the army."

"Jim liked."

"Jim enlisted agin. That's what he done."

Old Mag sat tilted back in her chair, her big bony hands, seamed with black, clasping her knee. "I reckon Jim's a officer," she said, after a long pause. "I reckon Jim's high up by now."

"Law, I reckon." The river, flowing on and on, was like the gentle downpour of spring rain, like the soft rush of wind in the pines. Ivy's throat was dry and ached. "How do you reckon, Mag, he knowed hit were a boy?"

"I don't have no idee on earth."

Ivy held the postcard close to the fire again. "Hit's writ fair."

Old Mag nodded.

"Jim were allays a good scribe," Ivy murmured.

Vaguely embarrassed, Old Mag took down her wisp of hair, holding the hairpins in her mouth, then twisted it up again. "Jim had a heap o' manners."

"Where do you reckon this here place is, Mag, where Jim's at?"

"I hain't no idee."

"Reckon hit's fur?"

"A right smart piece. Hit fur's as Californy."

"You reckon?"

"Might be yon side Californy, fer aught I know. Andy Weaver says—"

"Andy!" burst from Ivy, half under her breath. She understood everything now, saw Andy handing out the mail at the store. "Here, Mag, here's a card backed to you. Reckon you've caught you another feller. Want me to read it to ye? Why, God bless my soul, if it ain't from Ivy Ingoldsby's man! It's from Jim Ingoldsby, shore as you're born!"

"Andy 'lowed hit taken a week—right at hit—to git to this here place where Jim's at."

"A week! Fur as Californy!" ran through Ivy's mind. "Well, he hain't got him no other woman, nohow. 'Say howdy to Ivy for me!' 'Say howdy to Ivy!' 'Say howdy to Ivy!' 'The little fellow!' 'Some sweet day!' 'Say howdy to Ivy!' 'Say howdy to Ivy—'"

CHAPTER THREE

AS SHE LAY beside Enoch on the pallet, huddled close to him for warmth, Ivy tried to stop thinking, but the old question was again hammering in her brain: "Why did Jim leave me? Oh, Lord God, why did he do me that-a-way?"

Her childhood came back to her, the cabin, far from any others, in Rocky Hollow where she had been born, the seventh of twelve—born when laurel was in flower, so that her mother had named her for the rosy cloud of bloom she had looked out on through the little window beside her bed; for the "ivy" that came each May to lighten the deep shadows of Rocky Hollow—ivy, the first thing her mother's tired eyes had rested upon after the granny-woman had lifted her head from lower down the bed. "Hit's a gal, Mis' Buckles, another fine little gal!"

Ivy's thoughts dwelt softly on her mother, a kindly, dragged-out woman, often sick, but always struggling for a semblance of decency and order in the swarming cabin. Her mother would plant a few flower seeds every spring, zinnias or marigolds, touch-me-nots, and bleeding-hearts. "Seems like," she could hear her mother saying, "flowers keeps a body from bein' so lonesome." Ivy could see her mother squatting beside the branch that tumbled down past the cabin, straightening her back from time to time, trying to get enough clean clothes together so that some of the children could go to Sunday-school two or three times at least in the course of the year.

Ivy remembered the daily squabbles; remembered a brother killed by a falling tree; a little sister burned to death, little Dee, left alone in the cabin and trying to start a fire as she had seen the older ones do, by pouring oil on the green wood. She could still hear the screams of little Dee, a sheet of flame, running frantically towards the field where the rest of them were dropping corn. She could see herself on one of the steep slopes that wedged in Rocky Hollow, grubbing sprouts on a piece of "new ground"; she could see a stranger passing up the hollow and all of them stopping, her father and mother too, resting on their hoes or mattocks, staring after the stranger to whom her father had called down a low half-hostile "Howdy." Ivy could scarcely remember a time when she had not handled a hoe.

There were moments of delight Ivy remembered of her childhood; the time she had uncovered the pheasant's nest in the leaves; the little terrapin she had made a pet of; the Indian arrow-heads she had turned up with her hoe; times she had played house under a great sycamore that overspread the log spring-house, with acorn-cups for dishes, with tufts of moss, bits of broken crockery. Her childhood, when she thought of it, did not seem to her to have been an unhappy one. Her father, if high-tempered, had not been brutal, or only occasionally, when he was drunk and might beat her mother or kick one of the boys. There had been the fun of going up on the mountain every summer for huckleberries—the whole troop of them, and other families too—the fun of going down the river each spring to the sugar-orchard, sleeping in the sheds left there from year to year among the sugar-maples.

Then her mother had died, leaving her, the oldest girl at home, to mother the family till her father had married again, within the year. Then, in the spring that followed, back at the sugar-orchard, all of them helping make sugar and syrup again, and people coming to trade with her father for the thin sappy syrup, carrying it away in the buckets they had brought.

And then one day, as she had been carrying a bucket of sap to the fire, a young man standing in her path, teasingly, as if to block the way; a tall, straight, very clean young man, with very short hair, in soldier clothes, and the young man laughing: "Don't be scared! You've growed a right smart since the time I saw you last, at the burying-ground, when they put your Grandpap Buckles away. Well, you ain't gettin' any worse-lookin', I'll swear you ain't!" and then Jim laughing again—Jim was always laughing—"Ivy, I swore to Gawd, first time I ever laid eyes on you, I'd come and steal you some day!"

And then Jim and her "a-talkin'," while the sugaring went on, and Jim helping her as she trudged to and from the fire, or to and from the spring, some distance away. And then a dusk when Jim had caught her and kissed her.

She liked to dwell on the memory of Jim's going to town and bringing her back a pair of slippers, the first she had ever owned, town slippers to replace the clumsy outgrown shoes of her brothers which she had worn before, when she had worn any at all. She saw Jim and herself standing up before the preacher in the sugar-orchard, "of a Sabbath, the prettiest day hit were." She could recall in sharp detail the look and feel of that day, bluets twinkling up from the turf under their feet—those wee "forget-me-nots" her mother had loved—the mountains blue-black, ragged fringes of snowy cloud half hiding their tops; and a red-bird, like a drop of blood, against the bare ghostly branches of a giant sycamore on the river-bank, the red-bird whistling its throat out from the topmost branch of the sycamore.

She could still see Jim's father, Uncle Jake, hobbling down the steps to meet them, his unsmiling deep-plowed face, his faded and patched overalls hanging loosely on his once powerful figure—her and Jim coming through the gate at sundown, Jim laughing, his head high, her own cheeks burning. She had wanted to hide, to streak away like a rabbit when the dogs were after it. She could still hear Uncle Jake's harsh grating voice: "Proud to know ye, Ivy. I know your pap. Me an' him was raised up together." And then Aunt Jane, bleached and gentle, in her clean gray print, shyly, from the doorway: "I reckon you're plumb beat out, Ivy, honey. Hit's a right smart piece from the sugar grove."

She could still see Uncle Jake's and Aunt Jane's cabin as it had first looked to her—the two beds, in opposite corners, the few straight splint-bottom chairs, the wide boards of the floor white as she had never seen before; white spreads on the beds; a clock. Not ten miles from Rocky Hollow, but a strange new world. Someone passing every day, up or down the road; people to shout to and who shouted down to them: "How air ye? How air you-all? Reckon hit 'ull fair off?" Other cabins; Big Bill Byrd's down below, on the river; Doke Odum's on down the road; and up it, hardly more than half a mile in the opposite direction, the Philipses'.

Ivy liked to dwell on the memory of Jim's going to town and bringing her home a pink chambray dress and some pretty chemises. Jim was "free-hearted." Jim had money saved from his three years in the army; he had bought a cow and two shotes. Days of plenty. Jim had made the crop by himself. "Pap, you ain't a-goin' to raw-hide these here knobs whilst I'm here. Ivy, do you guess I'm goin' to have *my* woman workin' in the sun? Well, you've got another guess." Days of plenty—sweet milk every day, and butter on the table.

Then winter. Jim walking back and forth to town, twenty miles away, for something to do. Jim's money all spent. Jim sitting by the hearth day after day, smoking cigarettes, getting up to stretch himself now and then, yawning. Uneasy days. And then Jim going off to a logging camp, coming home every week or so with a sack of flour over his shoulder, shoes for Ivy and his mother. Jim laughing again, but talking, while at home, of the army, not such a bad life for a man. "A sight easier 'an loggin', or tryin' to grub a livin' off o' these here worn-out old knobs." Not a bad life, pool, movies—something to do of an evening.

And then bluets twinkling up from the grass again, redbirds whistling from the sycamores. Jim restless again. He had "quit off loggin'." He would look for a job in town. Maybe he would rent a house there, take them all into town to live; no more grubbing. And Ivy whispering to him at the gate: "Could you git me a few yards of nice domestic, Jim, ef your money holds out? An' some pretty soft flannel-cloth or like o' that? Reckon you know what I want 'em fer. I'll be down afore long."

And then a package coming in the mail; some little dresses, a hood, and a white coat, embroidered, everything very fine. But no word. Days of looking and waiting, the days lengthening out to months, the months to years.

"Oh, why did Jim do me that-a-way, never to show his face agin? Lord, I've been a good woman, to my lights. Lord, make it plain!" the plea went up from Ivy's heart as she tossed on the pallet, turning and turning, the straw in the mattress beneath her cracking out loudly in the still night. "Were hit because Jim couldn't stand fer his woman to have rough ways?"

Try as she would to thrust it from her, the old thought was back again.

"Don't talk so loud, Ivy, for Gawd's sake!" Jim would say. "What's the use yellin' like I was down at Byrd's, place of right beside you? I ain't deef!"

Aching from cold and weariness, struggling to sleep, Ivy only found herself more fully awake. The years kept passing in review.

Her own family had left her behind almost as completely as Jim had done. Her father, a few weeks after her own marriage, had moved to California, taking her younger brothers and sisters with him. Her older brothers and sisters were married and scattered. They were up in Virginia somewhere or over in North Carolina—vague regions, only a little less unknown than the California which had swallowed up her father. She rarely heard from any of them. . . . She had been abandoned to the mercy of Jim's old folks, and Jim's old folks had kept her with them.

Aunt Jane had been another mother to her, one from whom she had learned to strain the milk more carefully, to sun the crocks, to tidy the cabin according to a precept, "soon of a mornin'," unknown to Rocky Hollow, where if floor and doorstep were swept, beds were left to be crept into at dark as they had been crawled out of at dawn. Happy, almost radiant hours Ivy had known working beside Aunt Jane; hoeing; shelling beans to dry; at their patchwork together; picking out walnut kernels to be sold in town, each at a corner of the hearth through winter afternoons, little Enoch between them. Ivy had loved Jim's mother; loved her none the less that Aunt Jane had neither accused nor defended Jim, had never talked of him, even to the hour when Ivy had wiped the death damp from her brow and Aunt Jane had looked up with a last toothless smile. "Ivy, honey, you've allays been good to me. You won't have nothin' to study about atter I'm gone."

Once, it was true, when Aunt Jane had baked a little cake for Enoch in the shape of a man, and together they had watched his delight in it, Aunt Jane had said with a deep look: "You never see no comfort with chillun, Ivy, 'cept when they're round your knee." Again, when little Enoch had taken a sugar-spoon that Aunt Jane kept in a hidden place, and lost it, Ivy had witnessed the gentle old woman deeply disturbed till the spoon had been found. She had overheard Uncle Jake blustering at Enoch: "You tech that 'ere spoon agin, you little Hessian, an' I'll wear ye out! I'll put hit to ye proper! Your daddy brung that 'ere spoon to your gran'mam, an' she sets a heap o' store by hit."

Uncle Jake had been as irascible, as bitter-tongued, as Aunt Jane had been patient and charitable. Unruly to the last, the old man, when he came to die, had forbidden Ivy to send for the doctor. "Pay heed, Ivy, to what I'm a tellin' ye. The doctor 'ud take your turkeys fer pay. Ef he come agin, he 'ud take your cow. Hain't no need. My time's come. They 'ud rob ye of your last dust o' meal, fer all the mercy them fellers has got—Snodgrass or Slimp, no difference 'twixt 'em. There hain't no country doctors this day an' time. Country doctors has passed away, same as the bears useter be on the mountain. An' them town doctors—well, hit's them, them an' the lawyers, mighty nigh eats up pore folks." A violent coughing-spell had stopped him, but a moment later, between panting breaths, his raucous voice had sounded again: "Ivy, don't git me no coffin. Hain't no need. Doke Odum, he'll make ye a box. Jest wrop me in my windin'-sheet."

At the end, Uncle Jake had broken the long silence in respect to Jim. "He done ye wrong, Ivy. God knows Jim done ye wrong, but me an' his mammy—what time she lived—has tried to make hit up to ye, what little we could." At the end, Jim had been constantly on Uncle Jake's mind. Ivy had put her head down close to the old man's shrunken mouth. "I'd liked to saw my boy once more." Then, in the next rattling breath, his eyes suddenly opening wide and glaring at her: "Justice overtaketh every man."

Except Jim, there were only some distant Ingoldsbys, and Uncle Jake had willed the cabin and his few remaining acres to Ivy. With it he had given her, while he still lived, some solemn advice: "Whatsomever you do, don't let nobody git hit away from ye. If you've got ye a little patch o' land that's yourn, you've got your bread, an' ef you've got your bread, you kin live. You hain't beholden to no man."

She had her little patch of ground, but in the years that followed, Ivy had sorely missed Aunt Jane's riper experience. "Seems like my little turkeys is all so droopy. The turkey hens is so hateful, takin' em out in the heavy dew of a mornin'. Aunt Jane, she was the best hand with turkeys!" Instead of a flock to sell in the fall, there had been only two or three turkeys, and finally none. There had been fewer eggs to trade, too, than when she and Aunt Jane had tended the chickens together. Then, after the old folks were gone, there had been no one with whom to leave Enoch, still barely four. Climbing the icy knobs with her in winter, stinging, aching with cold herself, the little fellow would cry continually. And it was hard to trail him along, for miles, when she was going to mill, helping shuck corn up Troublesome, or helping make molasses down by Drowning Ford. Ivy worked well, so she had always found work to do, when there was work, and pay in kind. She and Enoch had lived, but it had been, for the most part, to bed on gnawing stomachs; or eating too much when it offered, and then Enoch with burning fever and out of his head, or Ivy sick, and terrified at the thought of what would become of Enoch if anything happened to her.

At last, after four years of this struggle, after months of thinking of little else, Ivy had decided on the move to town which Old Mag's daughter Martha, coming home to her mother's from time to time when work at the overall-factory was slack, had urged upon her. "You'll jest wear out afore your time, Ivy, ef you keep a-stickin' here in the knobs. There ain't but one thing in God's world fer you to do."

The Byrds had bought her chickens and cow, Ivy crying to herself softly behind the empty cow-shed as one of the Byrd boys had driven the cow away. She still felt the cow's soft flank under her stroking hand. "Soo, soo, Daisy!" It had been giving up something of herself to part with her cow and chickens. And when Uncle Abel Dillard had waited for her on the road above, Enoch and her household goods piled in the wagon-box, closing the cabin door behind her, taking one last look into the empty room, her throat had throbbed with pain, and, her hand on the worn latch, she had been all at once filled with desperate longing to remain in the cabin she loved almost as Enoch. But Uncle Abel had called: "Ivy, we'd best be a-gittin' started or we'll belate ourselves. Hit's a right smart piece fer my off mule to travel, hit lame." . . . Town beckoned. Her hopes, after all, had been high.

At Odie's—Odie was Old Mag's daughter, married to Rat Bunts—Ivy was to pay five dollars a week and help Odie mornings and evenings. After a week at Odie's Ivy had made up her mind that as soon as she earned enough, she would find another place to board.

Odie, who always had just had a baby, was expecting one, or was recovering from a miscarriage, sprawled all day in a rocking-chair, bestirring herself only as was absolutely necessary. Most of the household burden, including the care of each new baby that lived, had rested, since they were able to walk, on Odie's raft of frowsy though bright and pretty little girls. With Ivy's arrival a new order had begun. Ivy had been expected to start the kitchen fire in the morning, to cook the breakfast unaided, to put up a lunch for Rat, to wash the dishes—if they were washed before evening—in general, to set Odie's household upon its feet before she started to the factory, while a pile of unwashed dishes and unscraped pots and pans from the midday meal had awaited her return at dark, and the family wash had been saved for her to do, along with her own, on Saturday afternoons, with the ironing for such evenings as she was able to stand on her swollen feet. Even on Sundays she had had no rest. She had spent them in cleaning the cottage and in extra cooking. "Ivy, you sure are one grand cook," Odie had flattered her; "I never et such cake and pies in my life as yourn."

On Ivy's first Sunday in town, Rat, passing through the kitchen from the back porch where he had been shaving, had said to her out of the corner of his mouth: "Ivy, don't let her sweet-talk you. That slut 'ull work you to death if you give her a chance."

Next day Rat had borrowed ten dollars. He had wanted to borrow the rest of the small hoard left from the sale of her cow and chickens, but Ivy had held it back. "I hate hit the worst, Rat, but I hain't bought no outfit fer Enoch. I hain't bought ary book fer the child nuther—looks like school-books is allays so high—an' I don't know yit what I'm a-goin' to make from that 'ere piece-work."

Ivy looked back on her life at Odie's with loathing. Rat had constantly tried to see her alone. Then he and Odie had quarreled incessantly, calling each other, before the children, by obscene names. And it had been almost impossible for her to eat amidst such squalor, the house reeking with un-clean smells, and Odie's children dipping their filthy little hands into the potato-dish and the gravy-bowl. "Seems like I hain't got no stomick to eat victuals where's been fingered over," she had thought miserably.

Her work at the factory, too, had grown daily more unbearable. Be-fore, much of her work had been done outdoors and no two days had been alike. Now, all day long feeding a pair of overalls through a machine, with a dusty window beyond the machine, and through it, if she had looked off her work, a brick wall across an alley, and other dusty windows facing her.

If she had worked hard before, she had stopped to visit with anyone who passed. In the factory, at first, Ivy had stopped to talk to one girl after another along the row of machines where her own was, but they had been quick to warn: "Watch out, forelady's lookin'!" They had been anxious to resume their stitching of pockets and leg seams, and Martha had told her frankly: "You can't never in God's world make it at piece-work, Ivy, if you stop to talk," adding: "Don't none of 'em like to be stopped, Ivy. A body cools off like, when they stop, and it takes a right smart time, you know, till they can get up their speed again." Later Martha had cautioned: "Law, Ivy, you got to do more dozens a day 'an that, to live in town."

Ivy herself had begun to long with the whole strength of her being to return to the place whence she had come. Her thoughts had gone back to a hawk that Doke Odum had caught once in a trap and, chained to a stick, brought to show her and Enoch. She remembered the look of fear and anxiety in the hawk's eyes, the hawk's thrusting its head suddenly forward, looking off towards the mountains with its wide-apart far-seeing eyes. Ivy imagined she was the hawk. Following a line of white stitching across blue denim hour after hour, day after day, the eyes of her mind had always been looking far off, to the mountains—those mountains to which, like the hawk, she belonged.

One day Ivy had plowed the machine needle through her thumb. Soon after that, when she had been able to run her machine again, she and Mar-tha had been leaving the factory in the evening and Martha had startled her with: "Ivy, I'd rather take a beatin' as to tell you, but the boss man says he'll have to put somebody else on your machine. He 'lowed you wouldn't never do much good at piece-work nohow. *You* know, some folks cain't."

Though Martha's words had thrown her into a panic, Ivy had already decided that this was so. Martha was able to make eight or nine dollars a week, had once made twelve. Ivy had not made four.

There had been days of hunting for another job. During this time, everywhere told that work was scarce, Martha had said to her one day in her low, rather mournful voice, not looking at Ivy: "Why don't you get you a feller?"

Ivy had started, not sure she had heard aright, but Martha had gone on in a dull murmur: "I'll tell you the truth, Ivy, if ever I spoke it, I wouldn't never have got along on what I can make in the factory. You got to look at things sensible, Ivy. You ain't only got yourself to look atter, you got Enoch."

Not wishing to rebuke Martha, Ivy had made no reply. A little later she had found a job in a shirt-factory, the shirts cut, as the overalls had been, in New York and jobbed to small Southern towns where they could be finished by labor that was still cheap.

At the shirt-factory Ivy had missed Martha. She had talked to no one. She had stitched without stopping, lonely and discouraged, already beginning to be terrified at the thought of the future. Then a whisper had started of a lay-off.

"I don't know a thing more about it than you do," the manager had answered curtly when Ivy had asked him how long the factory would be shut down.

After a week or so Ivy had found work again, this time at a poultry-house.

At the poultry-house Ivy had picked fowls for shipping, from daylight till dark, long after dark, bent over a tub on the floor, picking, picking, in a gloomy airless room filled to suffocation with feathers and a sickening stench.

"I reckon I've died an' went to torment," Ivy reflected at times. The river and mountains, her cabin, and the steep fields under the open sky no longer filled her mind. A sort of aching vacancy had taken possession of it, broken now and then by an impulse she could scarcely resist to drop the fowl in her hands, jump up and scream, flee the poultry house and town forever.

Then one noon Martha had come to the poultry-house to tell her of a job she thought Ivy might get. An old lady, a widow woman, wanted a white girl, someone from the country—an easy place, only the old lady.

The big red-brick house with strange parts jutting out and springing up from it everywhere had awed Ivy at first glance. "Looks like a hotel!" she had thought, almost afraid to ring the bell. "Big as the jail-house, an' her all alone, pore soul!"

The old lady had opened the door herself. She was small, straight as a stick, and had spoken in a high childish treble, saying she was tired of niggers stealing everything she had, wanted Ivy to come at once. "Your little boy ain't troublesome, is he?"

The house was dark inside and smelled of cooking. Everything, including the old lady in her black dress, had looked grimy. Upstairs and down were doors and doors and doors, most of them shut, and short unexpected flights of steps covered with musty carpet that was threadbare in spots. Over the kitchen was a little room under a sloping roof, with a small window before which hung a tattered remnant of lace curtain, black with soot. "Hain't hit nice!" Ivy had responded politely to the old lady's announcement that the room was for her and Enoch.

From a side porch, letting her out, the old lady had called in her piping querulous voice: "When you come tomorrow, Ivy, go round to the back."

"Reckon the old lady didn't mean nothin'," Ivy had reflected. "Town ways is the curiousest ever I knowed. Seems like folks in town don't never make a body feel much welcome." Well, anything would be better than the poultry-house. She had better return next day with Enoch and their bundle of clothes, as she had all but promised.

She had set the table for three, on her first evening in the old lady's big house; inspected Enoch's face and hands, smoothed her own hair.

"Well, I reckon hit's ready," she had announced, flushed with heat, a trifle flurried and uneasy, but proud to show the old lady how well she could cook. "I won't brag on my biscuits—seems like I cain't never get useter cookin' with coal—but I reckon we'll have us enough to eat. I fried the ham, like you said, an' cooked us some grits—"

"Where would you like," she had asked, as the old lady still stood, looking hard at the dining-room table, "we-uns to set?"

"Sit?" A slight glaze had gathered on the old lady's eyes, but after a moment's silence, her lips clamped, she had piped decisively: "You and the little boy eat in the kitchen."

Suddenly Ivy had been filled with shame and fury. "I thank ye, I hain't no nigger! I thank ye, I'm good as you are!" she had wanted to blaze forth. But she had forced the words back.

"Ef you don't want me an' Enoch to set with ye," she had said, holding the pantry door open, her head high, her cheeks flaming now, and her throat hurting so that it was hard for her to speak, "me an' Enoch don't want to. We'll give ye our room, place of our company. Come, Enoch."

CHAPTER FOUR

READING TIME FROM the sun, Ivy knew it was close to midday. She had
finished scrubbing the floor with her scrub-broom and was squatting by
the hearth to examine the corn-bread baking in a small oven set in the
ashes, murmuring to herself: "Hain't no bread on earth tastes so good an'
sweet as bread where's baked in a baker," and thinking: "Jim might come
a-walkin' in 'most any day, an' I want ever'thing to look jest like hit useter
what time Aunt Jane were alive. Jim were allays perticular. Jim never had
no use on earth fer a sluttish woman." A step startled her, and, turning,
she half expected to see Jim in the doorway, instead of the tall, youngish,
loosely hung man in ragged overalls who was smiling at her with coarse
red lips only partly concealed by a thick stubby black mustache.

"Doke, you skeert me!"

The man took a loaded sack from his shoulder and placed it against
the wall. "You're easy skairt!"

"Have ye a cheer, Doke. Been to mill? How are ye?"

"Tol'able. Nothin' extry." He slouched into a chair and, picking up a
stick, began to whittle. After a silence: "How's yourself?"

"Well as common. How's Leoly and the chillun?"

"I hain't seed nothin' wrong with none of 'em," the visitor answered
facetiously, his bold black eyes beginning to roam over the room. "Say,
Ivy, did Andy charge fer bringin' you-uns in?"

"Doke, you allays want to know so much."

"An' him a-puttin' money in the bank, the son of a bitch!"

"Now, Doke, don't you start sech as that. You know good an' well, Doke, I don't like no foul-spoken man."

"Where's Enoch?" The visitor gave a stealthy glance around him.

"I couldn't see no peace till I let him go to the Philips'. He couldn't wait no time to git with Adam an' Simon Peter." Ivy's heart had begun to beat a little faster. Once, soon after Uncle Jake's death, Doke had crept up from behind her with his soft padding step and pinioned her arms. She had torn herself loose and pursued him with fury, but her eyes traveled now to the ax always standing, when she was alone in the cabin, at the head of her bed.

"I heerd you was workin' fer a rich widdy woman," the visitor remarked slyly, after a pause in which Ivy had taken an iron pot off the links, setting it on the heath. "Say, Ivy, I weren't a-aimin' to stay fer dinner."

"You're welcome," Ivy laughed, "to beans an' corn bread."

"An' hain't nothin' better. I kin eat beans twicet a day, three hundred an' sixty-five days in the year—But say, Ivy, what manner o' person were that 'ere widdy woman?"

"Law, she were nice an' common."

"Treated you-uns friendly?"

"Law, she treated us fine!" Ivy busied herself over the oven now, drawing it forth from the ashes and sliding off the lid with its covering of live coals, to examine the cornbread again.

"Most o' them town folks, from what I've heern, treats you like you's scum o' the earth, ef you're a-workin' for 'em."

"Law, I reckon."

From under the battered hat slouched over his brows Doke's glittering eyes were following Ivy's face. "Damned ef I wouldn't see 'em in hell afore I'd cook their filthy victuals fer 'em, them a-namin' hit to me that I hain't good enough to set at table an' eat by the side of 'em. You say the widdy woman didn't do you an' Enoch that-a-way?"

"Law, no."

Doke sprang from his chair with a roar of laughter. "Lord, Ivy, a feller kin see right through ye same as you're glass!"

"What makes you so mean, Doke?" Ivy flushed hotly. She had only told Martha what she had suffered during her weeks in the old lady's big grimy house. "I don't reckon," she thought now, "Doke's heern nothin'. Doke's jest so talkified."

Doke hoisted the loaded sack to his shoulder. Standing in the doorway, bending under its weight, he remarked with a grin: "Ivy, you orter let me learn you somethin' about lyin' afore you try hit agin."

"You'd best stay an' eat, Doke."

"I'll be pokin' along. The old woman cain't make her no bread till I git there with this here meal. Say"—he turned as he reached the porch, his black eyes sparkling with a mixture of malice and good humor—"say, Ivy, reckon you heerd about One-arm Press?"

"Law, yes."

"Pinned hit on him proper! Found old Press at the still, an' reckon he 'ull have to serve his term. Hain't nobody this time to pay his fine." Doke had put his load down again. "Bruce an' Dave, they was right there with their pap. But, doggone, them boys give the constable the slip. The boys, they beat hit to town an' joined the army."

Ivy stood in the doorway, her eyes resting idly on the river below, a long winding line of black between its snowy edges. She was thinking of Mrs. Philips, another wife left to make the living. "Hit's hard on Mis' Philips," she said. "A one-arm man were better 'an no man. An' now she hain't got nary man-person on the place, on'y Adam an' Simon Peter, an' they don't count, no more 'an Enoch. They hain't hardly took to the hoe yit."

"Say, Ivy, don't you stay up of a night a-studyin' about Mis' Philips. That old woman 'ull make hit. She's bootleggin'. She's a-packin' a gallon or two to town ever' week of the world. She totes hit in the basket with her butter an' eggs. But say," and Doke turned once more, after he had started, "you hain't got a little coffee, have ye, Ivy, that ye kin spare a feller?"

"Why, yes—"

Following her back to the lean-to with its cracks through which the snow had sifted, Doke's eyes swept it while Ivy took a small paper bag from the safe. She had caught sight of Doke's bare leg through a rent in his overalls. "Nary stitch underneath! Mighty nigh naked," she thought, "an' pore as a scarecrow!" She poured half the coffee into a cup, from which the handle had been broken. "Don't be in no haste a-payin' hit back."

"Doke, did your taters make?" she called after him when he had reached the gate.

"I had several—a right smart crop. But I tell you what's a fact, Ivy, we hain't got a God-blessed tater left of all I raised."

"Forevermore!"

"Hit takes a sight."

"Law, I reckon."

In mid-afternoon Ivy had dragged some young hickories down from the knob and was chopping them up for her evening fire. The great arch overhead was bright blue now, the river a clear translucent green.

"Law, the pretty sun!" she stopped her chopping to exclaim. The sharp sweetness of the pines, their aromatic life-giving fragrance, was wafted to her. Her thoughts ran back to the factory. It was this she had longed for at the factory, at the poultry-house, at the widow woman's—the boundless sky above, the clean sweet air, the mountains walling her in protectingly, the river below with its soothing, never ceasing murmur. Yet, even so, a little of the elation at being home had begun to wear off.

The truth was, she could hardly have chosen a worse time in which to come back. There was no work to be had. It was weeks yet till corn-planting time. Everyone was running out of food.

Perhaps she had been too hasty. . . . The widow woman had always been poking about in the pantry and icebox. "Ivy, what's become of that steak we had yesterday? I thought sure there 'ud be enough for dinner today," or: "Ivy, we ain't out . . . ?" of this, or that. "Why, where's it gone to?" The widow woman had seemed to begrudge every bite that she and Enoch ate. But there had been food. Now she had only the small stock of provisions she had been able to buy after she had paid Odie what she owed her—a few pounds of dried beans, some flour and meal, a little sugar and coffee, a piece of fat bacon.

But she would manage somehow. She always had.

"Jim 'ull be more 'an apt," she thought, as she chopped away, "to wait till the rough weather is done an' past. Jim 'ull be a-comin' in when ever'thing is a-gittin' pretty agin, an' green.

"There hain't livin' man kin say I've give in to him, an' him speak truth," she reflected now, in a matter-of-fact vein, but with grim satisfaction. "Many's the one, since Jim left, has named hit to me—good as named hit. But one thing's certain an' shore, Jim cain't put no name o' whore on me ef he comes."

Some stirring words from a hymn suddenly recurred to her.

There's a great day comin',
A great day comin';
There's a great day comin' by an' by.

Far over the knobs her nasal voice soared, high and exultant, drowning the strokes of the ax as she chopped and split.

Are ye ready? Are ye ready?
Are ye ready fer the judgment day!

CHAPTER FIVE

IN THE DEAD of night Ivy was awakened by someone calling. "Hello! Ivy!" The calling kept on. "Yes, I'm a-comin'." It was someone, she realized now, going the rounds, waking every cabin, and a little shiver ran through her. Ivy unbolted the door. The night was without moon or stars, but she felt the presence of someone standing inside the gate.

"Hit's Luke Diggs, hain't hit?"

"Yes."

"I reco'nized the voice."

"Mis' Dillard died an hour back."

"Law, me! Somethin' run all over me—I were afeared hit were Mis' Dillard. An hour back." After a silence: "What time is hit now?"

"Three o'clock, right at hit." The young man spoke in a drawling, curiously gentle voice.

"When are they a-aimin' to bury her, Luke?"

"Day atter tomorrow."

"The weather has turned off soft, Luke. Do you reckon—" She paused.

"The coffin cain't git here no sooner. Uncle Abel is a-goin' to town to fetch hit a Monday."

"Law, yes, the stores hain't open of a Sabbath, an' I reckon Uncle Abel wants to git him some things fer her—gloves' an' like o' that. He wants to put her away nice."

Ivy stood in the doorway, the muffled roar of the river sounding in her ears. "But hit's a right smart time to keep her. I hope hit won't git no warmer, Luke." They were silent awhile. "Where are they a-aimin' to bury her at?"

"Bane's Buryin' Ground."

"Hit's a pretty spot, an' the ground at Bane's, hit works mighty easy." After another silence: "Doke's a-goin' to dig the grave, I reckon."

"I reckon. Me an' Wash Byrd is a-tellin' folks."

"There 'ull be no school, do you reckon, Luke, till atter the buryin'?"

"I reckon not."

"People has respect to the dead," Ivy murmured. "Well, I thank ye, Luke, fer comin'. I'll go, soon as hit's day."

"They're a-lookin' fer ye. Everybody shore is proud, Ivy, to hear you're back," the young man added. "They're a-lookin' fer ye. Uncle Abel, he named your name—"

"Yes, I'll go. I'll do what I kin. I hope there 'ull be somebody as wants to do fer me when my time comes, an' I'm glad to do fer Mis' Dillard. Won't ye rest yourself, Luke?"

"I'll be goin' along. I've got a right smart o' travelin' afore me."

"Kin you see, Luke, an' you no lantern?" Ivy called after him.

A soft laugh returned. "I don't need no lantern, Ivy. I kin see of a night same as a varmint."

CHAPTER SIX

OLD MAG'S GAUNT sway-back figure towered above the stooped figure of another elderly woman halting beside her in the road above Ivy's cabin, a woman whose head, like Old Mag's, was bare, and whose light print dress stood out starchily below a black sweater she wore.

"Hain't ye ready?" Old Mag shouted down, a little impatiently. Old Mag was slightly arrogant when offices for the dead, in which she always bore an important part, were to be performed. "Ivy, hain't ye ready?" she called again.

"You an' Mis' Philips jest go on along," Ivy shouted back. "I'll be there directly. I have obliged to fix fer Enoch—somethin' fer his dinner."

Old Mag made a movement to proceed, but the other woman gave a slight detaining jerk to Mag's apron. "We'll wait," she called down decisively. "You don't need to fix nothin', Ivy. Let Enoch stay at my place whilst you're away."

"Mis Philips is allays so kind to a body," flashed through Ivy, "an' she's got plenty sand in her craw, too!"

"You're shore," she called back, "Enoch won't be no trouble to Novy?"

"Let the child go stay with Adam an' Simon Peter. He'll be no bother."

The river was still shrouded with mist, but presently, as the women walked along, bands of gold and blue appeared in the east. Though there had been snow only two days before, it was almost like an early morning in summer.

When they reached Doke Odum's, Leola appeared at the cabin door, a dirty child in her arms and other ragged dirty children peeping from behind her. Leola, her dusky hair hanging around her soft round face, returned a languid "Howdy" to the greeting of the three women passing on the road above.

Old Mag nodded backward after they had passed the cabin. "Leoly 'ull be down afore long, jedging from looks. I don't reckon Doke has ever give ye a copper, has he, Mis' Philips, fer all them young uns o' hisn you've brung afore this!"

Mrs. Philips's rather hard black eyes, set in a network of fine lines, had begun to twinkle. "I reckon I 'ull go," she answered evasively, "same as allays, when Doke comes a-peckin' on my door."

The women picked their way carefully along the rough road, Old Mag stalking a short distance in advance, and Mrs. Philips, her eyes bent on the ground, her smooth black hair shining like crows' wings in the morning sun, hobbling along beside Ivy. They said very little. With the solemn errand on which they were going it was not fitting to talk much. And Ivy herself was further subdued at the thought of those she should meet soon, of the others who would come to help, or to pay their silent respects to the dead woman. "I made my brags," she said to herself a trifle bitterly, "an' now I'm back agin!"

Close by the road a cardinal burst into a loud jubilant whistle. "The first I've heern," Ivy said. "Don't hit sound good?" When they had gone a little farther she called the older women's attention to a field they were passing: "Look, the grass is a-startin' to green!" She bent down some hickory sprouts, examining the tips of the branches. "Hickory buds is a-startin' to swell, shore as you're born!" Each new sign of spring drew some expression from her, but the older women continued silent except to remark, from long habit, on the footprints they came upon in the road. "This is Luke. . . . Doke's been along. . . . A mule's shoe—too small fer a horse. . . . Some varmint's tracks."

Opposite the Dillard cabin, which sat close to the road, was a rough shed, on the river-bank, its open doors revealing a small forge. The women halted in front of the shed, taking counsel together in subdued voices.

"She won't never in Gawd's world keep till day atter tomorrow, ef you ask me," Old Mag said, with a toss of her head.

"Reckon we orter name hit to Uncle Abel?" asked Ivy.

"We'd best say nothin'," Mrs. Philips decided. "Hit hain't a-goin' to stay like this." She pointed to the sky. "Mares' tails—apt as not hit 'ull weather afore night."

A slight young girl, mincing on high heels, received them at the open door of the cabin. Her hair was bobbed and her skirt, town-fashion, was knee length. To the women's whispered "How are ye, Bertha Jane?" she answered: "Well enough, I reckon," smiling and setting out chairs, though her eyes were red and there were yellow channels marked where the tears had coursed down her small heavily powdered face.

The floor was still damp from a recent scrubbing. A cat was curled on the hearth, and four small boys, nearly of a size and all in clean overalls, stood around bashfully in the dusky room, bare except for its two beds, the splint bottom chairs, and the home-made baskets hanging, together with some ears of corn, from the rafters. On one of the beds a white mound was outlined through the sheet that was drawn over it.

The women took their places in the circle of chairs around the fireplace, from which a half-burned log emitted a faint light. From time to time Mrs. Philips got up, went to the little front porch, and spat off it, into the road. Old Mag spat into the ashes. Old Mag took down her wisp of hair, holding the hairpins in her mouth, then twisted it up again. The little boys shifted their feet uneasily. A rooster crowed. The only other sounds were of the river's endless seething murmur through the open door and of Bertha Jane's quiet weeping.

When they had sat thus for some time, Mrs. Philips rose and pushed back her chair. "Have you-uns had breakfast, Bertha Jane?"

Faintly: "Yes, we have."

Mrs. Philips raised her eyebrows meaningly. "Wesley, Matthew, Isaac—all you boys, run out."

Ivy wiped her eyes, got up, and tiptoed, as though she might disturb the dead woman under the sheet, across the room to Bertha Jane, putting her arm around the girl's slight shoulders and whispering: "Don't cry, Bertha Jane! Your mammy's better off." Then she tiptoed out the back door and through the back porch to the kitchen. Near the stove sat a heavy-set man in blue overalls and a blue work-shirt, his head in his hands, a large round head, with scanty brown hair standing up like bristles. "How are ye, Ivy?" he greeted her in a purring womanish voice. "You have your health, I hope." His broad smooth face wore a curiously placid look, though his low brow was deeply furrowed. He was barely fifty, yet everyone called him Uncle Abel, as though he were aged. "Ivy," he said now, "I'm a poor widdy man!" His tears started afresh.

Ivy sat down on a bench beside the table covered with oilcloth, from which the breakfast dishes and some remnants of food had not yet been cleared.

The bereaved man lifted his head again. "I aimed to git her some squirrels, fer soup."

"Squirrel soup is the best," Ivy answered mournfully, "when a body cain't take nothin' else."

"Afore I could git her the squirrels, she were gone."

"She were a good woman, Mis' Dillard," Ivy murmured, after a pause. "She were peaceable. She didn't never say nothin' agin no one."

"She were a Christian, Ivy."

"Law, yes. There hain't nothin' to torment ye, Mr. Dillard."

"She brung up her children right."

"Law, I reckon."

"They've all professed but the least one—all but Isaac." After a pause: "She were the workin'est woman."

Ivy nodded. "She were a hard-workin' woman, Mis' Dillard. She allays kep' everything nice."

"Ivy, looks like the trouble that's on me is more 'an I kin bear."

"You're a-havin' one more time in *this* world, Mr. Dillard."

"Roosevelt, he died, jest when the boy were gittin' up to be some size. Short, I cain't look fer him to be no help to me, his leg took off in the mines; an' now my woman a-dyin' on me—hit's more 'an I kin bear!" He wept aloud.

Ivy waited awhile, then, starting to clear the table, ventured softly: "I reckon there 'ull be folks a-comin', Mr. Dillard. I'd best be a-gittin' these here dishes outen the way an' start a-fixin' fer dinner."

The bereaved man sighed deeply, but got up with an air of relief and, saying he would show her where she could find things, tiptoeing, led the way to the cellar, his boots creaking.

Ivy glanced around at the crocks covered with clean cloths or paper, at the glass jars filled with canned fruit or vegetables, at the barrels of sauerkraut and the piles of potatoes and parsnips. "Hain't them nice taters," she said, "an' you've got a sight of 'em, Mr. Dillard, hit to be March."

"Several," he said, "but they're a-sproutin' bad. Ivy, you take ye some when you go."

"I'm afeared you cain't spare 'em," Ivy protested politely.

"I've got plenty to do me an' you too," he insisted. "I'll jest fix 'em fer ye now, whilst I have hit in mind," and he started filling a sack.

"Now, don't you give me so many, Mr. Dillard. You'll rob yourself."

He went on filling the sack, picking out the largest and soundest potatoes.

"Well, I thank ye fer 'em, Mr. Dillard. I thank ye terrible."

"You're more 'an welcome." Suddenly he straightened his bulky figure, his overalls bulging at the seams from the heavier clothing that in winter he wore underneath them. "Ivy, I'm a pore widdy man!"

Ivy drew back a step. She was a trifle alarmed at the way in which Uncle Abel was looking at her. She turned towards the steps leading up from the cellar.

"Ivy," he detained her, "don't buy ye no seed taters. I'll furnish 'em to ye gladly, when hit's time to plant. Now I want to show ye the meat." Squatting, he untied the white cloth that covered a big crock, exposing a further covering of lard. "Sausage," he said. Then, pointing to another crock: "Spareribs is in the crock yon. Here's middlin'," and he opened still another crock, taking from it a big slab of fat bacon.

"Law, hain't hit fine!" Ivy exclaimed, examining the piece of bacon, though she continued to feel uneasy.

"Hit's fine meat—fine!" Uncle Abel turned the piece of bacon from side to side, with solemn pride. "Them hogs was kilt when the sign were in the head, an' the moon were a-fullin'." He replaced the bacon. "Cook plenty, Ivy. I'm a pore man, but I want folks to have the best I've got. I want 'em to have plenty."

Ivy moved back and forth to the step-stove, on which were several pots she was watching. She was alone in the kitchen except for the hounds stretched under the table, and the hens that came and went through the open door. She rolled out the crust for the pies she was making.

"Hain't no need," she thought, "to think hard on Jim. I reckon Jim is sorry fer the way he done, or he wouldn't never 'a writ. Jim 'ull git him work at a loggin' camp, like he done afore. He 'ull come home ever' two or three weeks. Jim hain't a-goin' to get mixed up in no liquor business. Hain't no Ingoldsby has ever made liquor. Jim is a-wearied of the army. Jim hones to see the mountains agin, an' to hear the old river a-talkin' of a night. Jim is a-honin' to git back to these here hills an' hollows where he were raised up, an' where his fathers was raised up afore him. Jim is a-gittin' older now."

She was placing a pie in the oven when Mrs. Philips appeared at the door. "Ivy," the older woman said, clearing her throat, "would you fix her hairs? You're a better hand at sech as that 'an me or Mag."

Ivy wiped the flour from her arms. Standing between Old Mag and Mrs. Philips, she held to their hands, peering down at the dead woman, her face uncovered now. "Don't she look sweet?" Ivy said, her tears flowing.

As she was combing the dead woman's thin, faded hair, Bertha Jane came down the ladder from the loft with a bundle in her arms. "Hit's yaller," Bertha Jane whispered chokingly, holding out the bundle, "but mammy, she named hit to me—she wanted to be laid away in her weddin' dress."

Ivy took the crumpled dress, shaking it out for the others to see, a coarse muslin dress that had once been white, a dress with a full, long skirt and a little frill around the neck.

"Law, me, her weddin' dress!" Ivy exclaimed. "Who would 'a thought—? Don't cry, honey! I 'ull soak hit in buttermilk. Buttermilk 'ull make hit white as the driven snow, won't hit, Mis' Philips?"

People had begun to come. Uncle Abel sat by the hearth, his head in his hands, rousing himself to greet each new caller: "I'm a pore widdy man!"

At noon-time Ivy announced: "Hit's ready." Uncle Abel sat for a moment or so as though he had heard nothing, then sprang from his chair. "Well, let's eat"; and he led the way to the kitchen. Kinsmen and others from some distance away had arrived. With the family, they filled the benches on either side of the long table. Ivy, her face flushed with excitement, passed back and forth behind the benches, to and from the step-stove, urging: "Won't ye have more? Why, you hain't hardly et a bite!" There was a platter of boiled beans, with bacon arranged in thick slices on top of the beans, a platter of sausage cakes, heaping plates of both corn-bread and biscuits, boiled potatoes, mashed parsnips, a big bowl of pickled beets, another of sliced raw onions. There were pies and various sorts of jelly on the table, coffee and buttermilk.

Bent over their plates, the guests, like the family, ate silently, slowly but diligently. From time to time different ones would sit back and rest, then start eating again, sopping up the last of the soup from their beans with a piece of corn-bread, polishing the plate, when they were through, until it shone as if it had already been washed, licking and sucking their fingers to clean them.

"I'm plumb foundered," Old Mag grunted as she got up from the bench. "I hain't et sech a meal—Lord knows when! I hain't been peert the enemy's durin' winter. Seems like I cain't keep more 'an a mouthful o' victuals on my stomick."

As the day wore on, more and more people came; timid women with rosy-cheeked flaxen-haired babies in their arms and rosy-cheeked flaxen-haired children, shy as rabbits, trailing behind. Young men came, in canvas leggings and khaki breeches left over from the war; aged men with wild hair, leaning on their hickory sticks; a handful of men in the prime of life. Across the road, in front of the little smithy, the men and boys, all in clean overalls and clean blue work-shirts—in their Sabbath cleanliness— gathered in little knots, whittling, talking together in low tones.

The women, their children clinging to them, on Old Mag's query: "Would you-all like to review the remains?" one by one approached the bed, looking down sorrowfully, speechlessly, at the dead woman, then stood around in the dusky room, giving way noiselessly as others arrived at the cabin.

"Don't she look natural?" Mrs. Philips would mutter to each one, out of the corner of her mouth, set tight, to hold the snuff-stick—"jest like she could speak!" Old Mag, with suppressed excitement, would whisper:

"Porest corpse ever I seed! Nothin' but the hide an' bones! But she never had no meat on her no time, Mis' Dillard." Now and again during the afternoon Ivy would leave the kitchen, where she was baking cake, so that there should be abundant food for those who would sit up through the night, and take her turn at receiving the callers. "Don't she look sweet?" Ivy would say each time she led someone to view the dead woman, moved each time to fresh tears. "An' don't you know," Ivy would whisper, "she's a-goin' to be buried in her weddin' dress! I've done put hit to bleach. Her weddin' dress! Hain't hit the pitifulest thing ever you heern?"

With Old Mag and Mrs. Philips, Ivy shared the importance of being in charge. Already she was losing a little of the smart from her brief, bitter stay in town. When one and another remarked: "Law, Ivy, you're a-lookin' plumb puny! Seems like town hain't agreed with ye much," Ivy could meet them lightly with: "I'm pore, but I'm peert." When Alf Bunts, half drunk, said slyly: "Well, Ivy, I see you're back in the sticks agin with us pore folks. Did ye quit off your job in town fer good?" she answered without hesitation, her head high: "Law, no, Alf, I hain't quit. I reckon I 'ull go back when fall o' the year comes. Hit were a fine place where I were a-livin' at—a widdy woman, an' her rich. Hardly a thing to do. Law, yes, the old lady treated us like we was kin. But a-comin' spring like hit is, I couldn't stand hit to be shet up in no town."

Towards the end of the day Ivy went out to the front porch and stood in the dusk. Those who had called through the day were gone. Mist was gathering on the river, and it was beginning to drizzle. Suddenly she was aware of Doke Odum coming up the road with his swift soft-footed gait, like a fox. "Where's the old granny-woman?" he asked abruptly, as he reached the steps. "Where's Mis' Philips?"

"Forevermore, hit hain't Leoly—?"

Doke nodded. "She were took a hour back."

Mrs. Philips raised her eyebrows when she saw Doke. She spat off the porch, into the road. "One goes," she said, "another comes."

The drizzle turned to rain. Ivy and Old Mag still stood on the porch, their eyes following the bowed figure of Mrs. Philips, her apron over her head, as she disappeared down the road, behind Doke.

"Hit allays rains," Ivy remarked solemnly, "atter a person dies."

Old Mag nodded. "Hit don't never fail. I've studied about hit a heap o' times."

Ivy had placed the remains of various dishes left from dinner and supper on the table, covering them with a white cloth. It was raining hard now and the steady downpour on the kitchen roof, together with the dim light from the one small lamp, made her sleepy. Her thoughts dwelt dreamily on Jim. "I've got Enoch, but he hain't enough. Seems like a woman has got to have her a man, an' him clost, to keep her from bein' lonesome." Suddenly an overpowering craving for the man she had known as lover and husband came upon her. "Jim done me wrong, ay, Lord! But ef Jim Ingoldsby was to come a-walkin' in, I couldn't never in God's world stand out agin him!"

Bolt upright in her chair, she woke some time during the night to a sound of voices singing mournfully. The wind had risen. She could hear the trees tossing. She could hear Old Mag's voice, above the wind, above the rain and the dull roar of the river, above the voices of the others:

I'm a-goin' home, I'm a- goin' home,
I'm a-goin home to die no more.

The mourners had started another hymn:

Jest as I am, without one plea,
But that Thy blood was shed for me.

Old Mag's voice rose again, higher and higher, wilder and wilder:

O Lamb of God, I come! I come!

The wind was tearing up the river now, howling and moaning, lashing itself to a fury, drowning the voices of the mourners and shaking the cabin. Ivy had jumped up to join the others in the front of the cabin when Luke Diggs was almost blown into the room, the door slamming behind him.

"I 'lowed you might be afeard, Ivy," he said, with a quiet reassuring smile that revealed his glistening teeth. He was a sturdy fellow, with deep dark eyes, with rich color and finely carved features. "Hit's a right smart storm," he said. "Hit's a-turnin' cold, too, an', Ivy, I see you're in need of wood."

"Luke Diggs," Ivy said to herself as Luke disappeared outside, "Luke is the on'y man-person ever I knowed where 'ud stir hisself to help womenfolks."

Returning with an armful of wood, the young man announced that the rain had turned to sleet. "March fer shore," he smiled. He dried himself at the step-stove and drank the hot coffee that Ivy poured for him.

"A body gits plumb faint," Ivy said, "when they set up of a night."

Luke sat with her for a while. The roar of the storm gradually died down, but the sleet kept slapping, like wet fingers, against the little kitchen window. Luke related some of his experiences during the war. "But I were never as skeert," he said, "of them shells a-bustin' an' like o' that as I were aforehand, a-studyin' about havin' to cross the water—fur as a man's eye kin reach, nothin' but water."

He left quietly as the door opened to admit a scrawny young woman about Ivy's own age, Luke's sister, but with no resemblance to him.

"Have ye a piece o' cake, Molly," Ivy said, as Luke slipped out of the room.

"Hit's nice," Molly said. "I reckon you made hit, Ivy." But suddenly, clutching her flat breast, she turned to face Ivy, staring at her out of her red-rimmed protuberant eyes. "Gid Rider an' Novy Philips is a-talkin', hain't they? Reckon they 'ull marry?"

"You cain't never tell," Ivy said.

"Allays a-studyin'," Ivy thought, "about marryin'. Pore old Molly!"

"Have ye another cup o' coffee, Molly, an' some o' this here dried-apple pie."

With an abrupt movement the girl gripped Ivy's shoulder, staring into her face again. "Ivy, I reckon Uncle Abel 'ull be atter ye afore long."

Ivy drew back, her face reddening. "Molly, how kin you name sech as that?—his woman, her hardly cold yit!"

"Hit won't be no time," the girl persisted, her weak but burning eyes still fixed on Ivy's face, "afore Uncle Abel is a-settin' out. Looks like a widdy man cain't never wait no time afore he's a-puttin' flowers in his hat, afore he's a-startin' to hunt him another woman."

It was Gid that opened the door now, Molly slinking out of the room as he entered.

"Molly Diggs is a-wastin' away," Gid laughed, "'cause she cain't git her no man."

"Molly, she's a-grievin' herself to death," Ivy said, "an' all fer that old drunken sot Alf Bunts, an' him a-gettin' him a new girl ever' change o' the moon."

"Molly, she 'ud take any man she could git," Gid said, sitting down at the table and beginning to eat hungrily of the dishes Ivy placed before him. "Boys, I wouldn't be left alone with that 'ere woman fer nothin' on earth."

Gid got up and stretched himself, smiling lazily, rubbing his stomach with satisfaction, then settled himself beside the stove, tilting back against the wall and thrusting out his long legs. "I'm a pore widdy man!" he mocked Uncle Abel, doubling up with laughter.

"Gid, hain't ye shamed!" Ivy tried not to laugh.

"Lord, Ivy, a blind man kin see—why, that old man is atter you right now!"

"Gid, quit off your foolishness! Hit's plumb shameful, his woman, her not put in the ground yit!" Ivy felt at once a little shocked, amused, and vaguely resentful. "You know good an' well I hain't got me no divorce," she murmured, "an' you needn't to think," she added, "I'm a-goin' to take my ducks, as the sayin' is, to no sech market, nohow."

"Hit's a-comin' day," Uncle Abel said, coming into the kitchen a few moments later, and Gid, with a mischievous backward glance, left Ivy alone with Uncle Abel.

Uncle Abel said he would feed his mules. He took his cap from the nail where it was hanging, pulling it down around his face. His cap was sprinkled with white when he returned. "Hit's a-snowin'," he said. "Hit 'ull be a rough trip."

"Law, yes."

Uncle Abel sat down by the stove, rubbing his leg, waiting for the biscuits that Ivy had put in the oven to bake for his breakfast. "I'm bothered a right smart," he said, "with this here leg a-crampin' on me. The veins is swole till looks like they'd bust. I've laid off to ketch me a eel."

"Law, a eel-skin is fine fer cramps," Ivy said.

"A body to bind a eel-skin around his leg, hit a-crampin', an' there hain't nothin' better."

"Law, no." Ivy poured a cup of coffee and placed it beside Uncle Abel's plate.

"Them rubber stockin's the doctor wants a body to wear," Uncle Abel said, "they hain't nothin' to a eel-skin, fer cramps."

"Law, a eel-skin is 'way yonder better, fer cramps."

"I'm a pore man," Uncle Abel sighed, between mouthfuls, "but I want to put her away nice. Ivy, you look atter things."

"I'll do what I kin, Mr. Dillard."

"I 'ull be in the dark, more 'an apt, a-gittin' in."

"I'll look atter things the best I know."

"Cain't no person do no more." Uncle Abel had risen heavily from the bench and was pulling on his mittens. "Ivy—"

Ivy was intent on setting knives and forks around the table for those who would eat breakfast when day broke.

"Ivy, you've had a right hard time a-gittin' along, hain't ye?"

Ivy tossed her head slightly. "I'm a-makin' hit, Mr. Dillard," she said. She kept on moving around the table, picking up the molasses-jug, then the sugar-bowl, and setting them down again. "I reckon I kin keep on a-makin' hit."

"Yes," Uncle Abel said, in his soft purring voice. "Yes—but a woman has need of a man, Ivy, same as a man has need of a woman."

With a sharp sense of relief, Ivy heard steps approaching, and Old Mag threw back the door, stalking into the room, lurching awkwardly from side to side. Old Mag was yawning; her eyes were hollow from lack of sleep. "Hain't hit most day?" she asked.

"Well," Uncle Abel said, "I reckon I 'ull be a-gittin' started."

Chapter Seven

IT WAS A few days after her return from the Dillards', and Ivy was busily papering the cabin with discarded newspapers she had collected in town. Enoch stood by to help, spelling out words in the papers that were low enough for him to read and studying the pictures that enlivened some of them. With newspapers tacked on the log walls, darkened with age and wood-smoke, the cabin seemed brighter and cleaner.

"Mammy," Enoch would stop her now and again, "you've got this-here one upside down. A body cain't read it this-a-way."

"Oh, shucks!" Ivy would respond impatiently. "Hit don't make no difference. Hand me them brads." She would change the paper, however, according to the little boy's suggestion.

"It ain't 'hit,' Mammy. It's '*it*,'" Enoch would correct her, and "Oh, shucks!" Ivy would say again. "You must 'a been settin' on a grindstone, to git so sharp—a little brat like you a-tellin' his mammy how she orter speak!" But in her heart she was proud of Enoch's increasing knowledge. It had been a bitter disappointment not to be able to enter him in school while they were in town. On the little she had earned, it had been impossible to buy Enoch both school-books and proper clothing. There was no use in sending the child to school now. Country school would soon be over for the year. Anyway, Enoch's feet were almost on the ground. Through the summer, of course, he could go barefoot, and by fall she would have saved enough, somehow or other, to buy new shoes and overalls for the little boy as well as his school-books. There would be a geography to buy in the fall. "Geographies, them's big books—I reckon they costs a heap," she was thinking, her brow unconsciously gathered into a pucker, as she stood on a chair, hammering the newspapers into place.

Early and late now she darned and patched her own and Enoch's few clothes. She had had little time to mend during her weeks at the factory and at the poultry-house, and at the old woman's big house she had hardly had a moment to herself from the time she was up in the morning till she had dropped into bed, dead tired, at night. Now she would sit by the small window in her cabin or on the little front porch, sewing stitch by stitch, in her slow painstaking way, making shirts for Enoch, perhaps, out of some remnants she had bought in town, or fashioning chemises for herself out of the flour-sacks she had been saving. "Them shifts a body kin buy in a store—they hain't no manner of account, fer wearin'."

Sometimes she would sit on the porch for an hour or more at a time, her hands idle in her lap, her gaze unfocused. The months in town had taken something out of her and she enjoyed these hours when she looked off vacantly towards the road or towards the river and the mountains, listening dreamily to the soft singing of the pines, to the endless murmur of the river, to the piping of the hylas, those "singing frogs" that had come with the first warm hazy days of spring.

But everyone now was beginning to get the ground ready for sowing and planting.

Both her garden-plot and the steep field across from her cabin, which she had always planted with corn, needed more, Ivy realized, than the shallow scratching with a hoe she had given them year after year. The earth needed to be turned up deeply again, as in Uncle Jake's day. Maybe, she thought one day, she could get Doke Odum to do a little plowing for her. . . . Best not go empty-handed . . .

She built a fire and made some potato soup, carrying a bowl of it, while it was still hot, down the road to Doke's cabin. Three or four rickety hound pups ran out from under the cabin as she came through the gate, and a swarm of shy and ragged children met her at the door.

"Leoly, I brung ye some tater soup," she greeted the young mother, lying back on a dirty pillow, the few days' babe at her breast, and in one hand a soiled and tattered magazine from which she had been reading, while other tattered magazines were scattered around on the dirty patch-work quilt that covered the bed.

"Git ye a cheer, Ivy," Leola responded languidly.

"Hit hain't so nice, Leoly, as I *have* made," Ivy apologized, "but I didn't have no milk. You don't supposed to make tater soup with water."

Leola turned her soft dark eyes towards the visitor and with her free hand, picking up the magazine, with its highly colored cover, which she had laid down when Ivy came in, held it out. "Ivy, did you ever read one o' these here 'confession magazines,' as they calls 'em?"

Ivy glanced through the magazine hurriedly, then replaced it on the tousled bed. "I hain't got no turn," she said, "fer readin'."

"The stories in 'em is grand," Leola said, a slight warmth creeping into her voice.

"I hain't no hand to read," Ivy said, "I don't never spend no time a-readin'." She took the tiny infant from Leola's arms, rocking it back and forth in the straight splint-bottom chair, crooning to it and smelling of its soft flesh. "Don't hit's little hide smell the sweetest!" she said. She seldom visited Leola except in time of child-birth or other illness. The squalid cabin was more repugnant to her even than Odie's. Its stench almost took her breath away. Then Leola—the moon-faced creamy-skinned Leola, with her soft unsmiling dark eyes, her inert unresponsive ways—Leola puzzled her.

Ivy set about cleaning up the cabin now, with the help of Ibbie, the oldest little girl. She swept both the cabin and the yard, washed a pile of dirty dishes she found, and then washed the children's faces and necks, covered with sores, and combed their matted hair.

"Leoly," she called across the room, "I 'ull jest rub some lamp oil on Ruby's an' Opal's little scalps—"

"I hain't a-carin'," Leola acquiesced in a far-away voice. She had resumed her reading, her snowy and swollen breast, as she suckled the new-born babe again, a patch of light amidst the dusk of the bed.

"Their hairs has got a right smart o' nits on 'em," Ivy called again— "little Noey's, too.—Hit 'ull kill 'em, shore as jedgment day, nits an' all," she encouraged the children, each in turn under her thoroughgoing hands. "Pore little young uns," she said to herself, "a-clawin' theirselves to death!" and aloud: "Cedar branches, to boil 'em an' take the water, hit's good, too, fer head-lice.—Hold still, Noey," as little Noah squirmed "—hit hain't a-goin' to smart ye more 'an a minute."

In the midst of her efforts Doke came in. "I reckon you're a-findin' a whole hog-killin' of little travelers, hain't ye, Ivy?" he rallied her. He had been up Josiah Creek, sent for to shave Uncle Rutt Bigg, who had died during the night. "Uncle Rutt were a-gittin' up in years," Doke commented cheerfully now, looking around for his banjo. "Uncle Rutt, he were risin' ninety." Sprawling by the open door, with holes gaping in his shoes and his bare bony legs showing between his overalls and his shoe-tops, Doke began to pick the banjo, his big bushy head resting against the doorjamb.

Guy, the oldest boy, who had been to mill on the mare, came limping in now, carrying a sack of meal on his hunched shoulder. A sallow, sullen boy, he dropped down by the door and began playing apathetically with one of the hound pups.

Little Noah crept up to his father, whispering something to him, and Doke straightway started singing in a loud voice, with great gusto:

> *Old Dan Tucker were a fine old man,*
> *He slapped his foot in the fryin'-pan,*
> *Combed his hair with the wagon-wheel,*
> *An' died with the toothache in his heel.*

Leola, in the dimmer and dimmer light, continued to read and to suckle the new-born babe intermittently, while Doke, after ordering Guy and little Noah to bring in some wood and a bucket of fresh water, went on picking the banjo, talking and joking with Ivy at the same time. "Ivy, I reckon Leoly 'ull waller in the bed long as them there confession magazines, as they calls 'em, holds out. I brung her home a whole corn-shuckin' of 'em, where the summer people had throwed 'em out with their trash. But I don't reckon I orter never let Leoly git a bait of 'em. Hit's like a dog a-gittin' a taste o' sheep.—You're a-goin' to stay to eat, hain't ye, Ivy?"

"No, Enoch's a-lookin' fer me, an' I don't want to be in the night a-gittin' my wood.—I'm glad, Leoly, you're a-mendin' up. Now, don't ketch ye a cold an' git the weed. Hain't nothin' worse 'an a bealed breast. Doke, ef you kin git around to hit, would ye plow my field, hit an' my garden-patch?"

"First chancet I kin git."

"They're a-needin' hit bad."

"Ef I live an' nothin' don't happen."

"They're a-cryin' for the plow."

"Ef nothin' don't happen to hinder me."

CHAPTER EIGHT

SOMETIMES SOMEONE WOULD pass as Ivy worked in her garden, hoeing or smoothing off the soil and gathering the stones that Doke had turned up with the plow into neat little piles. The passer-by would stop and visit across the garden palings, old palings, green with lichens, rotting away, fallen down in places.

"Ivy, you hain't saw my cow, have ye?"

"Law, no, Mis' Dodd."

"I 'lowed she might 'a come down apast here, a-seekin' her some green stuff."

"I hain't saw hide or hair of her."

"She hain't been milked sence day afore yesterday."

"Law, me, she 'ull be plumb ruint ef she hain't milked afore long."

"Ivy, Pernie Botts an' Shell Henson, they fit—hit were a week Wednesday. They fit till they was down, till they was bloody as hogs."

"The Lord help my time!"

"Hain't you heern?"

"I hain't heern no tell."

"Shell, he's bigged Pernie, an' Pernie, she named hit to him they orter marry, an' he denied her. But Pernie, she put son of a bitch on Shell, an' won't no man stand fer that."

"Law, no, won't no man stand fer that."

"Ivy, you've got a right good spot fer your garden."

"Law, yes. Hit hain't much level. Hit's right sidlin', but the sun hits hit so fair."

49

"Aunt Jinny Lowdy, she's got lettuce up."

"Forevermore!"

"Hit's up nice. Mis' Richardson, up Josiah, she's got fifteen little young chicks hatched out."

"I do know, hatched a'ready! Well, she 'ull lose a right smart of 'em. Hit 'ull turn off cold agin."

"There 'ull be snow agin. I've knowed hit to snow when onions was shoe-high. . . . Ivy, have you sowed your beets?"

"I don't never sow 'em till Good Friday."

"I hain't sowed mine. . . . Ivy, I see your peach-trees is a-buddin'."

"Law, yes, the buds is a-swellin'. I'm afeared they're a-goin' to put out, an' then git nipped. I was in hopes hit 'ud be a good year fer fruit."

"Well, I 'ull be goin' along."

"Won't you stay fer dinner, Mis' Dodd?"

"No, I 'ull be scramblin' along. I might find her yon side the ridge, in one of them fur hollers, or somewhars down in the bottom. . . . Ivy, you come to see me."

"Yes, you come agin, Mis' Dodd. You come when you kin stay all day."

Chapter Nine

AFTER DARK, IVY could see the glow-worms now, shining among the chips around her chopping-block. She could hear the turtles, their brief shrill song sounding ever and again above the sweet piping of the singing frogs. All the little living things of the woods and of the old fields, of the river and the full-flowing creeks, were waking up.

One day Ivy and Old Mag, bare-headed, each in her gingham apron, each with a sack and a short-bladed knife, hunted together, as they had often done before, up and down the rich shadowy hollows, along the little streams, beside the worn foot-paths and the rough deep-furrowed roads—tasting, smelling, searching for wild greens.

"Law, Mag, won't me an' you have us a good dinner today!" Ivy exclaimed, when she had almost filled her sack. The potatoes Uncle Abel had given her had been a welcome addition to her scanty, fast-vanishing store of food, but she craved something more—something green, with a bitter tang.

"Hain't nothin' better," Old Mag said, as, squatting every few feet, she went on digging and cutting "—hain't nothin' kin beat a mess o' squirrel's ear, hit mixed with tongue-grass, an' this here narrow-leaf dock."

On another day they went together to gather the tender young shoots of poke, and again to a stream some distance away where watercress grew abundantly. "Law, Mag, hain't these creeses the finest ever you see!" Ivy would keep exclaiming, reassured by each fresh manifestation of the bounty of nature. "Hain't they the nicest!"

On one of these excursions, homeward-bound, they sat down to rest when they had come to the parting of their ways. The bank on which they sat was starred with anemones. Blood-root everywhere held up its snowy chalice among the ferns, and spring beauties with their painted petals swayed daintily from the rocks in the gentle April breeze. Beneath their feet the turf was studded with violets. Here and there on the steep slopes, half wooded, half cleared, which hemmed in the hollow that opened in front of them, a purple-rose cloud—the flowering branches of red-bud—floated among the still naked woods. Below them, at the bottom of the hollow, a weeping willow, touched by the sun, stood forth, a cascade of foaming green that partly hid Old Mag's dilapidated log spring-house. A wild plum-tree whitened with its powdery blossoms the shadowy slope that rose behind Old Mag's cabin. No other cabin was in sight, but through a wedge-shaped gap in the intricately lapping knobs the mountains appeared, deep blue, with fragments of pearly cloud clinging to their summit.

There was no sound save the faint far-off tinkle of a cowbell, the exultant cackle now and then of one of Old Mag's small flock of fowls.

Ivy and Old Mag sat without talking, drinking in gratefully the sweet April air.

"Law, Mag, hain't everything pretty!" Ivy broke the silence. "Mag," she said, "I 'ud as soon to be a-layin' up in Bane's Buryin' Ground, as to think I had obliged to live out my time in town."

Old Mag nodded. "I couldn't never be satisfied, me, in nary town on earth."

"I 'ud sooner be dead, 'way yonder, the grave-vine a-growin' on my grave—I 'ud sooner be a-rottenin' in the ground, as to think I had obliged to set at a machine all day, shet up in one of them wearisome old factories, a-stitchin,' from day-light till dark, an' hit jest to live."

Chapter Ten

"LAW, ENOCH, LOOK—Mis' Byrd's golden bells and quince roses is both a-bloomin'," Ivy exclaimed, pointing to some shrubs, gay with scarlet and yellow blossoms, blooming inside the weather-beaten picket fence that enclosed a small yard around the Byrds' cabin. It was the first time Ivy had been to the Byrds' since her return from town.

"Mis' Byrd, she 'ull be a-thinkin' hard on hit," Ivy had reflected earlier in the day, "ef I don't go down afore long."

As she unfastened the gate, half a dozen hound pups ran out from underneath a low porch that ran across the front of the cabin, setting up a deafening clamor. At the same moment little boys and girls began to appear from everywhere, shy, tow-headed children with scarlet lips and cheeks and turquoise eyes; and a plump, comely, still rather young-looking woman, with fair skin and thinning fair hair, came to the door. She held a fat rosy-cheeked babe in her arms, and her light print dress was open, exposing a billowy bosom.

"Why, praise the Lord, ef hit hain't Ivy! Hit's a time an' a time since I seen you a-comin' through that gate. I've been a-studyin' about hit, Ivy—I 'lowed you was miffed. Well, come on in! I shore am proud to see ye! You young uns take Enoch down about the barn to play. Me an' Ivy wants to have us a good visit. Now, watch out about the river, don't git too venture-some, an' don't none o' you little fellers git to quarrelin'," she called after the barefoot troop that had started stragglingly towards the barn. "Children is the most precuriousest things," she said, setting out a splint-bottom chair for Ivy in the big, bare, dusky room, with its three beds, each covered with a patchwork quilt. "There hain't none o' my twelve like t' other, an' seems like they don't none of 'em never want to play alike." She watched them a moment longer from the doorway, still holding the babe to her breast. "Woodrow Wilson, he run a rusty nail in his foot, in deep, but hit's a-gittin' better." She indicated a boy about Enoch's size, limping after the rest. "I greased the nail with fat meat an' hidden hit, an' the fever went outen his foot right now."

"Law, I reckon. Hit don't never fail, ef you greases the nail good."

Ivy clucked to the babe, turning its bald head occasionally to smile at her foolishly, then ducking again into its mother's capacious bosom. Mrs. Byrd sat tilted back against the open door, where she could command the stretch of ground that lay between the cabin and the river. "Seems like I'm kinder skeary about the children," she said, "sence Buck got his eye put out with that there stick o' dynamite."

"Law, I reckon."

"Wash an' Buck, they allays keeps 'em some dynamite, to dynamite the fish, what time the fish hain't a-bitin', but I won't let none o' the little ones play with hit no more. Looks like I'm a-gittin' nervous. I hate hit the worst, Buck a-havin' to go all the days of his life, him with on'y one eye."

"Buck's got him a Ford, hain't he?" Ivy remarked after a pause, in which the gurgling sound of the babe drawing in its mother's milk mingled with the muffled gurgle of the river.

"Who were a-tellin' ye, Ivy?"

"Law, the country's a-ringin' with hit!"

"Buck, seems like he's awful well pleased with his job in town, an' Wash, he's a-wantin' to git to town now, but I hain't give in fer him to go. I cain't spare 'em both, their pap at the loggin' camp, an' him not a-gittin' home more 'an every two or three months. A man cain't make a livin' fer his family, Ivy, offen these here old knobs, an' a little bit o' bottom land—not the size o' ourn. Looks like a man has obliged to go away, to support his family, without he makes liquor. An' a woman," she added, after a silence of some length, "a woman cain't see no peace ef her man's a-makin' liquor. But hit's hard, hain't hit, Ivy," she said after another ruminating pause, "fer a man to have to go away from home to look atter his family?"

"I reckon hit is!"

Mrs. Byrd laid the baby, asleep now, on one of the beds.

"I hear Wash a-comin' by of a night, a'most ever' night," Ivy ventured at last, "him a-singin'." Her heart had begun to beat a little more quickly. She wanted to warn Mrs. Byrd that Godfrey Tipton had made threats against

Wash if Wash didn't stay away from his half-witted daughter, Theta, and that now Wash was making threats against Godfrey. "But I reckon I 'ud best say nothin'," she reflected. "Mis' Byrd, she won't never hear no cheep agin one of her children. Hit 'ud be fire to tow ef I was to name hit to her about Wash an' Theta."

"I reckon Wash, he's been to some frolic," Ivy said.

Mrs. Byrd's shining face had clouded. "I hope Wash, he hain't a-gittin' into no devilment, a-runnin' of a night."

Suddenly both women looked up, their faces brightening, as a tall slender girl, her flaxen hair bobbed and waving around her delicately modeled face, came in from the adjoining room. She had the scarlet lips of the younger children, their turquoise eyes, and their rosy cheeks, only hers were a fainter rose.

"Linsey," her mother said, "go fetch the quilt you're a-piecin'."

"Hit shore is a pretty pattern," Ivy said, examining the quilt with interest. "There hain't no pattern no prettier 'an the Ocean Wave. I'm a-makin' me a new quilt, too, what time I kin get—a Road to Californy an' Back."

"Linsey, go fetch your Windin' Blade an' your Lost Sheep—fetch 'em both," her mother suggested now, and, as the girl disappeared: "Linsey, she's patched her five."

"Why, Linsey's got her plenty quilts to marry on," Ivy laughed.

"Linsey hain't a-studyin' nothin' on earth about marryin'," her mother came back quickly, adding in an undertone: "Linsey, she's got an idee of boardin' in town this fall an' goin' to high school. Linsey's got very good primary learnin', but seems like primary learnin' don't satisfy a heap o' the children this day an' time."

Linsey took her place now beside the older women, and after a little further talk on quilts and patchwork Mrs. Byrd proposed they go look at the garden.

"Ivy, look at my onions. Hain't they a-growin' nice? I raised 'em big as a pint cup last year, an' I've got a right smart o' sets left from plantin' . . . Lord, Ivy, don't thank me! Don't nothin' never grow ef you thank a body fer hit!—I 'ull put the sets in a poke fer ye. But you hain't a-goin' to go yit," she added quickly, "you an' Enoch is a-goin' to stay fer supper. Why, bless the Lord, I hope I don't begrudge you an' Enoch a mess o' victuals!"

They walked towards the little log barn.

"Ivy, reco'nize that hen?" Mrs. Byrd asked, when they came to the barn-lot. "Hit's that nice old gentle blue, useter be yourn, an' she's a-wantin' to set. Ivy, you pack her along with ye, when you-uns go."

"Law, Mis' Byrd—"

"You pack her with ye, honey, an' the partridge rock over yon—she's one o' yourn, an' she's a-wantin' to set, too."

"Law, Mis' Byrd—" Tears stood in Ivy's eyes. "Law, Mis' Byrd, I 'ull pay ye!"

"You take you two settin's o' eggs when you go, an' don't name hit no more about no pay!"

Chapter Eleven

LATE ONE AFTERNOON Luke appeared at the gate holding up a string of small fish. "Yellow suckers, Ivy," he said with his quiet smile, "an' one of 'em's a red horse."

Ivy cooked the fish for supper, but a day or so later when she came upon Enoch hunting grampus for bait under the loose rocks in the garden, she said, without looking at him: "Hain't no use, Enoch, fer you to go a-fishin', without you want to throw 'em back in the river. Hain't no use fer ye to fetch no fish home. We hain't got ary speck of grease to fry 'em in."

Almost every night now, after Enoch went to bed, he would cry, saying he was hungry.

"Don't study nothin' about hit," Ivy would still him energetically. "You 'ull soon drap off to sleep," only to add a moment later, in a less sharp voice: "I reckon I kin git us some rations, somehow or other, afore long."

"Seems like my hairs is a-turnin' gray," sometimes she would say to herself, "a-studyin ef I kin make hit till I have some hens a-layin' an' stuff in the garden is a-bearin' an' I kin git me more work a-helpin' folks. But I 'ull go to see Mis' Philips," she thought, after one of these moments of despondency. "Mis' Philips, her cow's fresh. Ef the calf hain't a-takin' hit all, maybe she kin spare me a little milk."

It had rained gently all the night before. Mist still wreathed the tops of the mountains, the sky was shot with veiled opalescent color, and as Ivy climbed the ridge, banks of laurel and rhododendron that walled in the winding road sent down light showers of raindrops on her bare head.

She heard quail calling, a fresh dewy sound, startled and slightly anxious. The woods on either side of her resounded with the clear bubbling notes of the thrush. The fresh delicious scent of the rain-moistened earth was mingled with the faintly acrid scent of rotting leaves and logs, and the scent carried her back, half happily, half sadly, to her childhood in Rocky Hollow. She remembered other mornings like this; mornings when the pine-trees were shooting up their pale new growth, when the oak trees were beginning to uncurl their velvety new leaves, like tiny half-closed hands. She remembered other mornings when wild strawberries were white with bloom as they were now, when the burnished petals of buttercups shone, clear gold, in the grass, and the ferns were unfurling their fronds.

"I don't reckon heaven could be no prettier," she murmured to herself as she went along.

The flush of red-bud along the edge of the woods, vivid a few days since, was fading now, but dogwood blossoms lay like drifts of snow through the forest, while around the stumps of giant trees, the virgin timber which the loggers had cut years before, azaleas blazed in all their glory.

"Hain't no flower on earth no prettier," Ivy said aloud, breaking off a branch of the rosy azalea and twirling it in her fingers "—hain't none prettier 'an honeysuckle, without it's ivy."

Through rifts in the trees she could now and then catch glimpses of the river, farther and farther below, and across the river a tan or reddish patch was visible here and there where someone had cleared a little rectangular patch of steep land and plowed it, ready for corn.

After all, Ivy thought, things were not so bad as she had known them before. "The days is a-gettin' so much longer—a body don't hardly need no lamp oil. An' a body don't need no firewood, not of a day, ef they 'ull stir around. All a body needs, comin' the time of year hit is, is a little cookwood, an' they don't need much o' that ef they hain't got much o' nothin' to cook."

Mrs. Philips was churning on her little front porch.

"No, don't git me no cheer." Ivy sat down on the steps. "I come to see ef I could borrow your needle. I cain't sew with mine to do no good. Hit's bent, an' hit's rusty, too. Hain't that Gid an' Novy?" she asked, catching the sound of voices from inside the cabin.

The corners of Mrs. Philips's black eyes deepened into crinkles. "Novy's a-learnin' Gid to read. She 'lows she won't have her no man cain't read."

"Many a woman," Ivy said, "has learnt her man to read." She pictured Gid and Novy in the cabin together. All at once an image came up before her of an erect young man in soldier clothes, standing in her path, in the sugar grove, laughingly blocking her way. "Me in my bare feet," she thought, "an' them dirty." . . . Why should anyone tease her about an old man like Uncle Abel Dillard, an old man everyone poked fun at?

"I reckon," Ivy said, in an undertone, "Gid an' Novy 'ull marry this fall."

"I reckon."

"I reckon hit 'ull make a man o' Gid."

"I reckon. . . . Lord knows I'm a-hopin' so!" Mrs. Philips lifted the dasher from her churn to peer inside it, "Looks like hit's a-takin' the butter a time to come." Her light print dress stood out clean and stiff around the splint-bottom chair on which she was sitting; her black hair, parted like crows' wings to enclose her grim white face, shone with brushing, but a snuff-stick protruded as usual from a corner of her mouth, and her lips were stained. "Ivy," she said, in a low voice, "Ivy"—she glanced at the younger woman sharply, then dropped her eyes—"you hain't got no meat on ye this spring. I hain't never saw ye so pore."

"I'm pore," Ivy laughed, "but I'm peert!"

"I reckon, Ivy, you've saw a time sence you come back in."

"I hain't saw no easy time," Ivy laughed, nervously now.

"You hain't got no cow, Ivy, an' hit 'ull be a time yit afore your garden-stuff is ready to use on."

"Law, I reckon. Taters hain't even a-bloomin' yit."

"Ivy"—Mrs. Philips had stopped churning. "Ivy, me an' you's both got trouble on us."

"Law, yes, Mis' Philips, an' I were sorry to hear o' yourn."

"Him who listens not must feel. I named hit to Press agin an' agin he were a-gittin' too bold. Now he's a spendin' his time in the jail-house, an' Bruce an' Dave—I reckon you've heern—they has had to join the army to keep from gittin' there." She began to churn again. Accompanying the chug, chug of the churn and the swish of the milk was the muffled drone, coming through the open door, of Gid's voice reading, stopping to spell out words.

A hen flew out from underneath the cabin, cackling wildly. "A settin' hen," Mrs. Philips muttered, "is allays crazy, I reckon. Ivy—" she dropped her voice— "Ivy, could I git ye to pack a basket to town fer me, oncet or twicet a week?"

Ivy, her face suddenly crimson, gave a startled sidelong glance at the older woman.

"My feet's give out on me.— I 'ull pay ye well."

"Law, Mis' Philips, I hain't oneasy. I know you hain't in no ways short-handed—" Ivy continued to look towards the narrow stretch of plowed ground across the road from the cabin, to the woods whitened with dogwood on the ridge that rose behind it.

"There hain't no danger, Ivy, none on earth. You kin tote hit in amongst the butter an' eggs. There hain't nary person on earth 'ud suspicion—"

"Law, Mis' Philips—"

"Pore folks, Ivy, has got to do 'most any ways they kin."

"Law, yes, but seems like—"

"You're pore as a weasel, Ivy, pore as a granny-hatcher. An' Enoch, the child hain't a-lookin' right."

Ivy dropped her head on her hands.

"I know in reason, Ivy, you-all hain't a-gittin' enough to eat."

"Law, yes, Mis' Philips, we're a-gittin' plenty," Ivy sobbed softly.

The older woman resumed her churning. After a few moments she leaned over and touched Ivy on the shoulder, standing out bony and prominent from underneath her faded gingham dress. "You don't have to tote the stuff, Ivy, without you're a mind to. There hain't nobody a-goin' to make ye."

Ivy struggled to stop sobbing.

"Honey, my feet hain't give out on me as bad as I let on."

"Don't think hard on me, Mis' Philips," Ivy said now, almost wistfully. "—Howdy, Gid," and she turned quickly, blowing her nose and blinking her eyes to free them from tears, as Gid, in his puttees and ragged sweater, appeared at the door.

"When's you an' Uncle Abel a-steppin' off, Ivy?" Gid asked banteringly, as he lingered on the steps, lighting a cigarette. "I seen Uncle Abel was wearin' honeysuckle in his hat, a Sunday. He's settin' out fer shore."

"A body cain't help but like Gid," Ivy laughed, her eyes following him as he disappeared up the ridge road. The tension was broken, and Nova joined them now, bringing another chair.

"Hain't that one o' them there confession magazines?" Ivy asked, observing a bright picture on the cover of a magazine in Nova's hands and trying to act as if nothing had happened.

Nova nodded and smiled, her dimples coming into play. Tilted back against the cabin, she perused the magazine, her dress of bright yellow cotton pulled up above her knees, displaying silk stockings that ended in patent-leather slippers with high heels.

"Hit do beat all," Ivy thought, "how the girls is a-dressin' this day an' time. But I don't reckon there's none of 'em," she thought, "has got sech expensive clothes as Novy."

"Buck Byrd," Ivy broke in presently on the girl's reading, "Novy, Buck's got him a Ford."

Nova tossed her head slightly, a gipsy head of short black curls. Her dimples reappeared. "We're goin' to have a victrola."

"A victroly!" Ivy cried. "Forevermore!"

Mrs. Philips had picked up the churn to carry it into the cabin, but she stopped in the doorway. "A body," she said, half apologetically, "a body on'y has to pay five dollars down, an' five a month."

Nova had taken a small mirror from her pocket. She was rubbing something across her lips, when she looked up to find Ivy watching her. "Ain't it a sight," Nova laughed, with a saucy glance from under her long, blue-black lashes, "me a-usin' a lipstick, an' Mammy, her a-usin' a snuff stick!"

"Times is changin'," Ivy murmured. She was a little abashed. . . . Fords, victrolas, lipsticks. Everything was changing. She was a little resentful of all these new ways, these new things; a little scornful, but a little envious, too.

"Ivy—" Mrs. Philips stood in the doorway. "Ivy, you're a-goin' to stay fer dinner."

"Law, Mis' Philips, I must be a-goin'. I jest come to borrow your needle. Enoch, he's a-lookin' fer me."

"I've done sent Simon Peter to fetch Enoch."

Ivy sprang from the steps. Mrs. Philips held nothing against her. "You're bad as Mis' Byrd," she laughed, "Mis' Byrd, she would have me an' Enoch to stay fer supper, Tuesday was a week. We couldn't get shed o' her no earthly way!"

Chapter Twelve

"I DON'T RECKON," Ivy remarked, talking as much to herself as to Enoch, "we kin raise us enough corn fer our bread—not fer bread the endurin' year, but raisin' enough to feed a body's chickens beats raisin' none. An' hit's time we was gittin' hit in. Ef corn hain't planted by the time the top o' the mountain is green, hit 'ull do no good."

It was a warm breezy day, and now and then Ivy would stop to gaze up at the great billows of snowy clouds banked in the vivid blue above her. "Puts me in mind o' soap-suds, them clouds." She would stop to watch the slow wheeling movements of hawks sailing overhead, then dip her hand again into the bag tied around her waist and again drop three kernels in a place, drawing the dirt over them with her hoe.

The clear loud whistle of a bobwhite suddenly broke the stillness.

"I reckon," Ivy said, "the pa'tridges has got 'em a nest clost by."

Her mind was somewhat less burdened since she had had a day's work up Josiah Creek and another down by Drowning Ford. Mrs. Philips had promised her milk, too, as soon as the calf should be taken away from the cow, and had sent her a bundle of sweet potato slips. "Hain't no reason," she thought now, "fer me to git out o' heart. Enoch," she said, suddenly speaking her thoughts aloud, "I'm a-goin' to have us a cow agin, soon as ever I kin. There hain't nothin' on earth helps a body to git along like a cow, without hit's chickens."

Enoch went on dropping corn in the row below. "I 'ud a heap ruther," he said, after some time and just loud enough for his mother to catch, "to have a Ford, or a victrola, as ary cow on earth."

Ivy sniffed. "No need, Enoch, fer ye to be a-gittin' above your raisin'. Fords an' victrolys don't git a body nothin' to eat. I 'ull be well satisfied ef ever on earth we kin have us a cow agin."

The season advanced swiftly now. Blue spring daisies nodded by the wayside, along the creeks the cucumber-trees were starred with their great snowy blossoms, papaw bushes hung full of garnet bells, and Mrs. Dodd, hunting her cow, stopped one day to call down from the road:

"Ivy, strawberries is a-ripenin' fast. Molly Diggs has picked her enough fer a pie."

"Law, hain't hit the best, strawberry pie!"

"Ivy, I reckon there 'ull be several. I hain't never saw the like o' blooms. There 'ull be plenty, but there hain't been enough rain on 'em. The berries won't be no size this year."

"Law, no, but the least ones beats none."

"Pickin' strawberries, hit's wearisome ef the berries is small. Ivy, pickin' strawberries is the back-breakin'est job ever I knowed."

"Law, hit don't never weary me, not ef I'm a-fillin' my bucket."

But if Ivy spoke cheerfully, again she was anxious. She had borrowed from everyone, a little of this or that.

Others had come to borrow from her. Often she had been called upon to share the small store gained from her own borrowing.

The dry spell broke at last with several days of rain. Ivy shivered as she waited under a sycamore-tree to which a rough flat-bottomed boat was tied. She was going to the store to ask Andy for credit. There was no other way. "Blackberry winter," she said to herself; "there's generally allays a cold spell when blackberries is a-bloomin'."

"I reckon," she kept thinking, "some man-person 'ull be a-travelin' this way afore long, an' set me acrost." But finally she started bailing water from the boat and at length paddled across the swollen stream herself, fighting the current.

As she approached the store, she saw some men sitting on the river-bank, and when she drew near, she could see that they were eating with their fingers or pocket-knives from tin cans. A smell of the strong raw mountain liquor assailed her nostrils as she passed the men. "They're filthy as hogs. They've been a-wallerin' around a still," Ivy thought, "an' hit hain't nothin' on earth but singlin's they've been a-drinkin', from the miserable smell." They had been up all night, she knew. When the mash was ready, there was no sleep. But after their runs were made, they rushed to the store, half famished. Some of the men turned their faces away. Others greeted her civilly: "Howdy, Ivy."

Inside the store were a few old men sitting on chairs or boxes and several raw-boned bedraggled women, with snuff-sticks in their mouths, leaned against the counter, spitting alternately with the old men into the sawdust boxes provided for the purpose. There was no sound except of spitting.

Ivy took her stand near the women. "Is your hens a-layin'?" she asked in a low voice of the woman nearest her, seeing some eggs in a basket on the woman's arm.

"They hain't a-layin' like they was awhile."

Everyone was silent again. Ivy could hear Andy moving about energetically in an adjoining store-room. She heard creaking and splitting sounds that indicated he was drawing nails, prizing the top off a barrel or crate.

"Hain't hit cold?" Ivy asked at length, laughing nervously. "I reckon hit's blackberry winter."

"Ef the wind lays," an old man answered, "hit 'ull frost tonight."

"Then good-by fruit!" came jocosely from a door at one side and Andy emerged in his black suit, white shirt, and black tie, with a scoop full of sugar in his hand.

"Good God A'mighty, 'pon my honor, why, what in the world, if it ain't Ivy Ingoldsby!" but he turned immediately, with a flirt of his black coat-tails, to one of the women he had been waiting on, taking a live hen from her hand and weighing it. "Eighty-five cents comin' to you, Mis' Pippin. Now, what would ye like?"

For some time there was no reply, and Andy hopped around, waiting on other customers, who were each, like Mrs. Pippin, buying one thing at a time, with long, ruminating pauses between their purchases.

"White Mule," came at last, in a low hoarse voice, from Mrs. Pippin. "Ten cents' worth."

Andy cut a piece of tobacco and handed it to her. "Now what else, Mis' Pippin?"

When she failed to answer, he took the small glass lamp another woman had brought and filled it with oil. He waited on a little boy who had bashfully produced an egg from his overalls-pocket and asked for a candy heart in exchange. Then he turned again. "Now what else, Mis' Pippin?"

"Nickel's worth o' snuff."

"An' what else, Mis' Pippin?"

"I reckon that's all." Mrs. Pippin opened the package of snuff and inserted a fresh supply under her lower lip. Suddenly she added: "I 'ull take a pound o' middlin.'"

Andy disappeared, returning with a chunk of salt pork.

"Hit looks to me," Ivy said to herself, watching Andy cut off a piece of the bacon and lay it on the scales, "like shoulder meat. I don't believe hit's no middlin' at all."

Andy waited on another customer, then resumed, a little more persuasively this time: "Now, ain't there somethin' else, Mistress Pippin?"

"How much does that leave me?" Mrs. Pippin asked in her raucous voice.

"Fifty cents, Mis' Pippin. Now, what 'ull you have fer the rest?"

"I reckon that's all." Mrs. Pippin shrank back among the other women, and Andy turned to Ivy.

"I hain't in no hurry," Ivy insisted, feeling her face suddenly aflame. "No, I hain't in no hurry! Jest wait on the others."

"Ain't there somethin' else, Mis' Pippin?" Andy resumed.

"Got any thread?"

"Yes, Mis' Pippin."

"Is hit good?"

"Best I can buy. Now what else?"

"How much does that leave?"

"Forty cents."

Mrs. Pippin asked now for a nickel's worth of snuff and a dime's worth of coffee. Her trading was apparently finished when she drew four eggs from her pocket. "What you payin' fer eggs?" But at last she was through. "Reckon," she said, "I 'ull jest take a nickel's worth o' washin' powders an' the balance that's comin' to me in snuff."

As the crowd in the store began to thin out, Ivy's heart began to beat more and more tumultuously. She hardly knew whether she dreaded more to have someone overhear her asking Andy for credit, or to be left alone in the store with him, "him bad atter women, the way he are." But she waited until all the others were gone. To her surprise, Andy made the transaction easy. "Why, I reckon I can let you have a little credit, Ivy. I reckon you're good fer it. Come again, Ivy," he called after her, as she left with her burden of flour and bacon, a little sugar and coffee—all she could carry.

The sun had gone down, but the men whom she had seen outside when she entered the store and who had been in the store several times, buying more salmon and sardines, were still outside. Several of them were sitting on a bench against the store, their faces red and heavy, their heads wagging slightly. A few were still on the river-bank, sprawled on the wet grass. On a little level space between the store and the river, two men were walking shakily around each other, eying one another, each with a hand on his hip, and one of them muttering: "Now, I don't want to have no trouble with ye!" From behind the store issued the hoarse sodden cries of men already engaged in a drunken brawl.

Pausing on the platform outside the store, Ivy, her eyes down, was settling the sack of flour on her shoulder when one of the men on the bench leaned forward.

"Come kiss me, Ivy, an' I'll give ye a drink o' liquor."

"I'll give ye to understand I don't kiss men, an' I don't drink liquor."

"Hit's a God-damned lie, Ivy," and the man, rising stumblingly, started towards her. "You're the biggest bootlegger in the country."

Ivy dropped her load and, drawing back, faced the man, her cheeks on fire, her eyes crackling. "I don't thank no man, Alf Bunts, to blackguard me! You're a—you know what! That's what you are!" With a sudden accession of furious strength, she picked up her heavy load and almost ran with it, on up the river.

"Ivy, Ivy!" someone called from behind her.

It was Wash Byrd, running after her. He was staggering, his eyes were swimming, and he reeked with liquor. "Don't pay no attention, Ivy, to them sons o' bitches. They're all drunk. Want me to set you acrost the river?"

He untied the boat and paddled with spasmodic vigor, changing the paddle swiftly from hand to hand to keep the boat from being swept downstream. When they landed, he turned to go in the opposite direction.

"Why, Wash, hain't ye a-goin' my way? Hain't ye a-goin' home?" Ivy was still trembling, but uppermost in her mind now was the thought: "Wash, he's a-goin' to see Theta!"

"I'm a-goin' over the ridge—yon way," and he nodded in the direction of Godfrey Tipton's. He continued down the road, unsteadily.

Ivy stood stock-still for a moment, thinking. Then she placed her load on a near-by stump and ran after him, taking hold of the young man's sleeve. "Wash, come on home," she begged. "You hain't in no shape to go to Godfrey's!"

He turned on her angrily. "It ain't no affair of yourn, Ivy."

"Wash, come along with me! You hain't no business to go to Godfrey's, you drunk!"

"What's it to you?" With an oath he tore himself loose.

"Wash, Wash, don't go! There 'ull be trouble, shore as jedgment day. Godfrey, he—"

"I 'ull go, by God, ef I have to wade through blood!" Wash made an effort to pull himself up to his full height. His fair skin was deeply suffused with blood, and he spoke braggingly, with a swaggering movement of his shoulders: "I 'ull cut out every gut that's in him ef he starts any racket."

"Wash—oh, my God!" Ivy fell on her knees, grasping at him again, pulling at him with all her strength. "Don't go, Wash!"

"I 'ull shoot the son of a bitch ef he—"

"Wash, fer Jesus' sake—"

"I 'ull shoot, by God, long as I've got a load in my gun!"

Ivy wiped the mud from her knees. She walked back in a daze, picking up her load from the stump. It was almost dark. Enoch would be frightened. He would be wondering what had happened to her. . . . Everything seemed unreal. But over and over in her mind kept sounding: "Hit runs in the Byrds' generation to kill an' git kilt."

Ivy was frying potatoes for supper when she heard someone running through the yard. She dropped the fork in her fingers and flew through the cabin. Through the thick dust she made out dimly the figure of a man and heard the dull swish of the bushes as he broke down the slope below her garden. Her breath came in gasps as a cry rose from below, then another, a woman's voice shrieking.

"Pore Mis' Byrd!" Ivy sobbed, clinging to a post for support. "Pore Mis' Byrd! Wash has kilt Godfrey!

"Pore Mis' Byrd! Trouble's on her! Pore Mis' Byrd!" she kept sobbing convulsively through the hush that had settled over things. There was only the murmur of the river now, on and on; the tingle of a cowbell. On the mountains a forest fire was creeping along stealthily, a great red serpent winding its way across the side of the mountains, through the darkness.

PART TWO

IVY AND SHIRLEY

Chapter One

IVY HAD RAISED her eyes from her hoeing to follow a small splotch of white, the scut of a young rabbit that had just scudded by, when she caught sight of someone coming down the road on horseback. With the long vision of those who live much in the open air, she recognized the rider, while still some distance away, as Shirley Pemberton. She had sometimes in summers past gone to the Pemberton cottage with blackberries to sell or early apples.

Shirley, in riding-breeches, a small felt hat pulled down over her eyes, checked her horse below the field where Ivy was working. "How are you, Ivy?"

"I'm tol'able. How are you?" Ivy came a few steps down the slope, nearer the rail-fence that separated them. She felt ashamed of her patched and ragged dress, none too clean. "I hain't saw ye fer a time. I reckon you have your health."

Shirley waved her gloved hand towards the corn-field. "Why, it's almost straight up and down!" Her face was colorless, her mouth rather wide and full-lipped. "It must be hard," she smiled, "to hoe corn on such a steep slope."

"Law, no, hoein' corn on steep ground is a heap easier 'an hoein' hit on level ground. Hit don't make a body's back ache so bad. A body kin stand straight up to hoe ef the ground is steep."

"We're out for the summer," Shirley said.

"I 'lowed you was. Old Mag—Mag Rider—she were a-tellin' me she

71

cleaned up you-all's cottage. Hit's a right smart bit, hain't hit, sence you-uns has been here?"

"Several years. My father," Shirley said, hesitatingly, "isn't very well this summer."

"Your father's a-gittin' up in years, hain't he?" Ivy asked, after a pause.

"Oh, not so old!" Shirley smiled again, shaking her head, as if to shake something away.

"He's peert to his age," Ivy said encouragingly, "the peertest old man to his age ever I seen."

"My father wants to walk—every day he feels well enough—from our cottage up to his mountain land. He likes to walk, likes to go back there."

"Law, I've been a-berryin' a many a time on your pap's mountain land, where your pap's loggin' camp useter be."

"My mother won't be here—just my father and I. I wondered, Ivy, if we could get you to come and stay with us, at the cottage?"

Ivy's thin face suddenly took on a deeper hue. "Law, I couldn't leave Enoch!"

"Oh, just in the day-time—"

Ivy looked down at her feet, drawing the dirt in the corn-row back and forth with her hoe, absently. "I weren't a-aimin' to work fer no person, not the kind o' work you all has got—cookin' an' cleanin' up an' like o' that."

"There's very little work, and we'd pay you—whatever you think's right."

Memories of her stay at the widow woman's were surging through Ivy. "I don't reckon," she said, "I could suit ye."

Shirley's arm was outstretched as her horse nibbled at some leaves it could reach across the rail-fence. "You can cook beans and corn-bread, I'm sure."

Ivy eyed the young woman on horseback a little suspiciously. This was the longest talk she had ever had with Shirley. "I hain't a-braggin' on my cookin'," she said proudly, "but I kin cook plain victuals good as anyone, I reckon."

"Then you'd suit us perfectly. And Ivy," Shirley laughed now, a low laugh, friendly and disarming "—Ivy, can you make fried pies?"

"Law, I've made a many a one."

"My father thinks he'd like fried pies again. My father came from the mountains, you know."

"Law, yes, I've saw the very cabin, fer the world, 'way up on the head of Horse Creek, where your pap were born at an' raised up. But I don't reckon," she added suddenly, "I kin come. —She hain't a mite proud," she said to herself, but aloud: "I've got a heap to see to. The weeds in my garden is a-growin'—hit's a sight. Hit 'ull be a right smart spell, too, afore I kin lay my corn by. Then I've got my little chicks to tend to."

She should have whatever time she needed, Shirley said, to look after her own affairs.

Ivy dropped her eyes. "I don't know ef I 'ud be satisfied."

Shirley flecked a fly from her horse's flank. "Well, Ivy, I'm not *very* bad," she laughed, "to live with."

Ivy's face suddenly relaxed. "I reckon you hain't," she said, "an' I hain't no ill person to live with myself. I don't reckon," she said, good-naturedly now, "me an' you 'ud fall out."

Shirley smiled. She turned in the saddle, pointing with her crop to Ivy's cabin, snuggled among the gnarled old apple-trees. "What a nice place you have to live!" She gazed intently for some moments at the blue-green river, flashing in the sun, winding its way through the long, narrow valley that lay open before them, at the mountains beyond, with their filmy veil of blue, the afternoon shadows playing upon them.

They talked awhile longer. "Well, ef I'm alive, an' nothin' don't happen more 'an I knows on now," Ivy finally gave a reluctant half-way promise, "I reckon you 'ull see me a Wednesday."

Old Mag appeared an hour or so later. Martha was with her. Ivy was in the garden, thinning her rows of beets. Martha was looking even more fagged out than usual. The overall-factory, Martha explained in her lifeless voice, had been shut down again. "Boss-man said if we got us jobs anywheres else, we needn't to look for him to take us back in our old places, *you* know, when the overall-factory starts up again. Ivy, your taters is lookin' pretty."

Old Mag was stalking about, giving a cursory glance at the growing plants, and anything but careful, as Ivy observed with some anxiety, where she set her feet. "Ivy, your cowcumbers hain't a-lookin' so extry."

"Law, Mag, I'm afeared the sign weren't right."

"The time to plant cowcumbers," Old Mag said, "is in the sign o' the twins. lvy, my cherries is a-gittin' ripe. There 'ull be several. The trees is loaded. Ivy, my blackhearts 'ull be ready to pick on by the start o' the week." She wheeled abruptly. "Ivy, ef you want ye some cherries, you kin pick on shares."

They had started towards the cabin, and Ivy stooped down and picked up a little chicken from a brood outside the garden-gate, cuddling the downy chick in her hands, holding it against her cheek. "Baby chickens is jest so sweet, hain't they?—My first gang is a-featherin'." She dreaded to tell Old Mag that she had half-way promised to work for the Pembertons. Of course Old Mag scrubbed the cottages, tidied them roughly, preparatory to the arrival of their summer occupants, almost every year. But even Old Mag felt she lowered herself when she worked for the summer people.

"Lord 'a mercy, Mag," Ivy burst out now, "why, you-all jest come! You an' Marthy has got to stay fer supper. I hain't a-goin' to take no no."

She pulled some fresh lettuce and onions, boiled coffee, and made biscuits.

During supper they talked of Gid and Nova. "Gid, he hain't home more 'an to sleep," Old Mag grumbled, "sence him an' Novy's a-talkin'," Her dull sunken eyes showed a sudden glint of fire. "Gid 'ull have all he wants o' marryin', time Novy comes a-shakin' the meal-sack at him a time or two."

"I say marry!" Martha interposed with gentle scorn "—the boy ain't never yit earned him a pack o' cigarettes."

They moved their splint-bottom chairs to the porch and sat there through the long twilight.

"Wash Byrd, he's out on bail, ain't he?" Martha said, breaking a silence. "I heern his trial had been put off."

"His lawyers has saw to that," Old Mag said, with a shrewd look. She recalled that when the boy's pap had killed a man up Josiah Creek some years before in an altercation over a cow, Big Bill had had to serve less than two years.

"I'm in hopes," Ivy murmured, "Wash, he won't git more 'an a year an' a day."

She had said nothing to anyone of her talk with Wash an hour or so before the killing. "Godfrey," she reasoned, "he's dead. Pore old Godfrey, he were a good man! He never did no harm, none I ever heered tell on, to livin' soul. But Godfrey, he's a-layin' up in Bane's Buryin' Ground, an' hit hain't a-goin' to bring him back to life, me a-cheepin'."

"There's some of 'em says hit 'ull break Big Bill up," she said aloud now, after a long pause. "He's done mortgaged his place to Andy. Them lawyers is so expensive," and after another pause: "Pore little old Linsey! She won't git to go to no high school now. Hit 'ull take all her pap kin rake an' scrape to git Wash outen the trouble where's on him."

They sat again for some time without speaking. The scent of the earth, moist and sweet, filled the air. Sometimes an almost overpowering fragrance was borne to them on a wandering breeze—the fragrance of wild grapes in blossom, and of chinquapin blooms. Fireflies began to light the gathering darkness with their fitful sparks. The clanging of cow-bells reached them, and, faint and far off, the labored cry of a whippoorwill. The trees rustled softly. Down below, the river rushed on, softly, ceaselessly, on and on.

"Looks like it rests a body," Martha sighed, "just to hear the river, it and the trees a-rustlin'."

Another silence followed; then Ivy told of Shirley's stopping to see her.

"I seen her a-travelin' up my holler," Mag said, "I knowed in reason, Ivy, she were atter you, to work fer 'em." —"A sorry lookin' woman," Mag said, "that Shirley Pemberton."

"Law, her eyes is blue as a gander's," Ivy came back quickly. "Her hairs is black as a crow's. I think she's sweet lookin'. She don't paint herself, like some of 'em does, an' she's friendly."

"She hain't much to look at," Old Mag insisted. She stood up and spat off the porch.

"Well, maybe her looks 'ull bear acquaintance," Ivy said, a trifle resentfully. "An' she's friendly. She's jest common. She's mighty friendly. A body couldn't holp a-likin' her."

They sat again without saying anything.

"Old man Jesse Pemberton is bad off," Mag broke the silence. "I reckon this summer 'ull put him through. He's a-failin' fast. He's a wicked man, old man Pemberton. He ain't never professed."

A solemn hush followed Mag's words. Down below, on the river-bank, the Byrds' geese suddenly screamed out in the still night.

"I reckon," Ivy said at last, mournfully, "ef his time's come, old man Pemberton wants to die here in the mountains, where he were born at, where he were raised up, him an' the generations afore him."

Chapter Two

THOUGH IT WAS the long way round and she was already late, Ivy passed the Philipses' cabin, then Old Mag's, stopping for a leisurely chat at both places. When at last she started up the long flight of steps to the Pembertons' cottage, without offering any excuse for her tardy appearance, she called out, almost defiantly: "I reckon you 'ud about give me out."

Shirley, in a morning dress of light-green linen, was coming across the porch to meet her. Shirley smiled. "Oh, no!" she said.

She showed Ivy through the cottage, guiding her from room to room unhurryingly. Ivy had never before been farther than the door, and the cottage's simple but gay furnishings impressed her. "Hain't everything pretty!" she exclaimed, then beginning to warm under the influence of Shirley's reception, "I 'ud 'a brung ye a flower-pot, but I hain't got much o' nothin' bloomin', on'y some poppies."

Shirley said she liked wild flowers even better than those that grew in gardens.

"Do ye?" Ivy stretched her eyes.

They came back to the broad front porch. None of the other summer cottages, no cabins, were in sight, but in an oblique direction could be caught glimpses of the mountains, while below, broken by a succession of shallow rapids, the river rippled and shimmered. Across the river from the cottage rose a steep ridge completely covered with bushes as tall as trees and thickly set with rose-pink clusters of bloom among their dark glossy leaves.

Shirley waved her hand towards the ridge. "Isn't that rhododendron magnificent?"

"Law, hit's pretty," Ivy agreed, "but I hain't never heern," she added, "that name fer hit afore. I hain't never heern no one call hit nothin' but laurel."

Shirley pointed to some showy bright-blue spikes of viper's bugloss growing in the narrow strip of ground between the cottage and the river. "Aren't they the loveliest color?"

"Law, yes," Ivy said.

"But hit's plumb pitiful," Ivy thought, "her a-goin' on over them blue flowers! Why, them there hain't nothin' on earth on'y weeds!"

Shirley showed her now where the various supplies were kept, and, telling her they would not have dinner until her father got back from his walk, insisted Ivy was not to wait for meal-time if she was hungry, but to help herself at any time to any food she found in the cottage.

A thought of the widow woman flashed through Ivy. "I reckon," she said to herself, "rich folks hain't all alike, no more 'an us pore folks here in the sticks."

She felt more and more uneasy, however, as the dinner hour approached. She glanced around the high airy dining room, with its hanging baskets of ferns, its long, waxed table, its green chairs and green cupboards with bright dishes, yellow and green, ranged along their open shelves. With its big screened openings and with the hemlock-trees, like great ferns, waving their branches across the screens, the river glinting and sparkling through the hemlock branches, the room seemed almost out of doors. From a door that opened on the porch she could see Shirley, stretched in a lounging-chair, reading.

Yes, she remembered exactly the dishes and linen Shirley had told her to use, and where the silver was kept. But how many places should she set—? She felt her heart pounding. Would she be able to remain and work for the Pembertons, earn enough to buy Enoch's winter shoes and school-books, money for more hens, enough to start saving for a cow, enough perhaps for new shoes for herself and a new dress, or would her first day be her last?

Her throat was aching, but she stepped to the door leading to the porch and called in a loud resolute voice: "Shirley, how many places are ye a-aimin' fer me to set on the table?"

Still holding the book, her fingers marking the place, Shirley got up from the lounging-chair and came down the porch, joining Ivy where she stood looking down at the long, green table.

"This is where my father sits," Shirley said. "I'll sit here, and will you lay a place for yourself over there, opposite me?"

CHAPTER THREE

THE MONEY IVY was saving had grown into quite a little horde. Friends of Shirley or her father who stayed at the cottage over Sunday had given her money on their departure, unexpected gifts that filled her with joy and excitement—"tips" Shirley called them. Once she had made fried pies, to surprise Mr. Pemberton, and although, to her distress, he had barely tasted one, he had expressed his pleasure by a five-dollar bill.

Every evening when Ivy returned to her cabin, she looked to see if the money she had hidden was still there.

She began to think of ways to expend this money, ways outside of the bare necessities of life. She thought of a clock. Uncle Jake's clock had stopped running long since, and it was hard to judge time entirely by the light, especially on cloudy mornings. She thought of a rocking-chair. And more and more she thought of having her teeth filled. Maybe she could even afford a gold tooth, such as she had seen in the mouths of mountain folks who had moved to Montana or California and come back on a visit, "rich," from picking oranges or herding sheep. "I reckon them gold teeth is expensive," she thought, a trifle recklessly, "but ef money won't buy what a feller wants, what's money fer?"

The midsummer heat had come. Ivy was working hard. But her step was quick and light. On the whole, she was getting along better than she had ever done before. Almost her only fret at present was Doke's cow. Sometimes she was late in the mornings now, because she had had to mend her garden-fence again before leaving home, or make her garden-gate more secure. "But a body cain't bar agin a cow like that to do no good," she would explain to Shirley. "She kin lift a gate same as a person. She's nothin' but a aggravation, her a-eatin' all my cabbages, an' she won't be nothin' else long as the breath o' life is in her."

"I tell ye," she would complain angrily to Old Mag or Mrs. Philips, "I tell ye, ef I had me a gun, I 'ud as leave to shoot the sorry old critter as no, me a-workin' hard the endurin' day, an' a sight to do atter I gits home of a night, me a-needin' my sleep, an' then a-havin' to git up from the bed an' run her off! Of course, Doke hain't got no chancet to keep his critters up. He's done burnt all his fence-rails fer firewood. I tell ye, folks, there hain't nothin' a man won't do where burns his fence-rails. But Doke, he's got to do somethin' about that old cow o' his. I 'ud put the law on him, I 'ud take a writ, on'y I'm afeared he 'ud witch Enoch or burn me down. I do know Doke Odum is the aggravatin'est man on earth—I won't except none!"

One morning she found that Doke's cow had broken into her corn-field, ravaging the whole small patch. She set out Enoch's breakfast, but she could not eat her own. Bowing her head on the table, she wept bitterly. It was true, she was saving enough money so that she could buy what corn she should need for bread and to feed her chickens through the coming year. But she saw only one thing now—her corn was ruined. Corn meant bread. Corn meant life. Nothing must happen to corn.

Shirley's efforts to console her were of little avail. She asked to go home early. It was hardly later than mid-afternoon when she approached Doke's cabin, still seething with indignation, hot from her long walk in the July sun, and heavily laden with packages, food and other things that Shirley had insisted she take home. She was wearing some new low-cut shoes that she had sent to town for by Uncle Abel, and a dress that had been Shirley's, a cotton print of delicate design, but gay coloring. "I'm afeard you cain't spare hit," Ivy had protested, her heart beating high, when Shirley had given her the dress a day or so before.

Doke and Leola were in their yard, bending over a bedstead they had taken apart and brought outside. Some dirty patchwork quilts hung over the fence, and several badly discolored ticks, with wisps of straw protruding through them. The children were standing around, one of the little girls holding the baby. The hounds, running out from underneath the cabin began to bay, and Doke turned his head.

"Ivy," he greeted her with a good-natured shout, "the chinches has about driv' us out o' the house. Doggone ef they hain't!"

Ivy had stopped outside the gate, resting her packages against it.

"Doke," she called back, "you 'ull have to do somethin' about your old cow, an' not be long about hit."

Doke resumed his examination of the greasy wooden bedstead. After a moment or so he started down towards the gate, unhurryingly, his ragged overalls flopping around his bony legs, the children following at a distance, "Lord, Ivy, you hain't a-stoppin' jest to rare on me, are ye, jest to bless me out? Why, a feller don't see nothin' of ye sence ye heels hit by so fast of a mornin' an' of a evenin', both."

"Doke, I'm plumb wore out! She's et up the last blade o' corn I've got. I had the beautifulest bean-vines in the corn, jest a-startin' nice, an' them all tromped down too"—Ivy was almost crying with vexation. "I've been a-tellin' ye, Doke, an' now she's ruint my patch."

Doke's black eyes were roving over Ivy from head to foot. "Ivy, I hain't never saw ye so fine."

"Doke, you needn't to put me off with sech as that."

"Ivy, what you a-gittin' red as a beet fer?"

"Hesh your mouth, Doke! An' I wisht you'd keep them old bold eyes o' yourn where they belongs, they're bold as a mink's."

Doke ran his hand through his big head of bushy black hair, lazily. "Ivy, you must be a-wantin' a man!"

"Well, hit hain't you!" she blazed out.

"By God, no!" He added something half under his breath, while his eyes continued to travel up and down Ivy's sturdy though not ungraceful figure, from her new shoes and the silk stockings Shirley had given her to her hair, still brushed back smoothly from her low brow and coiled at the nape of her neck, but arranged, in imitation of Shirley's, a little differently from the way she had worn it before.

"Ivy"—a smile curled slowly around Doke's thick lips, vivid as blood under his bushy black mustache—"Ivy, you hain't heern nothin' from Jim, have ye? I 'lowed maybe you was a-lookin' fer Jim in, all them fine clothes."

In sudden fury Ivy dropped her packages, shaking her fist in his face. "Doke Odum, I 'ud like to knock out every brain in your head! I 'ull thank ye to mind your own business, you a-throwin' up Jim! I don't never want to lay eyes on Jim Ingoldsby agin long as blood warms my body."

"Oh, ye don't, don't ye?" Doke looked at her searchingly.

"Doke Odum, don't never on earth name sech as that to me agin!"

"I reckon, Ivy," Doke said, after a pause, "them fine clothes must be some of hern—"

"Hern—" Ivy glared.

"Some of hern she hain't no use fer, that girl you're niggerin' fer."

A choking sound issued from Ivy's throat.

"By Jesus, she don't need much o' none! I seen her in her canoe, hit were day afore yesterday, an' her naked, what you might say."

"You know good an' well, Doke Odum," Ivy shouted, her voice shaking, "them bathin' suits like hern is all the style. The girls is all a-wearin' 'em this day an' time."

"Oh, I don't reckon Shirley Pemberton is no different, Ivy, from the rest of them town whores."

"Doke," Ivy screamed, stamping her foot now in impotent rage, "Doke" she panted, "ef hit's the last word I say on earth, I 'ull—" She stopped, in sudden fright at the threat she was about to utter.

"I've fotched a many a gallon o' liquor," Doke went on imperturbably, "to them summer people, to them big rich folks from town. There's cottages I've went to, of a night, an' found 'em a-dancin' to a victroly, an' not a stitch o' clothin' on their naked bodies, bathin'-suits or nothin', on'y their nastiness—men an' women both."

Ivy's eyes started from her head. "Doke—!" The nails of her clenched hands cut into her palms. "Doke—!" she screamed. The children had backed away in fright. Leola came towards them.

"Doke, I've a notion to kill ye!" Ivy cried. "I've a notion to kill ye, you low-down—" A filthy epithet trembled on her lips, but she held it back. "Doke, don't never agin blackguard Shirley Pemberton in my hearin'!" Dry sobs had broken from her, between her panting breaths. "She don't have nothin' to do with them other summer people—an' you knows hit—more 'an to speak."

Leola, in her dark calico wrapper, stiff with soil, had stood by inertly, her white moon-shaped face, her soft dark eyes, alike expressionless. "Ivy," she said now, in a brief lull that had come, "I wouldn't take on so. Doke is on'y a-funnin'. He's on'y a-bein' mean."

Ivy made no answer. She darted another look at Doke, who, with his head turned away, had lifted a chunk of wood, laying it across the chopping-block under an apple tree near the gate. "Doke, you hain't fitten to take the name o' sech as Shirley Pemberton on them foul lips o' yourn!" She was still half sobbing. "Looks like you delight, Doke Odum, in mouthin' harm words agin folks where's decent."

"I say decent!" Doke gave a guffaw. He picked up his ax and began chopping. "You hain't a-talkin' about Shirley Pemberton's pap, are ye? I reckon," he sneered, between strokes with his ax, "the old man hain't got past scramblin' up to his camp of a day, has he?"

Ivy pretended not to hear. She could feel her fingers, like ice, as they came into contact with each other tremblingly gathering together her packages.

"I reckon old man Pemberton is still a-whorin', hain't he?"

"Doke, don't you start nothin' like that agin! I've tried to live peaceable with you an' yourn. I've took a heap. But I tell ye now, I hain't a-goin' to stand fer you a-blackguardin' the best friends ever I had."

Doke brought his ax up again. "Why, Lord God, Ivy, there hain't a soul in the country where don't know all about old man Pemberton."

Ivy said nothing. She could feel herself shaking from head to foot.

"Nan Buskill, she's up at the camp, jest where she's stayed sence way back yonder in loggin' days. Hit's over Nan that old man Jesse an' his woman, they fallen out. Nan Buskill, she's the cause o' Mis' Pemberton not acomin' here of a summer no more. Mis' Pemberton, she's jealous-hearted, I reckon."

Leola turned her soft dark eyes towards Ivy. A faint smile crept across her face. "Mis' Pemberton orter married the scrapin's o' the earth, like I done," she interposed in her listless manner, nodding towards Doke; "then she wouldn't never 'a been jealous."

Doke threw back his head, laughing uproariously. "Leoly, I wouldn't take nothin' on earth fer you!"

"You hain't good enough, Doke Odum," Ivy muttered, white-faced and still shaking "—you hain't good enough fer me to nasty my hands a-killin' ye!" She started up the path towards the road.

"Ivy," Leola called after her, gently yet detainingly, "you're a-gittin' fat as a bear. Looks like them Pembertons must be a-feedin' ye good."

"I'm a-gittin' plenty.—Doke, I hain't a-goin' to name hit to ye agin about that cow o' yourn." Ivy stood in the road, pausing before she turned towards home. "I don't want to have no racket with ye, but I hain't a-goin' to be wearied by your old cow no more. She's done ruint my com, but ef she breaks in my garden agin, I 'ull have ye indicted, shore as the jedgment day's a-comin'."

"There hain't a-goin' to be no next time," Doke called back, "an', Ivy, I 'ull pay ye fer every God-damned copper o' damage my cow has done ye."

"Keep them promises o' yourn to home," Ivy returned scornfully. "I don't think nothin' of 'em."

Chapter Four

IVY PUSHED THE DOOR OPEN. The cabin's dusky coolness met her—still smarting with exasperation and anger—gratefully. But as she went into the lean-to, a pile of unwashed dishes met her eyes, just where she had left them, and buzzing with flies that had come in through the lean-to window, without glass and with its rude wooden shutter only partly closed. "Enoch," she called sharply, "come here!"

She began storming half to herself: "I hain't never thought nothin' on earth o' folks where leaves their dishes one meal to the next. "—What do you mean"—she seized the little boy in her strong hands and shook him—"a leavin' them dishes where I told ye to wash?"

"I ain't a-goin' to wash no dishes fer no one," Enoch answered defiantly through his chattering teeth. "It ain't a man's work."

"A man! I 'ull show ye ef you're a man! Fetch me a hickory!"

"Don't whoop me, Mammy! Don't whoop me!" The little boy ran to the front of the cabin. "Mammy, you ort not to ask me to do sech as that," he whimpered, trying to escape her. "The boys 'ud make fun o' me. Washin' dishes is woman's work."

"I 'ull show ye!" Ivy flew outside, returning with a stout switch.

Kicking and fighting, Enoch struggled to wrest the switch from her hands.

"I reckon I've learnt ye somethin'," she panted, surveying him at last with mingled pity and anger where he lay crumpled up on the floor. "Me a-doin' man's work year atter year, sence the day you was borned, an' you a-tellin' me you won't do no woman's work! Hain't ye shamed?—

"Now, quit off your bawlin'! Go hack me some cook wood. You're plenty big to be a right smart o' help, an' hit hain't fer no little brats like Adam an' Simon Peter an' Woodrow Wilson to be a-tellin' ye what ye kin do an' what ye cain't."

She went on about her evening work. From time to time she would glance out the door. She could hear the little boy sniffling. In her wrought-up state she had whipped him, she realized now, too hard. She watched him bringing down the ax with a child's awkward and uncertain strokes. The pasty look Enoch had brought back from town had disappeared. "He's a-gittin' right chuffy," she thought, "he's a-lookin' good." But noticing how he kept shaking his hair back from his eyes, still red and heavy-lidded, she recalled that she had intended asking Doke to cut his hair on the coming Sabbath. Sabbath mornings Doke placed a chair in the road above his cabin and cut hair for any men or boys who came. He had never charged her for cutting Enoch's. "Doke, he kin cut 'em good, but I 'ull cut Enoch's hairs myself, atter what's passed," she said to herself. "I 'ull cut 'em ef they looks like they was cut with a pole-ax, afore I 'ull ask Doke!"

Still, if a person fell out with neighbors, inconveniences were bound to follow. "A body cain't hardly live to hisself," Ivy thought, as her anger gradually subsided. She began to reflect on the high words she had flung at Doke. It would have been better, she felt now, to have borne with Doke's evil tongue than to come home some evening to find only her chimney standing. "A many a cabin has been burnt to the ground, an' hit fer spite. Hit hain't no good to stay at outs," she decided at last. "Hit hain't no good to hold malice. Malice won't stand."

Her thoughts came back to Enoch. Only the day before, she had realized that Enoch might help with some of the tasks for which she had little time herself, now that she was working away from home every day, had a four- or five-mile walk each way to and from her work, and her garden to tend mornings and evenings.

Ivy and Shirley were in the kitchen, Shirley preparing a salad, while Ivy was stringing beans. Ivy had been recounting the troubles of a Mrs. Hawk, whose husband had deserted her some years before. "An' don't you know, Shirley, her young uns has took the whoopin'-cough, the last one. I've laid off to send her some polecat oil fer the young uns to take. Law, yes, polecat oil, hit's fine fer the whoopin'-cough, hit an' chestnut tea—you boils the leaves. Red-clover tea—hit's good, too.—Thallie Hawk, she's right shifty, she hain't no lazy-bones, but, law, me, she's saw a time, her no man, an' all that gang o' hern to feed an' clothe."

"Ivy, there are a great many women here in the mountains whose husbands have deserted them."

"Law, I reckon.—There's several."

"These men in the mountains don't respect women."

"Ay, Lord, they don't think nothin' of 'em."

"Whipping their wives-think of it!"

"The most of 'em," Ivy murmured, "don't hit their wives with nothin' on'y their fists."

"Fists!—Ivy, I hope you'll bring Enoch up to have different ideas about women and to help you all he can."

Though she had tried not to betray the fact, Ivy had been startled. After all, men were men! Some of them might treat their women badly, but men's ways in general were hardly more to be questioned than the ways of God. Nevertheless, Shirley's words had set her thinking.

Yes, mountain women had borne too much. There were men, it seemed, who did not whip their wives and knock them about. She had always thought, to be sure, that men had the same right to chastise their wives that she had to chastise Enoch. Where was the difference? She felt all at sea. . . . But Shirley had good learning. Shirley lived in town and had traveled to far-off places. Shirley had had a better chance than she to know the truth of such things. Anyway, she would bring up Enoch along the line that Shirley had pointed out. "I 'ull learn Enoch to be different," she thought. "I 'ull learn him to think somethin' o' women, more 'an jest to big 'em, an' fer the work they kin do."

Henceforth Enoch did the tasks she assigned him. Often he did them carelessly, but he never again refused outright to do the "woman's work" which—as Ivy realized, with secret pangs of sympathy for the little fellow—shamed him before his playmates.

Even so, her troubles with Enoch were not at end. Sometimes, as the summer advanced, it seemed to Ivy they were only beginning, beginning now, when almost everything else was going well, when the burden of existence had suddenly been lightened through Shirley's friendship, when life had never before been so pleasant and full of interest.

She came home one evening to find him smelling of tobacco. "I hain't a-workin' to buy ye 'baccer," she blustered angrily. "I don't use 'baccer myself in no way, shape, or fashion, an' I hain't a-goin' to have no little young un like you a-usin' hit. Now, hesh a-tellin' me about Adam an' Simon Peter! An' I don't want to hear nothin' about Matthew an' Wesley Dillard, an' about Woodrow Wilson Byrd—I hain't concerned with what none of 'em does. But ef ever I ketch ye a-smellin' o' them old stinkin' cigarettes agin, or o' chewin'-'baccer either, I 'ull thrash ye till ye cain't stand up, I 'ull fetch the blood!"

In her heart she did not want to whip him. She was still the Ivy of whom her mother had said: "Ivy, she's the tender-heartedest of all my children." And, besides, Enoch was growing stronger. It meant more and more of a struggle to conquer him. A few days later, however, when she found him again exhaling the telltale smell, she made him strip off his overalls. Always before, Enoch had yelled lustily at the very sight of a switch in her hands. But this time she whipped him till she was worn out before he would utter a cry of either pain or repentance. He was getting a man now, Ivy thought with a shudder; stoical, stubborn, ready to take what came, but have his will he would—a true mountain man.

Nevertheless, she tried not to worry overmuch. Everybody had worries, and she ought to be thankful, not only that she had a good place to work, but that she was saving money.

One afternoon towards sunset as she came swinging down the zigzag path towards her gate, filled with joy at the surprises she had in store for the little boy, she saw him seated on the porch step, gazing dreamily in front of him, as he often did, but with his face unusually flushed. "I hope an' pray the child hain't a-takin' no fever," she thought, "but I reckon hit's on'y the hot sun this time o' the year, an' him a-playin' so hard."

"Look what I brung ye!" she called gayly, before she had reached the corn-crib, holding up a bulging bag with one hand and with the other a good-sized package wrapped in paper. "Hain't Shirley the best, allays a-sendin' ye somethin'? This time she's sent ye a treat fer shore, a poke full o' oranges, like hit were Christmas, an' she sent ye a book, too—that's what ye like, with good readin' in hit, an' plenty pictures.—Law, Enoch, are ye sick? Why don't ye git up from the tread?" she cried out, when he failed to move from the porch step but still stared ahead of him, his eyes clouded.

All at once she caught a whiff of something. An icy hand seemed suddenly to have been laid on her heart But after looking at him steadily for a moment or so, she began to quiz him. "Where did ye get ye your dram, Enoch?" she asked, an instinct of cunning prompting her to appear good-humored. "I 'ud like to git me one myself!"

"Leola," the little boy muttered thickly.

Suppressing the wrathful cry that rose to her lips, Ivy forced a laugh. "Leoly! Law, me! I reckon her an' Doke's got plenty good sugar liquor, hain't they?"

Enoch nodded. A foolish, befuddled smile, painful to behold, overspread his flushed childish face. "I jest naturally likes the taste o' liquor, Mammy, an' I ain't a-goin' to say I don't. I loves it good as a cat loves cream."

Ivy questioned him further. Leola, she learned now, poured out liquor in a tumbler and gave it to Guy and Noah, bribing them thus to hoe the cabbages for her or to pick the bean-beetles off the bean-vines. It was not the first time she had offered Enoch a drink of the raw, powerful mountain liquor.

Ivy's heart sank. "Looks like I cain't see no peace on this earth." Even so, she could hardly realize what had happened. "Hain't ye retched an' heaved none?" she asked incredulously. "Hain't ye vomicked? Law, me, ef ever on earth ye teches a drap o' that miserable stuff agin, I hope to my soul hit 'ull make ye so sick you 'ull beg the Lord fer Him to let ye die!" —But it was really Leola's fault, not Enoch's. Suddenly turning on her heel, she ran down the road to Doke's cabin, delivering her mind to Leola in a shaking voice and no uncertain terms, though mindful not to go quite the lengths she had in regard to the cow.

It was hard now for her to keep anxious thoughts of Enoch out of her mind. She had no heart to sing hymns while she was working, as she had done before. When Shirley asked if she were not well, Ivy made the excuse: "I taken a hurtin' in my side," or: "I taken the headache awhile back." But after a few days had passed, again she was cheerful and lively. Perhaps what had happened was not so serious after all. All boys, no doubt, used tobacco on the sly and took a swig of liquor if they got the chance. It was Leola, that low-down Leola! If only Doke and his whole miserable, nasty family lived farther away.—

One Saturday afternoon Shirley had given her an extra dollar with her week's wages and she came home even faster than usual, fairly flying over the ground.

The door of the cabin was shut. Pushing it partially open, she saw that Enoch was stretched sideways across the bed in a corner of the room that faced her, his feet dangling over the side.

"Law, Enoch, wake up!" she called loudly from the doorway. "I don't like no big child like you a-wallerin' in the bed of a day." But she still lingered at the door to look back again at one of her hens, of which she had now a nice little flock. "Git up from the bed," she continued to call. "Me an' you wants to go to the river, to wash us fer the Sabbath day, an' we don't want to be in the night a-goin'." She stepped back now to the edge of the porch. "I believe my soul she's a-gettin' ready to lay! Her comb's as red as a rose, fer the world!" Then she proceeded into the cabin, but she had only taken a step across the threshold when she stopped stock-still.

"Lord God, he's drunk fer shore!" broke from her dry lips in a whisper.

She turned the little boy over from the pool of filth in which he was sunk. A deathly pallor was on his smeared face, and the long strands of his fair hair were plastered repulsively against his brow. As she bent over him, the poisonous fumes with which he reeked almost overpowering her, Enoch half opened his eyes, looking up without appearing to know her.

Ivy sank to the floor. "Pore little Enoch! Pore little Enoch!" broke from her in a sobbing cry as she rained kisses on his bare, soiled feet. "Have ye come to this a'ready?"

There was no anger in her. Again he was a tiny infant lying across her knees as she sat by the hearth, silent and shamed, in those first weeks after Jim had left her. He was the babe that had looked up wonderingly with his first flickering smile when he felt her tears rain down on his little face and wet it. And she saw him now, as in a clouded mirror, passing down the years. She saw him at the end of a long vista, in man's form, receding mistily in the distance until he became a mere speck, but still Enoch. She saw him skulking around the edge of a wood at dusk, his clothes soaked with winter rain, his face haggard with fear, wan with hunger. The law was hunting him. It was Enoch, her son, her baby, what the years had made of him, her poor little Enoch. . . .

Ivy washed him tenderly, making the bed up with clean sheets and a fresh quilt. "Ef his mammy turns agin him, who 'ull be fer him?"

Twilight came. Enoch still lay in a brutish stupor, snoring heavily. Ivy continued to sit by the bed, one of his soft childish hands in her own. "An' me a-aimin' to raise ye up righteous! Looks like I hain't a-makin' sech a good job of hit." From time to time she would take the cloth from his head, wringing it again out of cool fresh water. But she kept an eye always on the open door, lest someone should creep up unawares. No one should make a laughing-stock of Enoch.

Cool evening breezes blew down from the mountains, and the mists from the river began to rise. The river rushed on, on and on. Except for its soft ceaseless rushing the stillness was broken only by Enoch's rough, noisy breathing, by the quivering cry of a screech-owl now and then, by the peevish cheep of some bird that had been disturbed, by the distant cow-bells. In the stillness the river sounded louder and louder. Its muffled rushing became at length almost a roar.

The moon was full and its beams, pouring through the cabin's one small window, cast a pale silvery square on the bare boards on which Ivy's feet rested. The moonlight faintly illumined the second bed, always neatly made up, facing her from a shadowy front corner of the room, the chest of drawers in another corner, a black space where the fire-place yawned, and the splint-bottom chairs set here and there.

Her head throbbed. Since she had closed the door for the night, in spite of the freshness that came through the window, the low-ceiled room seemed suffocating to her. It was still permeated with sour and sickening fumes.

Ivy stood in the doorway for a while, breathing in the clean sweetness of the summer night. The trees looked ghostly. The mountains were mistily outlined through the white veils that shrouded them. Everything was enveloped in a strange and spectral beauty. She gazed down at the shimmering reflection of the moon in the river. "Looks, fer the world, like a pot o' gold had been drapt in the water," she thought. "Moonshinin' nights is pretty, but law me, law me!" she sighed, going back to her seat by the bed. She had wanted to bring Enoch up a good boy, a good man. A deep sadness, a feeling of complete discouragement, settled upon her. "Drunk, an' him on'y nine," she thought. But there must be a way to turn a boy from such evil, a way to make Enoch the man she had dreamed of. If only she could find a way. She racked her brain.

Suddenly she heard someone singing. It was Wash Byrd, coming down the road:

> *"Come, all of you good people,*
> *And listen while I tell*
> *The fate of Kinnie Wagner,*
> *A lad we all knew well."*

The song, with its mournful minor cadences, rolled and echoed through the stillness of the summer night:

> *"They went to get poor Kinnie,*
> *The whole town was alarmed;*
> *But little did they know*
> *That Kinnie was well armed."*

She heard Wash break down the slope below her garden. A little shiver ran through her. The muffled swish of the green bushes brought back the night that Wash had killed Godfrey. The young man's voice came from below now:

"It happened on the river;
The law was all around;
They opened fire on Kinnie,
He shot three of them down."

Though the song was mournful, there was something wild in the strain
that vaguely excited Ivy:

"They tried poor Kinnie Wagner.
Upon this murder case,
The judge looked at the jury;
They turned pale in the face."

Poor Kinnie! He must spend the rest of his days behind prison bars.
But in the midst of her sorrowful reflections Ivy thought, with a touch of
amusement: "Reckon Wash Byrd, he thinks he's Kinnie! But he hain't kilt
no five men, like Kinnie Wagner done. He hain't no call to brag!"

Big Bill was home now. He had quit his job at the logging camp. There
was more money in liquor than there was in logging, and he needed money
to get Wash off with a light sentence for killing Godfrey.

The night wore on. Ivy thought of all the men she knew, up and down
the river, up the creeks, in and out the hollows. How few there were who
had not been mixed up with liquor, who had not been in jail! Where was
the man she could lay before Enoch as an example? Of course there was
Luke, though people said of Luke: "Looks like Luke, he hain't hardly a
man—he don't never raise no hell." They said: "Luke's quair. Luke Diggs,
he hain't all there."

When it was daylight, Ivy brought a cup of tea to the bedside. "Here,
honey, I want ye to take a sip o' this spicebush tea." Then patiently, bit by
bit, she drew from the little boy the information she was after. Enoch and
the other boys stole through the woods, by various secret trails, and spied
through the bushes at the men working at their stills. They hunted until
they found the places where the men stored their liquor after each run,
pouring some out from the half-gallon jars into their own bottles, hiding
the bottles and drinking from them as much and as often as they dared.
Stealing liquor, drinking it, was fun, like making whistles from pawpaw,
making grape-vine swings, fishing with grampus, only it was more fun.
The boys played they had their own stills, like grown-up men.

Ivy had been thinking, thinking, hour after hour.

"I hain't a-goin' to rare on ye, honey," she said now. "Seems like my
heart 'ull bust—I'm a-sufferin' death, fer I don't want ye never to be no

low-down drunken sot. But I've been a-studyin' about hit the endurin' night, an' you needn't to be afeared, I hain't a-goin' to frail ye—looks like hit don't do no good. Honey," she said, after a pause, gazing into the pallid face against the pillow, "you've allays wanted a pet."

Enoch's heavy lids suddenly lifted.

"Seems like I never afore could git enough victuals fer me 'an you an' a pet both. But ef I was to let you have a little dog—"

"Law, Mammy!—"

"Aunt Jinny Lowdy, up Josiah, she's got a fice where she wants to git shed of—"

A shamed smile broke over the little boy's face.

"Hit hain't no old hound. Hit's a nice little fice, white with a black spot on it somewheres. She calls hit Spot. But, Enoch"—Ivy fixed his eyes with her own—"ef I let ye have hit, fer yourn, you've got to swear on the Good Book never agin to tech a drap o' liquor." She crossed the room, returning with a cheap, worn Bible that had been Uncle Jake's. "Place your hand upon it," she directed solemnly.

"Enoch, don't make no mistake," she warned him, after a silence of some length, during which she continued to look into his eyes steadily,— "Ef ever you breaks your word, so help me Lord God, I 'ull tie a rock round the little dog's neck and drap hit in the river, afore your eyes."

Chapter Five

UNCLE ABEL DILLARD, on his way to town to peddle snap beans, tomatoes, and early cabbages, halted his mules one morning above Ivy's cabin. It
was still early. Ivy was coming out of her gate, starting to the Pembertons'.

"I reckon, Mr. Dillard, you-all is well."

"Tola'ble. Well as common. I'm a-lookin fer Short in from West Virginy. Short, he got some person to write a letter fer him, a-tellin' us he's
got him his wooden leg. The company never charged him a copper fer hit,
an' they give him seventy-five dollars aside, fer him to come home on."

"I do know!"

"When he gits the balance where's comin' to him of his conversation
money, as they calls hit, I reckon hit 'ull sum up somewheres around two
or three hundred dollars."

"Two or three hundred, law, me! I reckon," Ivy laughed, "Short, he 'ull
be a-buyin' him a Ford.—Well, I must be a-travelin' along."

"Ivy, I hain't much, me. My fevered leg, hit's a botherin' me agin, an'
I've been troubled a right smart here lately with the rheumatiz."

Ivy contemplated the bulky figure on the wagon-seat. "Allays a-
gruntin'," she thought, "but don't never fail to eat hearty!"

"A nutmeg," she said, "to wear hit on a string around a body's neck,
hit's fine to keep off the rheumatiz."

"Yes," Uncle Abel said. "I reckon, Ivy, you have your health."

"Law, I'm a-feelin' fine," Ivy answered briskly. "But I hain't no hand to
give up. There's folks where gives up to a gnat's bite."

Uncle Abel picked up the lines, still gazing down, a little sadly, at Ivy, standing straight and vigorous beside the wagon, in her fresh light-colored summer dress. "I've been a-aimin' to git me a nutmeg—"

For the second time Ivy started to move on. But, not to appear uncivil: "I reckon, Mr. Dillard, you've laid your corn by, but did ever ye see sech a sight o' rain?"

Uncle Abel shook his head. "The rain, hit's done a heap o' damage.—Ivy, I reckon you're well tickled with where you're a-workin'."

"Law, I'm pleased to death! I hain't hardly a thing on earth to do. Well, tell Bertha Jane to come to see me. I'm home of a Sabbath evenin' generally allays, without there's preachin'."

"Yes, you come, you come to see us, Ivy. The moon 'ull youth today," he called back, after the mules had started. "Then hit 'ull fair off."

True to Uncle Abel's prediction, with the coming of the youthful moon, rain ceased. Again through the river's glassy blue-green depths the flat ledges of rocks on its bottom could be seen. Noons blazed with heat, but mornings were cool and misty. The fields were whitened now by Queen Anne's lace, its delicate lacy blossoms, mingled with yellow daisies, everywhere fringing the roadsides. Butterflies hovered ecstatically over the lavender blossoms of wild bergamot. The flaming stalks of the cardinalflower were beginning to appear in swampy spots, to cast their blood-red reflections in coppery pools here and there in the woods. Here and there a clump of hollyhocks glowed against some cabin chimney. There was no more hoeing of corn to be done. Corn was laid by. Patches of oats that this one and that had sown were cut and gathered in shocks. Men who had hayfields had deserted their stills and were busy haying. Full midsummer had come. And in spite of all the fears—"Blackberries won't be no 'count. They 'ull rotten afore they ripens, they 'ull be too sour"—blackberry bushes were bending under a weight of luscious fruit.

In overgrown fields, along the fence-rows, everywhere now were the blackberry-pickers. Mountain folks who had moved to town now came trooping back, on foot or packed in dilapidated Fords, eager, from long habit, to reap their share of the rich harvest which belonged to everybody. Martha, only recently called back to the overall factory, had quit her job and come to help with the picking and canning. Old Mag's daughter Belle, long settled in town, arrived with her seven children; Odie, bringing her frowsy brood and finding her mother's cabin overflowing, took possession of Ivy's.

Everywhere now the talk was of how many gallons of berries different families had secured, of how much canned stuff in general they were putting up. The Byrds had put up twenty gallons of cucumber pickles, the Dillards a barrelful.

All this talk made Ivy uneasy. And her mind was no easier from the fact that she was saving money. Provisions for the coming year meant to Ivy, not money, but visible rows of glass jars filled with canned fruit and vegetables, a goodly array of crocks neatly covered with cloth or paper.

She redoubled her efforts. Until far into the night, bent over the little step-stove in her dimly lighted lean-to kitchen, Ivy was canning berries that Enoch had picked, or making jelly; canning tomatoes or beets. Early and late she was stringing beans, which she would spread on the floor in her loft, leaving them there until they were dry enough to put in bags and hang in the sun until frost came.

At the Pembertons, too, there was more to do than there had been at first. More men were coming from town and staying to dinner.

But Ivy was strong. Never had she been more content. Though there was much cooking to do at the Pembertons' now, and piles of dishes to wash, there was also much praise. Shirley commended her constantly for her neat, clean ways, and the visitors, as well as Shirley and her father, declared they had never eaten such beans and fried chicken, such com-bread and blackberry pies. Ivy's eyes had grown perceptibly brighter. Above everything else, she felt uplifted in associating with people whose superior refinement she had been quick to discern. A feeling of elation, almost of exaltation, filled her. "Jim learnt me a heap," she thought at times, with a stab of excitement, with mingled confidence and anxiety, "but ef he was to come, I reckon he 'ud see I've learnt a heap sence. I hain't the same."

Over all these happy, breathless, exhilarating days hung, none the less, a shadow. When she saw Shirley starting out to walk, alone, as Shirley often did now, she would think: "Pore soul, trouble's on her!" She had heard folks say that Shirley's father and mother lived as strangers in the big house in town with the marble pillars, and that the young man Shirley had intended to marry had been killed in the war. "He looks kinder sad," she would think, dusting the young man's picture in its silver frame on Shirley's desk and reading her knowledge of the young man's fate into his face. And now Shirley's father—his face was more ashy every day. She would watch Shirley, smiling but tense, follow her father to the top of the steps as he started on his daily walk, a tall man, unstooped, but depending now on a stout hickory staff, such as the old men in the mountains used. Shirley would utter some word of caution in her pleasant contralto voice, and "My best friend!" her father would say, a mischievous gleam m his sick eyes as he patted her arm, "my best friend!"

At first Ivy had stood in awe of Mr. Pemberton. She had great respect for age. Then, too, Mr. Pemberton talked very little. His quietness impressed her. But now he would often come and, his hands clasping his hickory staff, sit for some time on the kitchen porch, where she was busy paring potatoes or picking chickens. His mouth was slightly awry, and he talked with an effort, yet he often spoke now of the old days, the days when only a few made liquor, and the mountain men were busy getting out the big virgin timber under his direction. It was logging, folks said, that had given Jesse Pemberton his start. He would chuckle over amusing remembrances of those days, over oddities of various mountain folks they both knew. Before long, Ivy was pouring out tales of her own, to which he listened with a quiet smile, an occasional encouraging question. "Uncle Abel Dillard, he's got power to stop bleedin'. He says them words from Ezekiel, *'And when I passed by thee, and saw thee polluted in thine own blood, I said unto thee when thou wast in thy blood, Live; yea, I said unto thee when thou wast in thy blood, Live.'*—Mis' Dodd, where lives up Stony Branch, she's got the power, too." Ivy felt free, too, after a time, to ask Mr. Pemberton's opinion on various important matters. There was one question in particular that tormented her. "Some folks says the world is flat, an' some of 'em says hit's round. I've studied about hit a heap. The Scriptures says, Mr. Pemberton, that four angels is a-standin' on the four corners of the earth. And ef there's *corners*, sir, how *kin* the world be round?" As the days went on, she talked to him more and more freely, sometimes a trifle vauntingly. "Law, Mr. Pemberton, there's a heap a ways a feller kin do to make a livin', ef he's shifty an' got resolution."

One morning as he sat in his accustomed place, quietly watching her while she peeled some apples, then shucked the corn for dinner, removing the silk from between the kernels in her slow, painstaking way, something prompted Ivy to tell him of her experience in going to town, of how she had sold her cow and chickens in order to get the money to go, and of how she planned to get another cow as soon as she had saved enough. She dwelt on her failure at piece-work, and on how she had rejoiced to get back again to her cabin.

Mr. Pemberton sat looking off at the mountains, blue as though some blue flowers were growing upon them, a few wisps of pearly clouds still clinging to their summit. "Folks like you and me, Ivy, don't belong to towns and factories. We belong to the mountains."

Ivy looked up from the ear of corn in her hands. There was a tone in Mr. Pemberton's voice she had not heard before. His face, with its stubble of white beard, was more ashy, 'she noticed, than usual. "Pore man, he hain't got long!" Something seemed to melt within her. "I don't reckon, Mr. Pemberton, I 'ull never be much o' nothin', me, but jest a mountain woman."

But, in spite of these words, Ivy was aware that she was improving in more ways than one. In the past she had thought very little about her appearance. It was with but small discontent she had worn her patched and faded dresses year after year, her threadbare coat, her clumsy broken shoes. And nothing had given her less concern than the knowledge that, at twenty-six, her face had begun to be lined and care-worn. But now, all at once, things were different. She was happy and having plenty to eat. Then Shirley had given her, not only dresses, but all manner of things. When she went to preaching now, on the first and third Sabbath afternoon of every month, she wore a silk dress, a dark-blue dress with white dots sprinkled through it, and a long string of scarlet beads. Nova Philips and Essie Byrd stared at her over their hymn-books, and the older women stroked her dress with their rough, big-knuckled hands. "Law, Ivy, honey, you're a-lookin' good!" When she went to the store, Andy exclaimed: "'Pon my honor, Ivy, why, what in the world? You're gittin' better lookin' every time I see ye!" He pressed her less to pay her bill. Doke waited at the gate, "Good God, Ivy, I never seed nothin' to come up with hit! You hain't a-gittin' too proud to speak to us pore folks, are ye, Ivy?"

Ivy began to study herself in the looking-glass in Shirley's bedroom with greater interest. She began to want Jim to see her in these clothes that Shirley had given her. Jim had failed to appear as the spring days had succeeded one another, as summer had succeeded spring. "Reckon Jim couldn't git him no furlough," she told herself, "or maybe Jim's term hain't up, ef he's a-aimin' to quit the army fer good an' all."

She fixed now upon fall as the time of his coming. "When the trees has turned, an' them all red an' yaller, afore the leaves has commenced to drap; the summer farewells all a-bloomin', an' everythin' a-lookin' pretty. Hain't no time nicer 'an fall o' the year, without hit's spring . . . Ef Jim comes in the fall, the corn-field beans 'ull be ready to use on. Jim, he useter delight in corn-field beans. . . . Ef Jim comes in the fall, folks 'ull be a-makin' apple butter. They 'ull be a-makin' sorghum, a-havin' the fresh new molasses, an' them so good! . . . 'Say howdy to Ivy' . . . 'Some sweet day' . . ."

Chapter Six

FOR MORE THAN two months now Ivy had been going back and forth to the Pemberton cottage. But one morning she arrived to find Shirley hurriedly packing her clothes and personal belongings. On the previous day Mr. Pemberton had undertaken the long walk to his old camp, as usual, but word had come that he had been taken ill there, apparently a complete collapse. Shirley had sent to town for a nurse and was starting for the camp herself on horseback, leaving Ivy to send various things after her by wagon and to close the cottage for the summer.

When Shirley was ready to leave, she said that it all depended upon how she found things, whether she would need Ivy at the camp. Would Ivy come if she sent?

"Law, Shirley, I 'ull come to ye day or night ef ye needs me! Enoch kin stay at Mis' Philips of a night, an' Mis' Byrd or Linsey 'ull feed my chickens."

Shirley gave her the remaining supplies in the cottage. It took several trips to carry them all home, and Ivy came and went now by the long way, stopping to gossip at both Old Mag's and the Philipses' cabin. She had only seen her neighbors in hurried snatches for some time past and was eager to hear all that had been happening.

It was the middle of the afternoon, the day after Shirley had left. Ivy was carrying home her last load. Old Mag was gathering some small knotty peaches from a tree overhanging the narrow grass-grown road that led down the hollow past her cabin. "They hain't much," Mag said, "an' they hain't ripe, but I 'lowed they 'ud make me a little peach butter—beats lettin' some feller steal 'em."

"Law, yes, they're handy to the road, an' looks like there's a sight o' travelin' this day an' time." Ivy laid her heavy packages down on a bank sparsely covered with laurel and blackjacks that ran along one side of the road. "I'm plumb give out," she said, dropping down beside her packages, pushing back the fuzzy ringlets that had formed around her forehead, and wiping her warm face with the skirt of her dress.

The two women enjoyed a leisurely visit together. As Ivy started to leave, Old Mag remarked that the coming Sabbath would be her birthday.

"How old 'ull ye be, Mag?"

"I hain't right certain. Hit's fifty or sixty, one or t'other."

"Law, Mag," Ivy cried on a sudden impulse, "I 'ull have ye a birthday dinner! I've got plenty rations, an' I've hardly saw ye the endurin' summer."

Old Mag demurred. Finally, however, Ivy drew forth the promise: "Well, ef I'm alive. Ef I'm able to hold up. Ef nothin' don't happen more 'an I knows on now."

Ivy, on her part, made the dinner conditional on Shirley's not sending for her to come to the camp. "But I don't reckon she 'ull send afore the Sabbath, nohow."

Before she reached the top of the ridge that separated Old Mag's acres from the Philipses', Ivy had decided to ask Nova, so that Gid should be sure to come, and also to ask Mrs. Philips. There would be no preaching on the coming Sabbath—so much the better, they could sit at table as long as they wanted to. . . . Of course Old Mag was still resentful of Nova, but it would be a good thing to bring them all together, the marriage only a few weeks off now. "Hain't no need, nohow, fer Mag to take on. Hain't no need her a-grievin' herself to death. A feller has obliged to take what comes."

As Ivy climbed higher, a light breeze sprang up, fanning her warm cheeks, stirring the pines, and wafting their perfume to her. Big brown butterflies sailed along beside her, pausing to feast on the rich purple blossoms of iron weed growing tall and rank by the roadside, then fluttering on to sip at the softer purple of the neighboring thistles. When she neared the crest of the ridge, her packages had grown heavy again, and she put them down, stopping in the shade of an apple-tree, for the sun was still high, and resting against a rotted broken-down rail-fence that ran in front of the old Minton place.

Facing her, a little way back from the road, stood the deserted Minton cabin, the ground around it densely covered with periwinkle. Mosses and lichens patched the dipping roof of hand-hewn boards. Wild grapevines had draped a curtain partly over the staring window, and Virginia creeper clambered over the crumbling chimney, along the ridge-pole, and hung in streamers from the eaves. Old man Minton was in the insane asylum. The rest of the family had moved to California, and the deserted place offered all sorts of riches to those who invaded it. Its overgrown apple and cherry-trees still bore fruit. The steep slopes below the cabin, forming the sides of a deep bowl, had grown up in wild-plum thickets. From the upper rim of the bowl chestnut and walnut-trees showered down nuts, while at the bottom an ever-flowing spring bubbled out from the rocks. In dry weather folks carried water, often a mile or more, from the Minton spring. Even the Minton cabin, with wide gaps between the logs where the mud that chinked them had fallen away, served its uses. Wandering cows chewed their cuds in the dilapidated lean-to at the back of the cabin, with its cool dirt floor, and lovers found a trysting-place in the same rude chamber.

Ivy's eyes rested absently on the mountains. Shadows were lying deep on them, floating like islands, great irregular splotches, on their plumy sunlit sides. From where she stood, she could catch only a glimpse of the river, a blue pool, it seemed, sunk in the green, far below her. She heard the mingled chirping and creaking of grasshoppers and crickets buried in the sea of long, feathery grasses that waved gently all around her. Chickadees were chattering in some near-by bushes. A cicada suddenly set up a shrill drumming that seemed all at once to intensify the heat. But a moment later the cool, soothing note of a dove came from the woods. The dove's plaintive note, over and over, carried her back to those spring days, long past now, in the sugar orchard, to those wild sweet days. . . . Underneath her buoyant cheerfulness was this strain, at once vague and poignant, of recurrent sadness, of loneliness, of hunger for that human and earthy yet glorified love of a man for his woman, of hunger for Jim. . . .

But as she rested, contemplating dreamily the scene that was spread before her, in the midst of other thoughts, plans for the birthday dinner were forming. She would have none of the newfangled dishes she had learned from Shirley, but just boiled and fried things, such as every body was sure to like.

Some slight rustling sound from within the deserted cabin suddenly arrested her attention.

"Well, hit hain't nobody's business but theirn," she thought, as Nova and Gid appeared at a corner of the deserted cabin, coming from behind it, Gid in his secondhand puttees and khaki breeches, in a light shirt and a gaudy striped neck-tie, with his slicked-back hair, towering above Nova in the bright-yellow dress that barely reached her knees. They were occupied with each other, Gid brushing something from the back of Nova's dress. Nova, suddenly seeing Ivy, stopped short, then started to run back.

"You-all is jest the ones, fer the world, I were a-wantin' to see," Ivy called out in a loud, reassuring voice.

She saw them exchange some words out of the corners of their mouths. With a defiant toss of her black curls, Nova came forward now, hobbling along on her high heels across the matted periwinkle, Gid a step behind her. Nova's eyes remained downcast and she was blushing visibly underneath her thick coat of powder and paint. But Gid, before they reached the rail-fence, had begun to talk and joke with Ivy. He lit a cigarette, then stooped down and crawled through the fence, helping Nova through.

Ivy explained about the dinner.

"I reckon, Ivy"—Gid blew out a column of smoke—"you 'ull have Uncle Abel."

"Go 'long!" Ivy laughed. "You'd best be a-lookin' atter your own affairs, place o' throwin' up Uncle Abel to me!" It was good to have a little rough fun again, to laugh and shout if she wanted to, at the top of her voice. "One-eye Buck's come in," she said.

Gid nodded. Nova's long, black lashes, sweeping her cheeks, quivered slightly.

"Buck, he's quit off his job in town," Ivy said. "He's come in to help his pap an' Wash make liquor."

"He's brung his Ford," Nova murmured, showing her dimples and lifting her eyes to throw a saucy sideways glance at Gid.

"Law, yes!—Gid, you better watch out," Ivy went on teasingly. "Buck, he 'ull be a-takin' Novy to ride. He 'ull be a-stealin' your girl from ye!—Gid, you hain't mad, are ye? you a-lookin' so sour! Why, I don't never fly mad when you teases me about Uncle Abel. Hit's tit fer tat."

Gid knocked the ash from his cigarette, deliberately. "Buck Byrd has done made his brags," he said, throwing his head back, and the corner of his mouth curling disdainfully. "He's made his brags he's goin' to break up me an' Novy."

"Forevermore!" Ivy shouted, staring in astonishment. "Law, I was on'y a-funnin', 'cause Buck an' Novy useter keep company, awhile back, afore you-uns started talkin'. I never thought one time o' him a-tryin' to part you-uns."

"Well, Buck better not start no trouble." Slipping his hand around to his hip, Gid flashed the tip of a revolver into view.

"The Lord have mercy!" Ivy screamed. "Law, Gid, you hain't a-carryin' no weepons on ye? You hain't a-carryin' no gun fer Buck?" she repeated incredulously.

"By God, I hain't a-takin' no chances," Gid answered, importantly.

CHAPTER SEVEN

THE RIVER GLITTERED and flashed in the morning sun. A light breeze blew through the open doors, bringing the fresh pungent fragrance of the pines to mingle with appetizing smells issuing more and more strongly from the lean-to. Ivy, bustling about, busy with a dozen things, kept exclaiming to herself: "Did ever a body see sech a pretty day?" She had had no word from Shirley. No doubt Mr. Pemberton was better. . . .

Almost before she knew it, the birthday party had grown to its present proportions. Besides Mrs. Philips, she had asked Bertha Jane Dillard. "Of course, Bertha Jane, she's dry. She don't never have much o' nothin' to say. But, pore little old thing, she don't never git to go nowheres sence her mammy's gone, her sech a sight o' work to do!" After Bertha Jane, it had occurred to her to ask Short, just back from the mines. Then Molly Diggs, happening along on the way to the store, she had asked Molly. And in the midst of her preparations on Saturday morning, who should appear but Luke, his teeth gleaming, the color coming and going in his bronzed cheeks, Luke holding up a pair of squirrels he had shot. Luke had said: "Ivy, I brung ye a mess o' squirrels fer to-morrow." And there had been nothing to do but ask him. Well, there would be plenty for everybody.

Molly was the first to arrive, in a dark-blue calico, sprigged with white.

Ivy herself, not wishing to outshine her guests, fearful also lest with so much cooking she might drop something on her, had resisted the temptation to wear her silk dress and had put on a plain green linen that Shirley had given her.

"Law, Molly, hain't hit the nicest!" she exclaimed delightedly at sight of the bright new tin cake-pan Molly had brought as a birthday remembrance for Old Mag.

Molly helped her move the table from the lean-to into the front of the cabin and to spread the white table-cloth that Shirley had given her. "I believe, Molly, hit belongs jest a leetle mite the fur way."

Molly leaned over, examining the table-cloth with her staring, red-rimmed eyes. "Why, laws a mercy, Ivy, them's roses a-runnin' along hit!" She ran her red bony hand over the satiny damask, picking up a corner of the cloth to smell of it.

"An' good as new, fer the world," Ivy said, flying back and forth to the step-stove, so that nothing should burn. "Hain't more 'an two or three broke places, an' them darned nice." She had gathered a cluster of wild lilies, arranging them in a glass fruit-jar. "I 'ull have me a flower-pot fer the dinner-table, same as Shirley allays done." She placed the jar in the center of the table. "Hain't no flowers on earth no prettier 'an these here leopard-spot lilies!"

Lifting the cover from a frying-pan, she pierced with her fork one piece after another of the frying ground-hog, while Molly sniffed pleasurably. "Whistle-pig, Molly! Parbiled hit first, same as I done the squirrels. Gid, he went plumb to the mountain fer hit. Law, Molly, hain't hit nice? Jest so tender! Falls to pieces ef you teches hit!"

Ivy began to cut corn from the cob now, standing at the shelf that ran along the outside of the little back porch. Molly, her mouth full of snuff, pared the potatoes, stopping from time to time to step to the edge of the porch and spit.

"Mis' Byrd's a-goin' to have another baby, hain't she?" Molly said, suddenly dropping her voice to a whisper and bringing her burning eyes close to Ivy's.

"Law, yes, an' hit 'ull be a girl this time, her a-stickin' out in front so fur. When hit's a boy, they carries 'em all around more."

Molly resumed her paring, but soon started whispering again. "Ivy, had you heern about Pernie Botts? Pernie, she kilt her baby, a-stompin' on hit."

Ivy drew back and stared. "Forevermore!"

"Pernie were in the bed an' she felt the baby a-comin', so she jumped up an' down right hard on the floor. She busted hit's skull."

"The Lord have mercy!" Ivy screamed.

"Pernie, she mashed hit's face till you couldn't tell hit were nothin' human."

"Law, Molly, I hain't never heern nothin' to beat hit in all the days o' my life!"

"Well, Shell, he bigged Pernie, an' Shell, he denied her when Pernie 'lowed they orter marry."

"Don't make no difference—I don't see how no woman a-livin' kin kill a little baby, hit hern, an' them so sweet!"

They were still pursuing the subject when a noise warned them that Enoch was returning. Ivy had sent him for extra chairs and dishes. He was coming down the path, a big basket in one hand, a bucket in the other, followed in single file by Adam and Simon Peter, each carrying a splint-bottom chair on top of his head, with Enoch's little dog bouncing in and out of the procession, barking and nipping at two half-grown hounds that had followed the Philips boys.

"Mis' Philips sent ye some sweet milk," Enoch announced breathlessly.

"A gallon ef hit's a drap!—Now, don't you boys nasty your clothes. Hit's a right smart spell afore dinner."

She was setting the table a few moments later when Enoch announced that Short Dillard and Bertha Jane were approaching.

Ivy ran to the gate. "Forevermore! Why, Short, you're a-walkin' good, hain't ye? Bertha Jane—" but she stopped short. It was the first time she had seen the girl since her mother's death in the early spring. "Law, honey, how are ye?"

"Well enough, I reckon," Bertha Jane murmured huskily. Her short ill-fitting dress hung on her loosely, its vivid pink intensifying the pallor of her small childish face. Smiling shyly, she held out a bunch of marigolds and zinnias mixed with some sprays of sweet fennel. "I didn't have nothin' else. Reckon hit 'ull do?"

"Law, honey, ye couldn't a brung nothin' on earth no nicer! Look, Molly, this here flower-pot Bertha Jane brung fer Mag's birthday."

Short, a heavy-set youth, whose broad amiable face was still bleached from his weeks in the hospital, and who was walking with a stick, limping heavily, now proffered the tin bucket he was carrying. His father had found a bee-tree and taken sixty pounds of honey from it.

"Land o' livin'—sixty pounds! Well, I thank ye terrible, Short, you an' your pap, both.—Now, Bertha Jane, you jest set here an' rest. No, there hain't a earthly thing fer ye to do; Molly's a-helpin' me, an' looks like you're kinder out o' breath.—What do you reckon ails ye, Bertha Jane?"

Bertha Jane smiled faintly. "Hit's the tubercles, I reckon."

"Do you reckon—? Are ye a-spittin' blood?"

Bertha Jane nodded. "An' Mammy, she had 'em."

"Law, yes, hit were the tubercles kilt your mammy, I reckon. They're ketchin', folks says—law, me!"

Ivy rejoined Molly in the lean-to.

"Uncle Abel," Molly whispered, with a snicker, "he's bound to git ye—a-sendin' honey!"

Ivy held up a warning finger. "Don't ye name hit, Molly, afore Short an' Bertha Jane, him their daddy!"

All at once a furious barking and yelping was heard. A big bony mongrel belonging to Luke had dashed into the yard, starting a fight with the other dogs, as Luke himself appeared from one direction, and from another Gid was seen, coming down the ridge, twirling two chairs above his head, with Nova, a blaze of red, mincing along the road, a few steps behind him.

Ivy, Molly, and Bertha Jane had all run to the door.

"Hain't her dress pretty?" Bertha Jane murmured, gazing wistfully at Nova, almost at the gate now, carrying a vanity case, her red organdie dress standing out crisp and dazzling.

"Yourn is a heap prettier," Ivy whispered. "I never did like no red dress!"

"Good God A'mighty!" Gid shouted, imitating Andy Weaver's familiar sniffle, as he peeped over the heads in the doorway. "'Pon my honor! Why, what in the world?" He set the chairs down inside the cabin with a loud clatter; then, striking an attitude, surveyed the already loaded table while the others stood around to admire his foolery.

"Ivy, are ye a-aimin' to give me an' Novy a infare as fine as this here?"

The word "infare" set everyone shrieking. Jokes were cracked and a rough and tumble frolic started, even Short, though handicapped by his artificial leg, to which he was not yet accustomed, entering into the boisterous fun.

In the midst of the hubbub someone reported that Old Mag and Mrs. Philips were coming. Yes, there they were! Old Mag, her bare head high in the hot noonday sun, stalking along a little in advance of Mrs. Philips.

"Don't Mag look nice!" burst from Ivy, as the two women drew nearer, Old Mag in a new dress of lavender gingham, barred with white. Ivy took a china bowl decorated with roses from the chest of drawers, holding it up for the others to see. "Seems like a berry-bowl allays comes in handy."

She forced Mag into a chair.

"Well, I do know!" Mag panted, glancing at the festive table. "Ivy, ef you hain't the beatin'est woman!" She was smiling broadly, but in her embarrassment took down her wisp of hair, holding the hairpins in her mouth, then coiled it up again.

Nova had brought a small silk handkerchief, her mother a red-bordered face-towel; and Luke drew forth a paper bag of stick-candy from one pocket, two oranges from another. The berry-bowl, the cake-pan, Bertha Jane's bouquet—all the gifts were showered at once into Mag's capacious lap.

Old Mag took up one thing after another, handling the gifts tremblingly. She tried to speak. It was no use. Her head dropped on her breast.

"Ef she hain't a-blubberin'!" Mrs. Philips's keen black eyes were filled at once with amusement and a little concern. The others had backed away, but Mrs. Philips placed her hand on Mag's shoulder "Law, Mag, you must git your countenance! Ivy done hit to please ye!"

Mag lifted her head. The tears were streaming down her furrowed, weather-beaten face. She raised her hand helplessly, the big-knuckled, seamed, and coarsened hand of one who has done much outdoor work, trying fumblingly to wipe her wet face with the back of it. "I hain't never done nothin' to deserve sech as this!"

"Law, Mag"—Ivy had found her voice—"there hain't no kinder person a-livin'! There hain't no free-hearteder—to what ye've got!"

Mag shook her head. "I hain't no good woman!" She looked around from one to the other, humbly, heart-brokenly. Her dull, cavernous eyes blinded with tears, she reached down, trying to pull up her skirt, weighted with the birthday gifts.

In a flash Gid recovered himself. Picking up the small square of silk, Nova's gift, he forced it into his mother's big, clumsy hand. "Here, use this, old lady, an' no more bawlin', without ye want me to lick hell outen ye!"

Old Mag burst out laughing, the others, in sudden relief, all joining in.

Luke insisted now that they should follow the usual custom. "Come, folks, we must put Mag under the table, so she won't stop a-growin'!" There was a wild scramble, Old Mag, by no means feeble, pushing them off, and everyone roaring with laughter. Finally Mag's gaunt frame was stretched out on the floor, Ivy jerking down the skirt of her dress, disarrayed in the tussle, and skrieking at the same time that the others should save her table, which was rocking back and forth, threatening to crash any instant.

"Well, you-all kin set down," Ivy announced at last. "I reckon the last one o' ye is starved to death."

Everyone continued, however, to stand around awkwardly. Mag and

Mrs. Philips and Molly all sought the front porch to spit again. Nova opened the vanity case to dab her face once more.

"Mag, you set here," Ivy broke the hush that had fallen, indicating a chair at the top of the table, facing the front door, "an' Gid to the side o' ye. Mis' Philips, you set yander, opposite Mag. The balance kin set where they likes."

Mrs. Philips and Old Mag both stroked the white cloth. "Law, Ivy, hain't hit nice!" Both of them, as Molly had done, picked up a corner of the cloth and smelled of it.

Fresh fun was created when Nova, showing her dimples, slipped into the chair on the other side of Gid from his mother. General joking was resumed now and dishes that were on the table began to be circulated.

Rosy with the heat, dripping with perspiration, Ivy bustled back and forth to the lean-to, passing food that the table had no space to hold and urging her guests to help themselves liberally. "Law, I don't want nobody to be in no ways bashful!"

She was conscious of a vague sense of relief. Here, among her own people, there was no strain for fear she might do or say the wrong thing, something that would betray her poor rough upbringing in Rocky Hollow.

And how proud she was! She saw the room, almost as though she stood outside of it, as a picture she would hold in her mind unforgettably—her two high tightly stuffed beds, like fat pincushions, shining out, each from its corner, in the freshly washed bed-spreads, the bunches of herbs hanging from the rafters, Uncle Jake's clock on the chimney-shelf, the table extending almost from door to door, beautiful in the white cloth Shirley had given her, with the jar of wild lilies, with the gay flowers Bertha Jane had brought, resplendent with bright-colored jellies and pickles—then, everyone in clean Sabbath attire, and vivid patches where Nova and Bertha Jane sat in their scarlet and pink dresses—a living picture that glowed softly in the tempered light, that threw off enchanting odors, odors of steaming food mingled with the slightly suffocating sweet of the lilies, with the aromatic scent of the fennel in Bertha Jane's bouquet. . . . Oh, if only Jim should step in now!

The big platter of string-beans and potatoes boiled with bacon soon needed replenishing. Mounds of soda biscuits, toppling pyramids of corn-bread, dishes of fried corn and fried cabbage, fried squirrels, the fried whistle-pig, bowls of gravy, of stewed tomatoes, of raw onions—all melted away until Enoch and Adam and Simon Peter, who were stationed about the table, eying it hungrily as they waved their green branches to keep the flies away, began to look at each other in consternation. But still Ivy plied her guests with fresh food and drink. "Bertha Jane, have ye another glass o' sweet milk.—Law, Mag, your coffee's plumb cold—let me pour ye some hot.—Luke, ye hain't a-settin' back a'ready? Why, you hain't hardly began!— Molly, try them spiced beets. They're fine, they hain't a mite stringy.—Law, Gid, you an' Novy is lovesick, I reckon—you-all hain't eatin' a bite!—Mis' Philips, help yourself to the honey, an', Short, would ye pass the cheese?— Hain't none o' ye tasted the jelly—there's apple an' plum an' blackberry."

The lean days of spring were over, almost forgotten. Now, in the day of plenty, folks could eat to repletion, gorge themselves joyfully.

"Ivy, everything's grand!" Mag helped herself for the third time to fried cabbage. "Lord a' mercy, I'm a-eatin' a sight—fer me!—I've had a right smart o' indigestion here lately, an' I don't know what on earth's a-causin' hit."

But although the whole meal was praised, nothing else called forth such enthusiasm as the whistle-pig. Everyone agreed that no other wild meat could compare with it, unless perhaps coon—everyone except Short Dillard. "Law, people, ef you wants somethin' good, hit's mush-rats! Hain't no eatin' on earth 'ull tech young mush-rats!"

"A heap o' folks thinks polecat is mighty good eatin'," Old Mag added to the discussion, "but phew! a polecat, hit allays tastes to me like hit smells."

The noise of eating at length began to subside, the clatter and click of dishes and cutlery grew gradually fainter. The river could be heard once again, a dull murmur. Everyone was sitting back to rest, before starting on the pies and cake, for which they had made their plates ready, when a warning "Hello!" told them that Doke Odum was descending from the road.

"In the name o' God, hain't you folks done eatin'? Why, the cows is a-comin' home!"

Doke's overalls—one patch laid upon another, innumerable shades of faded blue—for once were clean. He was freshly shaven and a pale bluish rim around the edge of his black bushy hair showed that it had been recently trimmed. "No, thank ye, Molly, jest keep your seat—I've had my dinner." Standing at the foot of the table, his battered hat in his hand, Doke's eyes roved over it with good-humored envy. The table was somewhat disordered now, the cloth splattered with gravy and spotted with coffee, but it was still abundantly supplied with tempting dishes, while the blackberry and apple pies and the coconut cake were only starting to be passed.

Molly finally prevailed upon Doke to take her chair, and soon he was completely at home. "Mis' Philips, retch me that spoon o' yourn, ef you're done with hit. Hain't no need to nasty up another.—Short, I heern the company give ye seventy-five dollars. By God, anybody where wants 'em kin have both o' my legs—fer that!"

"There's some of 'em said I orter git a right smart more," Short explained, after the laughter had died down, "but I couldn't find out nothin' fer certain. They made me sign some papers, an' I asked 'em to read the papers to me, so I could tell what I were a-signin'. But they said they never had no time. One of them fellers in the office, he said: 'You're a nice bird! Think we want to rob a pore miner?' That there's jest the way he spoke hit. There's the very words he used. Then I asked the doctor ef any more money were a-comin' to me, but, boys, he shet me up proper! Well, sir, there's the shortest-spoken man ever I seed—I don't bar none! Short as piecrust."

Bertha Jane leaned forward when her brother had finished, her small pallid face dyed crimson. "Short," she said, smiling shyly and clearing her throat, "ef he gits two hundred, he's a-goin' to git us a parlor-set."

"The Lord have mercy!" Old Mag and Ivy shouted in unison. "A parlor-set!"

By the time Ivy sat down she was too tired to eat. She lingered over her plate, resting, trying to swallow a few bites. The others were moving about, yawning, stretching themselves, belching unashamedly, patting their full stomachs.

Molly and Mrs. Philips at length started washing the dishes. Luke and Doke had taken up their stand in the shade of the corn-crib, where they could hail any passer-by, leaning against it, with Short seated on a bank near by, all three of them whittling lazily.

All at once, Ivy remembered the tooth-brush which she had placed conspicuously on top of the chest of drawers. One day, some weeks before, when she was complaining of toothache, a woman from town, spending the day at the Pemberton cottage, had recommended the use of a tooth-brush. Ivy had answered, a trifle resentfully: "Birch twigs, to chew 'em, is way yonder better to clean a body's teeth." But now she called out: "Don't you-all want to use my tooth-brush? A tooth-brush is way yonder better 'an birch twigs to clean a body's teeth."

She was showing the brush to Gid and Nova, who had come inside from the porch—"Hain't hit a nice un? I paid a quarter fer hit"—when Luke announced softly from the doorway, smiling and raising his eyebrows: "Ivy, there's a stranger come to see ye!"

A stranger! Suddenly Ivy felt weak and dizzy. Her heart seemed to be missing beats. She looked out the door, the others craning their necks. No, it was not Jim.

"What's his business?" she asked dully.

"I couldn't tell ye. He asked ef this were where Mistress Ivy Ingoldsby lived. But I reckon he's a-settin' out," Luke added, in his gentle drawling voice, a gleam of mischief in his soft dark eyes. "He's a-wearin' flowers in his hat."

Gid emitted a snort.

The stranger was standing against the paling fence, outside the gate. Turning as Ivy came towards him, he eyed her with unconcealed curiosity. A tall raw-boned man, he wore a new-looking suit of clothes and a broad-brimmed black hat with two or three short-stemmed zinnias thrust through the band.

"Is this Mistress Ivy Ingoldsby?" he inquired in a deep rumbling voice, looking Ivy boldly in the eye.

"Yes, sir."

"My name's Yancy. I'm a widdy man, a grass-widdy man. I live yon side the mountain, in Shady Valley."

Ivy held the gate open. "Won't ye come in, sir?"

"I kin state my business with ye here." He eyed her again unhurryingly. "Ef ever I saw ye afore, I don't know hit— but I've heern tell o' ye."

"Ye say ye have?"

"Big Bill Byrd—me an' him worked togither, loggin'—Bill, he were allays a-braggin' on ye."

"Won't ye come in, sir, an' have ye a cheer?"

The man glanced towards the cabin suspiciously. "Hit's best to see ye to yourself.—I'm a-huntin' me a wife—Bill, he 'lowed you was the workin'est woman ever he seen."

"I hain't no lazy-bones," Ivy admitted, with an embarrassed laugh.

"My woman, she died on me, hit were two years back. I got me another, but this here last un—well, she were a powerful hand to waste, an' I tell ye what's the truth, a woman kin throw out more by the window with a spoon 'an a man kin throw in at the door with a shovel."

"Law, yes."

"Looked like me an' her couldn't make hit." He spat, waiting some time before he resumed: "Me an' her's parted. Well," he said explosively after another long pause, "seems like I wasn't much satisfied with her, nohow.

I 'lowed I 'ud git me a woman this time where hain't a-gittin' up in years. How old are ye, Ivy?" he asked abruptly.

"I were twenty-six last May."

He studied Ivy's neat, vigorous figure in the green linen dress appraisingly for a moment or so. "You're stout, hain't ye?"

"Law, I hain't in no ways weakly," Ivy laughed nervously.

"Bill Byrd, he said you was savin', an' kep everything nice."

"Law, I hain't no nasty woman!"

"Four o' my children is married, but I've got five little fellers, an' a man cain't do no good a-lookin' atter hisself an' young uns."

"Law, no." Ivy had dropped her eyes again.

"I hain't no hard man to fix fer, more 'an I wants biscuits fer my breakfast. There's fellers where's satisfied with nothin' on'y beans an' corn-bread. But I wants my wheat bread, me, of a mornin'."

"Yes, sir."

"I hain't no braggart, nobody cain't put no name o' braggart on me, but I've got me a good house."

"Law, I reckon," Ivy breathed, more and more embarrassed.

"I don't want no house so fine a man cain't spit in hit, but I've got me a good sound house, two rooms. I put me some new oak boards on the roof here lately an' hit don't hardly leak a drap." He spat again, deliberately. "I've got me a good gang o' chickens—I've got several, forty or fifty, I reckon, an' I've got two nice fat shotes where 'ull be plenty large to kill afore Thanksgivin'." The stranger looked around him. "Ivy, ye hain't got ary pig to your name, have ye?"

"Law, no, sir,—shotes is so expensive, to buy 'em, this day an' time, an' I never did keep me no sow."

"I've got two cows, or *did* have. I sold one day afore yesterday, but I kep' the best un, her fresh, an' the milk jest a-pourin'."

Ivy caught a titter from the cabin.

The stranger came nearer, bringing his red hatchet-shaped face with its prominent nose close to hers. "I 'ull buy ye a dress, an' a new pair o' slippers."

Ivy drew back. "Thank ye, but I've got plenty clothes."

The stranger gave a short laugh. He looked at her with astonishment. "You say ye have—? Well, I reckon ye wouldn't mind to git ye a new outfit, nohow." He stood a long time now, looking down reflectively at the river, off at the mountains. "Well, Ivy, I thought I 'ud come to see ye. I think you'd suit me, an' we orter marry."

"Law, mister," Ivy burst forth now, her cheeks flaming, "I've got a man—me an' him hain't never been divorced!"

The stranger nodded. "I know ye hain't got ye no divorce, Ivy." He drew out a thick roll of bills. "I come prepared to git ye one."

"Thank ye, an' I wouldn't doubt hit, sir, you 'ud make a good man fer some woman where's a-wantin' to marry, but I'm a-makin' hit by myself, a-makin' hit good, an' atter the man I had, the way he done me—law, I don't want no man on earth! But won't ye come in, sir, an' rest yourself? Won't ye have some dinner?"

The stranger put the roll of bills back into his pocket.

"We've done et, but you've come a fur piece, sir, an' I know I kin find ye a bite o' somethin', ef hit hain't no more 'an a snack."

"Well," the stranger said at last, thoughtfully, and looking off into the distance again, "well, I reckon there hain't but one thing fer me to do." He dropped his head, letting it hang for a moment or so, then threw it back with a jerk. "Well, good-day to ye. Ef you should change your mind, ef you should take a notion to write, my name's Jack Yancy, Shady Post Office. I think you 'ud suit me tol'able well. Well, good-day. I 'ull be a-goin' along. I 'ull be a-travelin' back over the mountain." He climbed the path to the road, pausing at the corn-crib to remove his hat and wipe his forehead. "Hit's a warm day, gentlemen, sort o' close like."

"That were old big-mouth Jack Yancy," Mag exclaimed, as soon as the stranger was out of ear-shot, "nobody *but* him; useter live somewhars over around Poplar Tree, an' so ill nobody on earth cain't live with him."

"Jack Yancy," Doke nodded, "that's him! Kilt his woman, the first un, a-kickin' her in the belly when she were in the family way."

"Hesh your mouth, Doke!" Ivy said.

"'My name's Yancy,'" Gid started rumbling. "'I'm a widdy man, a grass-widdy man. Ivy, I think you 'ud suit me good. We orter marry.'"

Everyone was roaring with laughter by this time, and Ivy began to repeat what the stranger had said to her: "Them was the very words he said. That there's jest the way he spoke hit."

CHAPTER EIGHT

IN A LONG, low building, set close to the ground, a building in which the loggers had once taken their meals, Mrs. Buskill still made her home. Obliquely behind it was a two-room cabin that had served in the old days for Mr. Pemberton's sleeping-quarters and office. He lay there now at night, with Shirley and the nurse in the adjoining room. Through the day his cot stood in front of the cabin, in a little level space shaded by wide-spreading beech-trees.

Ivy had been at the camp now for more than a week. Mrs. Buskill cooked the meals with the aid of two half-grown nieces from back in the mountains somewhere, shy little girls who came every day to carry water, prepare vegetables, and wash dishes. The trained nurse, a pretty young woman whose painted cheeks flamed out above her snowy uniform, gave the sick man such care as he required, or would permit, and, to Ivy's surprise, she found herself with very little to do.

She talked to Mrs. Buskill, churned for her, helped her in any way that offered. At night she slept with Mrs. Buskill.

The nights were cold, so close to the mountains, with fall already at hand. Shaking a little under the quilts, her surroundings strange, at first Ivy had found it hard to sleep. She missed the soothing murmur of the river. Here was only the rustling of the beech-trees to break the thick black silence, a sudden rush of wind from the encroaching mountains, the eerie cry of some little "shivering owl." As she lay beside the gentle old woman, sleeping soundly, snoring now and again, Ivy mused on talk she had heard. Into this very bed Jesse Pemberton, long ago, in the days before she herself was born, had slipped every morning after Hawk Buskill, his foreman—dead long since—had risen to start the loggers to work. Now that Mr. Pemberton and Mrs. Buskill were old, it was hard to believe such tales. "Ay, Lord, a heap o' times, love, hit's endurin'," Ivy thought, and again: "But who kin say that sech as that is true?—People has sech evil tongues."

For the first day or so Ivy had tried to be of use to Mr. Pemberton. She had gone out over the knobs and gathered lobelia, making an infusion to lighten his labored breathing. She had parched salt in a skillet, pouring it into a meal bag, and sought to place the bag of hot salt against his feet, "them cold as a frog, pore man!" But the nurse had rejected all her suggestions, and now she had to content herself with waving a green branch slowly back and forth over the cot. She continued to watch the nurse's deft competent movements with admiration and envy, mixed with a strong feeling of hostility, since the nurse had suggested, rather peremptorily, that Ivy call Shirley "Miss" Shirley. "She don't call me 'Miss' Ivy, do she?" Ivy had retorted angrily.

It was after this incident that Ivy had told Shirley she felt she was not earning her wages and ought to go home. "It's worth more than the wages," Shirley had said, "just to have you around."

So Ivy had remained. Yet she missed the innumerable tasks, indoors and out, that filled her usual day. In the warm afternoons, when Mrs. Buskill, in her gold-rimmed spectacles, was reading a newspaper, she scarcely knew how to occupy herself.

Soon, however, she began to find interest in the many people who were coming. Doctors came. A barber made the long trip twice a week to shave the sick man. Young Jesse, with a hang-dog look on his red bloated face, rode out every day or so to sit for a while by his father's cot, father and son alike embarrassed and speechless in each other's presence. Business men came for long, confidential talks, and mountain men who had worked for Mr. Pemberton in days past—they were coming, too. From in and out all the hills and hollows, from up the shadowy creeks, from little hidden clearings, men and women were coming to pay a last tribute to one of their own who had gone out of the mountains and become a rich and important man. They were proud that old man Jesse Pemberton, when his time came, had elected to return and die in their midst.

Ivy would meet these visitors at the spring-house as she spied one little company or another approaching. While they refreshed themselves with long draughts from the spring, she would answer their inquiries in a hushed voice: "Law, he's bad off!—No, he don't complain of no misery, but, law, he's bad as a man kin be, him to be alive!"

One and all, the mountain folks brought offerings: pawpaws, beginning to turn yellow now; a few sweet potatoes which they had grabbled in their patches for, as it was not yet time to dig the main crop, and which they had scrubbed till they shone; a little basketful of wild gooseberries; some late "roasting-ears" gathered before frost could catch them; a flask of choice apple or blackberry brandy; a small string of fish; squirrels for soup.

Motionless, immaculate, in his soft fine light-gray woolen suit, in his white shirt without a tie, in his gray cap, Mr. Pemberton would hold out a limp, transparent hand to each in turn, calling the visitor unerringly by his name and addressing to each a few smiling stammering words. "Well, Uncle John, I reckon it's time for me to go. I'm like a tree that's made its growth—I've done all I came here to do." Sometimes, in spite of Shirley's or the nurse's protests, he would insist on settling the disputes that were being brought him to be settled, just as they had always been before. He would hear both sides of the quarrel. Perhaps it was the heirs to a property who had been wrangling among themselves, and he would decide to whom the flock of turkeys should go, to whom the bedstead, to whom the yearling or milk-cow.

The visitors would stay all day, squatting around on their haunches, or sitting on the benches that Mrs. Buskill had had carried out and placed under the trees. Silently they would watch the nurse coming and going with the thermometer, the hot-water bag, a cup of broth. Hour after hour they would gaze sorrowfully at the gray figure on the cot—numb, icy, dead already save for the vibrant mind, still ticking, ticking.

At dinner-time they would follow Mrs. Buskill into the long room where the loggers had eaten more than thirty years before—everything unchanged, its long tables covered with oilcloth, benches along their sides, the window openings without glass. They would partake of the cornfield beans, boiled with bacon, of the fried ham and fried apples, the biscuits and corn-bread, which Mrs. Buskill prepared daily in sufficient quantities for all who might come.

Waving her green branch back and forth, Ivy would hear the sick man direct Mrs. Buskill in his low painful stutter: "Nan, cut a piece of middling for Uncle Rutt Grubb. Give him some flour and coffee to take when he goes.—Better fill a sack with onions and Irish potatoes for Aunt Jenny Lowdy—they've had a good deal of sickness and didn't raise much."

Ivy would walk out slowly over the knobs with those who were leaving, knobs that had been sown in grass after they were robbed of timber and that were beginning to sere now in mid-September. She would follow along with them over the worn trails leading in and out among the knobs, discussing how much longer Mr. Pemberton might last and what his chances were for the life everlasting. "Ivy, I heern his wife sent a preacher to see him," some would say, and others merely ask: "Ivy, have he saw a preacher yit?" shaking their heads when Ivy answered: "Law, no, he won't let no preacher come on the place!" Once she cried out boldly to some questioner: "No, he hain't never professed! But ef sech as Mr. Pemberton is a-goin' to torment, hit's somethin' fer folks to be a-studyin' about!"

On the morning that Senator Timberlake was expected, Mrs. Buskill sent out to one of the herders and had a lamb killed for dinner. From the lamb, Ivy concluded that this was no ordinary visitor.

"Law, hain't his hairs pretty!" she whispered to Shirley, at first sight of the senator's profuse crop of silvery hair. "White as the driven snow, fer the world!—But he looks peert to his age, an' hain't he got the most manners!" She brought him a gourdful of fresh water—"I reckon, sir, you're a-perishin' fer a drink"—and contrived every possible errand that would bring her close enough to observe the ruddy-faced, carefully dressed, and courtly man whose slightly protuberant eyes beamed goodwill. Finally resuming her seat beside the cot, she began again to wave the green branch back and forth.

In a low but sonorous voice the senator talked of dams at this point and that on the river, using the words "water power," "option," and "millions" again and again. Mr. Pemberton lay with his eyes closed, occasionally asking a question.

Ivy had heard talk for some time past, vague rumors, of a big dam to be built. The dam would mean that folks' cabins all along the river, little homesteads where their fathers had lived before them, would be swallowed up. The water would reach 'way up Troublesome, 'way up Grandmam's, as high, some folks said, as Ivy's own cabin. A sharp new pain shot through her heart now. "Hit 'ull ruin me ef the dam's built, hit 'ull mighty nigh take my life!" All at once her cabin, the few acres that Uncle Jake had left her, seemed almost as dear as Enoch. . . .

But the senator was speaking of something else. "Why, the second unit of the Grossberg concern, that alone will give employment," with a sweep of his arm, "to thousands upon thousands of these poor mountain people!"

Mr. Pemberton half opened his eyes. The senator cast a pleasant, understanding glance in Ivy's direction. "Poor, but no finer people living! Pure Anglo-Saxons, no foreign admixture!" Suddenly the senator began to talk of workers somewhere else, his low rolling voice becoming more and more impassioned as he went on. Exactly who and where these workers were, Ivy was unable to understand. The senator said they were filled with hatred of their bosses and had but one thought—to burn down the factories that gave them their daily bread. The senator paused, looking off through an opening in the forest, towards the mountains, wild and somber, very near. He ran his fingers through his luxuriant snowy hair. "Think of what a labor supply we have in these mountain people of ours, a supply that's hardly been touched! All they need is a little training—"

Mr. Pemberton opened his eyes more widely. A searching, quizzical, faintly amused look had appeared in them. "Senator," he stammered, "just between us—sometimes I wonder if they'll really be any better off—our mountain people here—when they're herded together in a lot of mill-towns."

"Better off—! My God, man! What chance have they here? What chance would you have had if you'd stayed on Horse Creek? What have they got to interest them, to say nothing of support them? Tragically monotonous lives! But think what it will mean to these people when they can all have a chance to work every day in the year at good wages! Think what it will mean to them to have nice little homes in town with all the conveniences! Think of the lives of these mountain women, like Ivy here—fine, smart, good women as there are anywhere in the world—grubbing out sprouts, hoeing, plowing—!" The senator's deep voice was filled with emotion. "God never intended that a woman's hand should be put to the plow!"

"Law, Senator," Ivy burst out, unable to contain herself longer, "I hain't never plowed, but I 'ud a heap ruther to hoe an' to clear the filth off o' new ground as to work in ary factory on earth!"

The senator stared at her.

"I couldn't never be satisfied in no town on earth," Ivy kept on. "Seems like nothin' don't never happen in town, like here. An' I wouldn't work in one o' them old hateful factories agin—not ef you was to give hit to me!"

"Well, well!" the senator said, at last.

It was two days later and Ivy was watching beside the cot while Shirley and the nurse ate a hurried supper. Since early that morning there had been a change. The sick man was restless.

"Is it dark?" he asked now, though his eyes were wide open.

"Why, no, sir," Ivy said, "hit hain't dark! Hit's bright day. Hit lacks a right smart o' sundown."

He asked Ivy to draw the bill-purse from one of the inside pockets in his coat and, extracting some bills from it, held them out to her. "I believe there's a hundred, Ivy. I want you to get a cow with it."

"Law, Mr. Pemberton," Ivy cried chokingly, "don't give me all that! I'm afeared hit's more 'an you kin spare," she said, "an hit don't take no sech big amount, nohow—"

"Ivy, take it. Get a good one."

"Law, Mr. Pemberton, I kin git me a good un fer thirty dollars!"

"Take the money. Put it away."

"Ye ortern't to give me nothin'," Ivy protested sobbingly. She wanted to ask about the dam, if it were surely going to be built. But it was too late now—a waxy look had settled upon Mr. Pemberton's face, and the death damp already dewed his brow. Ivy took the bills, gazing on them incredulously through the thick mist that clouded her eyes; then, wrapping them in her handkerchief, she thrust the wad into her bosom.

"Ivy—I want to thank you—for what you've done—"

"Oh, sir, you-uns has done twice—yes, thribble, fer me," Ivy sobbed softly, "whatever I've done fer you-uns . . . I won't never forgit ye, Mr. Pemberton!"

Part Three

"Some Sweet Day"

Chapter One

IVY HAD PUT her cabin to rights and scrubbed the floor with her hickory scrub-broom. She had been glad to go to Shirley; yet how good it was to be back again! When she went to the door, she could see, down below, a gray-blue spiral of smoke curling up from the Byrds' chimney. Enoch's little dog trotted around at her heels. She heard her hens cackling and singing about, caught the river's murmur. . . .

She could hardly walk under her apple-trees without crunching the fallen fruit, it lay so thick. Squatting, she picked the apples over, throwing the best of them into some gunny-sacks she had brought for the purpose, and munching one apple after another. The tempered late-September sun felt good to her back. She sniffed delightedly the rich fruity scent of the many broken apples, oozing with juice, buzzing with bees.

Suddenly she was aware of a man coming down the road. "One-arm Press, ef hit hain't!—Well, he hain't a-losin' no time," she said to herself, guessing that the sack on his shoulder was full of sugar. "I reckon he's a-goin' down to Doke's. More an' apt him an' Doke is a-fixin' to make liquor togither."

"Law, Mr. Philips," she called now, as the one-armed man left the road and descended the grassy bank that separated it from Ivy's fence.

He held out his left hand for Ivy to shake.

"Won't ye come in, Mr. Philips, an' set awhile?"

"No.—No."

"You're fat as a bear," Ivy said. "Looks like they treated you good."

"Tol'able.—Tol'able." He smelled slightly of liquor.

His drooping sandy mustache was moist with tobacco juice. Otherwise, he was fairly neat, in a faded woolen suit of butter-nut brown. "Some fellers is allays a-kickin', but a man's got no cause to kick ef he gits his coffee an' biscuits of a mornin' an' his beans an,' a piece o' corn-bread of a night." He talked in a friendly fashion, yet somewhat impersonally, as though his thoughts were somewhere else. "Two meals is plenty when a feller hain't workin'." The grass was still sparkling with dew, but, selecting a spot that looked dry, he laid his sack on it.

Picking up some apples, Ivy held them out across the paling fence. "Here, have ye some wine-saps, an' that there's a smoke-house apple, the old folks useter call 'em yaller—meated, an' hain't no better apple grows on earth."

One-arm Press dropped two of the apples into his pocket, biting into a third, while Ivy continued to munch on hers.

"You didn't have to stay no big time, did ye?"

He shook his head. "The jedge," talking between bites, "he give me as light a sentence as he could, I reckon.—Well," he laughed, with a significant glance from his rheumy eyes, "I reckon Jedge Blount is well pleased—I reckon he's well satisfied fer me to be out agin. He hain't had a drap o' decent liquor, he says, sence he sent me up."

"Forevermore!"

"I tell you what's a fact—hit's a crime the liquor some o' these fellers is willin' to put on a fine gentleman like Jedge Blount, an' sech as him. Useter be there wasn't nothin' *but* good liquor—good corn liquor—come out o' these here mountains. Why, when I first started, 'way back yonder, there wasn't on'y two or three of us fellers owned stills. But now with every God danged-" He stopped short. "Excuse the language," he said. "But with so many of 'em a-messin' around with liquor—sugar liquor—this day an' time, the most of hit 'ud make a dog puke. Nothin' on earth but nasty slop. Miserable, sorry, stinkin' stuff—half water," he ended contemptuously.

"Law, I reckon."

Ivy had but a poor opinion of liquor-making in general. Nevertheless, she listened with interest and a certain respect. No one knew more about the business than One-arm Press.

"Ivy, ef hit won't make ye mad, I 'ull give ye some sugar."

"I say make me mad!" Ivy laughed.

"Run git ye a piggin."

Returning, Ivy unfastened his sugar-sack, a little awkward for the one-armed man to manage, and poured some out into the bowl she had brought. "I thank ye fer hit," she said.

"Well, I 'ull tell ye, Ivy"—settling himself against the fence, and starting on another apple—"I 'ull tell ye—hit weren't never meant fer men to make no livin' offen this pore miserable soil we've got here in the mountains. Where they've got deep rich dirt"—he reached down, as if he were picking up a handful of earth, motioning off what he was describing—"where they've got a good clay subsoil, a feller kin raise enough to feed him. But these old wore-out knobs an' these mountains, I tell ye they're on'y fitten to feed the wild critturs—the varmints. A man has obliged to do somethin' or ruther, besides tryin' to raise him a little stuff, without he wants to starve to death, him an' his family both."

"Law, yes," Ivy agreed, in a low voice, eating her apple down to the core. She could name a few men, two or three at any rate, who had made a living off of their little patches of land—if not a very good one, at least as good as those who fooled with liquor were making, what with the fines they had to pay and one thing and another. She had not done so badly herself—she had made it, somehow or other, year after year. No need, however, to speak of this.

"But I hain't never saw no bad time in jail myself," One-arm Press was saying now. "Me an' the jailer's good friends. Looks like we orter be," he added laughingly "—I've stayed in his house plenty times!"

The talk worked around at length to a mention of Wash Byrd. Wash had been sentenced at the fall term of court.

"I'm glad," Ivy said, "Wash didn't git no more 'an a year 'an a day."

One-arm Press looked thoughtful. "Well, you know the blood, Ivy." He gave a hitch to his shoulder from which the arm was missing, an arm that Big Bill Byrd had slashed half-way off in an altercation over a hound years before. "You know the Byrd blood!—But pore boy! Pore boy! He didn't know what he were a-doin', him drunk. He didn't go to kill Godfrey, I don't reckon, but Godfrey a-pickin' up his mattock the way he done, hit were him or Godfrey.—Pore boy!"

He stood for a while without saying anything, then shouldered his sack of sugar. "Ivy, you're a-lookin' good. Don't know as I've ever saw ye a-lookin' better. You've been a-stayin' with the Pembertons this past summer, hain't ye?—Old man Pemberton were a fine gentleman."

"Hain't no finer," Ivy said sadly, and after a pause. "They taken his corpse to town."

"I reckon ef the old man 'ud had *his* way, they 'ud put him away here in the mountains."

"Law, I reckon."

"They had a long piece in the paper, I heern some of 'em a-sayin', about the funeral."

"I knowed in reason," Ivy sighed, "they 'ud put him away grand. I reckon the flowers was a sight on earth."

"They put him away in a steel casket.—Well, Ivy, you come to see us."

"Yes, you-all come.—Mis' Philips an' Novy, they was good to Enoch what time I were gone.—Gid an' Novy's put off their weddin'-day, hain't they?" she called after him as he started down the road.

"Yes.—Yes," he called back, without turning.

Ivy went back to gathering apples. "An' they 'ull make the best apple butter, them so juicy, the cider jest a-gushin'—"

There had been a big racket—all Ivy knew thus far was from Enoch— when Nova refused to go to the magistrate with Gid on the day set for the marriage. "Hit do seem strange, her an' Gid so lovin', Novy a-callin' him 'dearest darlin'—"

She refilled her sacks, pouring the apples into a pile that was to be made into apple butter; then, bringing a basketful of beans, she sat down on the porch, resting her feet on the step and began stringing beans. Enoch's little dog, curled up close beside her, snapped at a fly now and then.

It was a beautiful day, the air full of life, full of the sweet spicy smell of the pines. There had been no frost as yet. "The river takes the frost up," Ivy thought. She glanced down at her garden. Above the wilderness of weeds with which it was overgrown at this season, the wild morning-glories lifted up their cups, an enchantment of color, hundreds of blossoms, still glistening with dew, rose and milk-white and sapphire-blue. Below, the river danced and dimpled and laughed. . . .

"Looks like a body orter be well pleased," Ivy thought, "ef he hain't got nothin' on earth but jest his health, ef a body's able to be stirrin' around."

She carried the beans into the cabin. "I hain't so crazy about pickled beans," she said to herself as she packed the beans in a huge stone crock, layer upon layer, sprinkling salt between, "but hit's best to have 'em more ways 'an jest dried, when beans is most of a body's livin', an' looks like my beans allays spoils so bad ef I can 'em—the cans is allays a-spewin' out."

Uppermost in her mind, however, was the thought of the money Mr. Pemberton had given her. She was keeping this knowledge to herself. It was hard to resist folks who came to borrow. She was increasingly tortured, too, by the fear that the money might be stolen from her. Her cabin was far from secure from pilfering fingers. She had missed little things in the course of the summer, gone all day, and Enoch away at play.

Once her dearest desire had been to buy Daisy back from the Byrds. But now she reflected, a little resentfully: "More 'an apt Daisy won't never be fresh agin."

It was at the time Wash was hiding from the law after he had killed Godfrey, before Big Bill had come home. Ivy had watched the cow down in the Byrd's field, cavorting wildly about, heard her bellowing. "Ef Mis' Byrd, she didn't want to take the pore critter to the bull herself," Ivy was thinking now, as she set out some cold sweet potatoes on the table in the lean-to for her solitary dinner, some left over beans and com-bread "—ef she didn't want to drive Daisy to no bull herself, an' ef she were 'shamed to ask Woodrow Wilson, him so young, what were to hinder her a-askin' Linsey an' Essie? A woman ortem't to be strange afore her own daughters. Law, I'm good as Linsey an' Essie Byrd, an' I've driv a cow to the bull a many a time, an' hain't no worse fer loin' hit. But Daisy, she's ruint now, them not tendin' to her, a-lettin' her heller the en durin' sixteen days, an' nothin' to put no quietus on her."

Well, she could find a cow somewhere, up or down the river. She wouldn't be in too big a hurry.

In the afternoon, armed with a broom and dustpan, she started for the church. The preacher had asked her to sweep the church after each preaching day. He would pay her fifty cents for each time. Before she reached Doke's cabin, she heard a victrola.

Doke was sharpening an ax, Noah turning the grind stone for him; but, seeing Ivy coming, he came padding up towards the fence with his loose-jointed loping gait. "Lord God, Ivy, what's that there you've got in your hand?" pointing to the dustpan.

Ivy explained its use, adding that Shirley had given it to her.

"Some of 'em says the old man left a million dollars. Others says there won't be much o' nothin', time them rascally lawyers gits done milkin' the estate. But I don't reckon Nan Buskill is a-wearyin' herself. Nan, she's got money in the bank an' plenty land the old man give her."

From the gleam in his eye Ivy could tell that Doke was hoping to provoke her sooner or later to an angry outburst. But she was on her guard.

"Doke, you've got ye a victroly, hain't ye?" she asked lightly.

Doke removed his battered felt hat, scratching his bushy head. "Ivy, why don't ye git ye one? They on'y costs a feller five dollars. You don't need to pay no more, without you're a mind to, an' you kin see a heap o' pleasure afore the company comes an' takes 'em away. Everybody is a-gittin' things that-a-way here lately—cook-stoves an' victrolys an' Lord knows what all."

"Law, I reckon," Ivy said.

"Short Dillard, he's got him his parlor-set, dog-gone ef he hain't!"

Ivy nodded. "I seen Uncle Abel a-haulin' hit home from town."

"Ivy, what's your rush? Come on in! I 'ull play ye a new piece, one about Kinnie Wagner."

Ivy shook her head. "The days is a-gittin' shorter, an' hit takes a right smart time to sweep the church, all that chewin'-gum an' them there old cigarettes on the floor." She started to move on. "Seems like folks hain't got respect to the church-house this day an' time." Suddenly she remembered she had not caught sight of Leola above the huddle of dirty children in the doorway. "I reckon Leoly an' the children is well," she called back, inquiringly.

"Well as common—on'y the old woman. Leoly, she hain't nothin' extry. She's in the bed."

Ivy paused. "What's a-ailin' her?"

"I jerked her teeth fer her, day afore yesterday. They wasn't no 'count. They was all a-rottenin'. I jerked 'em fer her raw, with my hog-ringer, the last one—"

"Land o' livin', I bet hit hurt!" Ivy had hardly spoken to Leola since the day she had found Enoch smelling of liquor Leola had given him. "I 'ull stop to see Leoly," she called now, "as I come past a-goin' home."

Thinking of Leola brought back the ambition she had once had of having her own teeth attended to, especially of having one or two gold teeth. One day, with something of a shock, she had overheard Shirley and a friend ridiculing such a display. . . . Well, it would leave more money for other things.

She was reverently dusting the pine pulpit and the highback chair where the preacher sat when she heard the children coming from school. She went outside and stood in the grove of great white pines that surrounded the church, chatting with one little group after another, asking after the children's parents. All the children were eating apples or pawpaws.

Her heart leaped with joy when at last she saw Enoch with three or four other boys coming along between the high dense banks of laurel and rhododendron that shadowed the road on either side. In his new overalls, his new cap, and good strong shoes, his books under his arm, the little boy looked so nice, so fair and rosy and sweet, she longed to kiss him. Taking him aside, she warned him she would be late. "But I drug some good poles down to the road afore I left. You hack 'em, Enoch. Have me a fire in the cook-stove aginst the time I git there, an' have some fresh water, so I won't be in the night a-gittin' our supper."

The sun was setting, the river glowing like a burnished rose, when she locked the church door behind her. A sharp wind had arisen and was blowing straight down from the mountains. Ivy shivered in her summer dress. "Hit 'ull frost tonight, ef the wind lays," she thought anxiously, wishing she had gathered the green tomatoes that remained in her garden.

She made her way through the swarm of ragged, filthy little children, smiling a shy welcome at her, to Leola's bed. Guy, the lame boy, and little Noah were occupied with the victrola, set close to the one small window, while Ibbie and Opal, the two oldest little girls, were working around the step-stove in another dusky corner, from whence arose the grateful, somewhat purifying odors of boiling coffee and frying bacon.

Leola was lying, face out, half covered with dark-colored dirty quilts, the few-months-old babe pressed greedily against her breast. She was moaning faintly.

"Law, Leoly," Ivy exclaimed, with difficulty suppressing a cry of horror, "I hain't never saw sech a face on livin' human!"

"Git ye a cheer," Leola urged, in a low voice, between her moans. Her face was a bruised, pulpy, purple-red mass in which the features seemed to have all run together.

Heating a shovel, Ivy held it near to Leola's swollen face. "Here, Leoly, hit 'ull draw the misery—I know you're a-sufferin' death!" When the hot shovel brought no relief, she wrung cloths from hot water, applying them tenderly. The children looked on silently, except Guy and Noah, who kept winding up the victrola, playing the same record over and over.

"I hate hit, Leoly, to leave ye," Ivy announced at last, "but night's a-fallin'. I 'ull come tomorrow," she promised. "I 'ull bring ye some soup—somethin' you kin eat. I'm glad, Leoly," she said in parting, "you-all has got ye a victroly."

"Hit passes the time," the suffering woman murmured. Her groans were a little farther apart now. "Thank ye, Ivy," she said, "fer comin'."

Doke was returning from the store, carrying a case of half-gallon fruit-jars, further proof that he had gone into partnership with One-arm Press. He held Ivy at the gate for a moment, bringing his face in the gathering dusk close to hers.

"Ivy, did ye know that Novy's a-slippin' out of a night, a-goin' ridin' with One-eye Buck, in Buck's Ford?"

"Law, me!" Ivy breathed. All at once she felt strongly perturbed. "I'm afeared there won't be no weddin'!"

Doke gave a low whistle. "Better be!"

Ivy drew back a step, but Doke thrust his face into hers again. "Ivy, Novy orter lace herself when she steps out," he whispered, laughing huskily—"she's a-lookin' chuffy!"

Chapter Two

THE RIVER AND mountains were still lightly veiled with mist. Bareheaded in the soft golden sunshine, Ivy was digging potatoes, stopping to rejoice over each hill that gave a satisfactory yield—"Law, my taters has made theirselves good—I 'ull have several!"—stopping to watch the little lizards lazily sunning themselves on upturned stones here and there, to watch the birds that everywhere now were gathering together in flocks.

After she had carried the potatoes to the cellar, she sat down on the porch step. The warm hazy air made her feel sleepy. She wished she could sit here all day, elbows on her knees, chin against her hands, just dreaming. . . .

But when she had sat for a while, one thought after another began to arouse her from her half-dozing content. Leola's sufferings in the last few days recurred to her with painful intensity. She thought of Bertha Jane. Bertha Jane's small pinched face, smiling shyly as she displayed the parlor-set, came up before her. "Pale as a corpse—! reckon she's not got long!"

On the Sabbath just past Gid had professed. The church had been full to overflowing, Old Mag holding her head high, as Gid, white-faced and big-eyed, towering above the preacher, had confessed his sins and asked for the prayers of all present. Nova, in her flaming red dress, had sat with downcast eyes, occasionally lifting her long, black lashes, a slight smile dimpling her face from time to time. What did it mean, trifling with the man she had promised to marry? "Novy, she's a ruinin' herself with folks, the way she's a-doin'." And Doke was right—Nova was beginning to show. "Her allays so flat, an' now her breasts is a-puffin' out like pones!"

Ivy's thoughts drifted. At last, with an effort, she forced herself to go inside.

She was chopping green tomatoes for chow-chow, cutting them with the sharp edge of a tin can which she had devised for the purpose, when a voice from the road startled her: "Ivy! Oh, Ivy!"

Looking out the door, she saw that it was Big Bill Byrd, followed by One-eye Buck. To her amazement she saw that each of them was carrying several large paper-covered boxes. They deposited the boxes inside the cabin, then stepped back on to the porch, Big Bill, a red-faced good natured-looking man, explaining that he and Buck had been at the store when the mail-man brought them.

Buck was wearing a light-colored checked suit. He looked, Ivy thought to herself, "fine as a lawyer." Despite an eye from which the sight was gone, he was a handsome youth, not as tall as his father, but yet of good stature, with fair soft hair, clean-cut regular features, and skin as fair and delicately tinted as that of his sister Linsey, whom he resembled.

"From Shirley!" Ivy thought, gazing at the boxes heaped on the cabin floor, her face flushed. "Wouldn't no person else on earth 'a sent me sech as that!"

Big Bill had dropped down on the porch step and, removing his hat, was wiping the sweat from his forehead.

"Law, Mr. Byrd," Ivy cried now, "you hain't a-goin' to set on no tread! Here, take ye a cheer," she insisted, bringing another chair for Buck.

The men started taking chestnuts from their pockets. They offered some to Ivy, and all three sat cracking the nuts with their teeth, spitting out the hulls as they talked. "Buck," Big Bill said suddenly, "didn't Andy give ye some letters fer Ivy?"

"I like to forgot!" With a teasing smile Buck felt for the letters in an inside pocket, drawing out some other letters first and a photograph of a girl, which he flashed on Ivy, but replaced before she could tell whose picture it was.

It was a rare thing for Ivy to receive any letters at all. But two at once—! One of the envelopes had a black border. Ivy examined the postmarks and then let the letters lie in her lap, while she went on talking, cracking and munching chestnuts. "I reckon, Mr. Byrd, you-all 'ull be a-pullin' fodder afore long.—Have ye dug your taters? I've dug mine—my Irish taters, I dug 'em this mornin'. But I'm a-goin' to let my sweet taters lay in the ground till frost is on 'em good. Hit makes 'em sweeter, don't hit?—Yes, I reckon I 'ull git to make my apple butter next week. I've laid off to have me a apple-parin'. . . .

"But you-all hain't a-goin', are ye?" she cried, as Big Bill, after a visit of some length, got up to leave. "Why, you hain't set no time at all! Stay an' have dinner," she urged now.—"Well, how much do I owe ye, Mr. Byrd? Nothin'? Well, I thank ye fer packin' 'em to me, I thank ye terrible, but you-all 'ud best stay fer dinner."

As he fastened the gate behind him, Big Bill called back, his eyes beaming: "Ivy, some of 'em was a-tellin' me that Jack Yancy, from yon side the mountain, come over to git ye—"

"Law, Mr. Byrd," Ivy returned laughingly, "folks teases me till my life's a misery!"

"Buck," she shouted, when the two men had reached the road, "did ye quit off your job in town fer good?"

Buck wheeled around. "I'll say I did! They puts too much *on* a feller in them there factories!"

Of the black-bordered letter all Ivy could make out was "Dear Ivy" at the beginning. But she had seen several specimens of Shirley's handwriting and knew it for hers. "Shirley hain't no sech extry good scribe," she thought now, "an' her with good learnin'." No doubt, however, Enoch would be able to read Shirley's letter for her.

The other letter, on pink paper with gilt edges, she read without much trouble:

> *Piney Flats R # 2*
> *Mrs. Ivy Ingoldsby*
> *Kind friend Guess this will Be verry much surprise to Get a letter from me. first I will tell you just why I am wrighting to you I was in Kings Mill and old friend of mine was talking to me and insisted that I wright you and I hope this will not be intruden on you: first guess you would like to Know my pacition I have Been maried and my wife has gone home to Glorry leaving me with 3 children so I am verry lonely. I cant Be Satisfy any more Singel. well guess you would like to Know something as to my Reputation so Mr Abe Pippin the man I was talking to in Kings Mill could tell you all about me. I worked at Black mt saw mill when he worked there. I would love to corspond with you and I hope some sweet day to meet you face to face: well Guess I will close for this time so if you would like to corspond to me I will apreciate it:*

ans soon from
Hop Harlow
P. S. Say Ivy I would like to talk to you. Excuse all Bad
Wrighting and Take all mistakes for Love don't think hard on me
for wrighting you.

"Hop Harlow! Who's him? I never heern tell o' no sech person." Ivy laid down the letters and started to unwrap one of the boxes, her fingers trembling a little as she untied the cords. What had Shirley sent this time?

She lifted out one dress after another—all so nice, none of them worn, to speak of. There were sweaters and gloves and hats—everything imaginable, and in one box a winter coat of some soft velvety material, lined with silk. Ivy thought of the faded threadbare coat hanging in the loft above her, the only coat she had ever owned, and a lump came in her throat so that she could scarcely swallow. She looked at the things she had spread out on the bed, at the dresses she had draped, one on top of another, over her splint-bottom chairs. Tears blurred her eyes as she gazed at the strange array, first in one direction and then another.

In one pile she had laid the undergarments, among them two night-gowns of pale-pink silk delicately trimmed with lace. Ivy held the night-gowns up against herself. She slipped one over her head, then pulled it off hastily, almost with shame. . . . She had never removed more than her shoes and outer clothing when she lay down at night, except in hot weather, when she slept in her shift. . . .

She turned the coat round and round. It emitted an odor of moth-balls mingled faintly with some perfume that Shirley used. Ivy buried her nose. Finally she put the coat on, rubbing the cuffs against her cheeks, to feel the softness of the fur. She looked at herself in the square of watery glass hanging above her tin wash-basin on the back porch, twisting about, trying to get every possible view of herself.

All at once she saw herself standing before Jim in this coat, in one of these fine dresses. If Jim failed to come, why not go to him, she and Enoch? Jim should see that she was no longer the woman he had left, that he had no cause now to be ashamed.—Where was this Fort Omaha? It was a far-off place, far as Montana, far as California. No matter! She had the money! Yes, yes, yes, yes! "Say howdy to Ivy." . . . She sank down beside the bed, clinging to the footboard, torn by wild sobs. "He done me dirt, but I hain't never loved no one else, an' oh, God, there hain't no woman on earth kin be satisfied, year after year, an' her no man!"

CHAPTER THREE

———— ✦ ————

JIM MIGHT COME, of course, at Christmas-time, if he had not come before. Better wait, Ivy thought, until after Christmas, wait and see. . . .

It was only a little more than a year since she and Enoch had set out on that other venture, one that had turned out so disastrously. But this would be different. She pictured—her heart at times beating to suffocation—Jim returning with her and Enoch, coming back home to the mountains. If Jim were unable to get his release at once, then she and Enoch would return ahead of him. The thought of staying for any length of time—longer, indeed, than was absolutely necessary—in the strange place where Jim was, frightened her more than the thought of the journey itself. Other mountain folks had traveled on the train. None of them had failed to reach their destination. "Folks is generally allays so kind," she thought, as she pictured herself asking directions in the course of the journey. It was not as though she were one of those mountain women who had never been anywhere, never even been to town.

As for money, she must be as careful and saving as ever. At present she was in great demand, helping one family after another make their apple butter, their cider and molasses, and earning pay in kind. Then later on she would gather walnuts, pick out the kernels, and sell them. Oh, there would be many little ways—better to start with more in her purse than she needed than not enough.

Occasionally she felt a qualm at planning to use the money Mr. Pemberton had given her for another purpose than the one he had intended. But she quieted her conscience with the reflection that Jim would

139

buy a cow when he came. Jim had saved money, all these years in the army. Jim was free-hearted. . . .

There was a thing, however, that troubled her.

One evening she was preparing supper, and Enoch was recounting to her the day's happenings at school, which ordinarily she found of intense interest. "Woodrow Wilson, he missed four words in the spellin'. . . . Teacher give us the sixteenth verse of the third chapter of John to learn afore Friday. Said he 'ud whoop them where don't git it letter-perfect. . . . Neff Torbett like to busted the teacher's eye with a book he throwed at him. Neff, he give Mr. Cartright some sass about the 'rithmetic lesson, an' Mr. Cartright were a-fixin' to cut him a hickory, but Neff, he said he wouldn't take no lickin' from no teacher on earth. Told teacher he 'ud cut his guts out first—them was his words."

Ivy continued to answer absently, "Well, I do know! . . . Law, me! . . . Forevermore!" Her thoughts were far off. They sat down to the table. Ivy kept her eyes on her plate. Her cheeks were hot with embarrassment. "Enoch," she began, "I didn't have no sech good chancet to go to school when I were a child as you're a-havin'—"

Enoch had heard this before. He made no answer. He helped his plate again from the dish of green beans cooked with corn cut from the cob.

"I know good an' well," Ivy said in a low voice, hesitatingly, "I don't speak proper. I acknowledge to hit."

With his knife half-way to his mouth the little boy paused and looked at his mother wonderingly.

"Enoch, I wisht you 'ud learn me to speak proper."

Enoch went on eating. He crumbled a piece of cornbread into the soup from the corn-and-beans on his plate. "Mammy," he said, at last, deliberately, gently, yet protestingly, "Mammy, you allays flies mad when I tries to learn ye—"

"No, honey, no!" she broke in pleadingly. "I won't no more! I promise ye! Ef you 'ull learn me to talk like folks where has good learnin', I won't never quarrel on ye fer hit agin!"

Chapter Four

IT WAS A warm blustery evening, with the sound of leaves scurrying along the ground. Ivy fretted a little that the moon was in the last quarter and rose late. The road would be dark and some of those she had asked might not come. She lit her small glass lamp with its cracked chimney and placed it on the chimney-shelf. The women would bring their own paring-knives. Everything else was in readiness, the splint-bottom chairs, her own and those she had borrowed, drawn up in a circle around the fire-place, although the evening was too mild for a fire.

The sudden frantic barking of Enoch's little dog announced that someone was approaching. Ivy peered through the open door. It was not yet completely dark and she could distinguish the form she saw as Mrs. Byrd's, flanked by the slim figures of Linsey and Essie, hobbling along on their high heels.

"Law, Mis' Byrd, I were afeared you couldn't never make hit on earth!"

"My legs is a-swellin' so bad I like to never got here," Mrs. Byrd called back in a cheerful voice, "but, goodness gracious, Ivy, looks like I don't never git to go nowhere, an' I were bound to come!"

In a fresh calico dress, the light-colored apron tied around her waist, throwing her enormously distended stomach into prominent view, Mrs. Byrd made her way into the cabin.

"I 'lowed you 'ud be down afore this," Ivy said, helping the unwieldy woman into a chair.

"I made sure," Mrs. Byrd said, trying to recover her breath, "I 'ud be down afore this."

Linsey and Essie had stopped on the porch, waiting for others to come. It was the first time Ivy had seen their mother since Wash had been taken to the penitentiary, and Mrs. Byrd laid a plump hand on Ivy's arm now, gazing up at her sorrowfully, tears swimming in her blue eyes, with their tender and benevolent expression. "Ivy, hain't hit the worst?"

Ivy sat down in the chair next her.

"Looks like," Mrs. Byrd said gently, gazing into the fire-place, a cheerless black expanse, "looks like a body cain't do nothin' with the young folks this day an' time—they're all so wild."

Suddenly she turned and placed her hand on Ivy's arm again. "I hate hit the worst," she said, in a hushed confidential tone, "ef Buck is the cause o' trouble 'twixt Gid an' Novy."

"Law, I don't reckon nobody, without hit's theirselves," Ivy returned cautiously, "knows how things stands 'twixt Gid an' Novy.—O' course, Novy hain't a-treatin' Gid right," she added a moment later, "but Gid an' Novy is both spoiled.

"I reckon," Ivy said, after another pause, "their mammies is to blame. Old Mag an' Mis' Philips hain't neither one of 'em never made Gid an' Novy do a earthly thing where they didn't want to. Mag an' Mis' Philips a-hoein' an' weedin', an' Gid an' Novy a-settin' in the house, a-playin' the victroly! Novy, she hain't never worked in the sun, what's to say worked, a day in her life, I don't reckon."

"Novy, rared back on the porch," Mrs. Byrd laughed softly, "a-readin' them there confession magazines! Looks like a body orter find somethin' better to do with idle time 'an to spend hit a-readin', now don't hit?—Well, Ivy, I wants my girls to have things nice, too—slippers an' pretty dresses an' like o' that, an' hit like to taken my life," she sighed, "fer Linsey, her with a turn fer figgerin', not to git to go to no high school; but I've raised up my girls to work—" She paused to take breath. "Ivy, *you* know that!"

"Law, yes, Mis' Byrd," Ivy murmured. Spot had started barking again, and Ivy bent back in her chair so that she could see out the door. "I reckon that's Mis' Philips an' Novy a-comin' now, them with a lantern."

The blink of yellow light drew nearer and nearer.

"Ivy," Mrs. Byrd said—a last hurried confidence "Ivy, ef Buck's a-tryin' to part Gid an' Novy, I hain't upholdin' the boy in hit. Why, bless the Lord," she whispered, half laughing, "I 'ud a heap rather fer Gid to have Novy as fer Buck to have her! Novy won't never make no wife fer no pore man!"

Paring slowly, their broken-bladed paring-knives moving almost in unison, the women dropped curl after curl of apple-skin into their laps and, quartering the apples with a dexterous movement, cast the pared quarters into crocks at their feet that were waiting to receive them. Now and then someone in the circle would get up to refill her apron with apples, to empty it of refuse, or to grope her way fumblingly through the darkness of the lean-to out to the back porch and return with a gourdful of water, offering it to the others: "Hain't none o' you-uns parched fer a drink?" One woman after another, cutting a slice from the apple she was paring and holding it against the blade of her knife, would lift it to her mouth, and a constant crunching accompanied the low hum of singsong voices as women sitting next each other visited together, discussing those matters with which their lives were engrossed.

"Is your hens a-layin'?"

"They was, but they've done quit."

"What's Andy a-givin' at the store fer eggs?"

"Andy's a-givin' twenty cents at the store, fer eggs."

"Is your cow a-mendin' in her milk?"

"She's a-mendin' in her milk now she's got on good pasture, but, law, she don't give much. I hain't hardly a-makin' a pound o' butter a week."

"Did ye raise ye a good crap on your new ground?"

"We raised us a right smart crap, but, law, the corn on our new ground, hit's late. I'm afeared frost 'ull ketch hit. New ground, hit holds back so."

"I'm a-aimin' to put my sweet taters down in pineneedles, to keep 'em."

"Hit's all the way a body kin do, to keep 'em. Sweet taters, they rots so bad."

"How's Mis' Rutter—have you heern?"

"Mis' Rutter, she hain't no better. She's bad off. She has to be turned in the bed."

"How's Bertha Jane Dillard—have ye saw her here lately?"

"I hain't saw her fer a time, but they say she's a-failin' fast."

"Law, the tubercles is bad!"

"Law, yes, the tubercles is bad.—I hain't hardly a-lookin' fer Bertha Jane to last till snow comes on the mountain."

"Thallie Hawk's eldest gal has got her a job in town. Had you heern?"

"I hain't heern no tell of hit afore."

"I heern some of 'em a-sayin' the Bunts gal has quit off her job at the knittin'-mills."

"Law, I reckon. They puts too much *on* a person in them there factories."

"Some says they're a-aimin' to build the dam, some says hit hain't nothin' on'y talk."

"I don't see why they want to build no big dam nohow, to flood us all out."

"Law, no! Why cain't they be satisfied with jest some little dams, where won't ruin folks?"

Ivy would often interject some lively remark into this sober interchange. "Law, Aunt Sally, you're a-beatin' the balance of us all to nothin'! Look what Aunt Sally's got done! Hain't she the beatin'est hand to pare?"—"I declare to goodness, Molly Diggs, I hain't never goin' to ask ye to no apple-parin' agin! You're a-eatin' your weight!" As the evening wore on, the dimly lighted cabin resounded to more and more rough merriment, and the sound of continual giggling and whispering came from the shadowy corner where Linsey and Essie and Nova had secreted themselves. They were tossing parings over their shoulders and scuffling good-naturedly as they jumped to see what youth's initials the parings had formed in falling. As she came and went, attending to various matters, Ivy caught snatches of the girls' talk. She caught Essie's sigh: "Well, I hain't a-havin' no luck with the parin's, but I reckon some sweet day I kin git me a man to lay up agin my back," and Nova's retort: "To lay up agin your belly, you mean!"

Ivy glanced from one laughing, black-eyed, painted girl to the other. Nova, with her dimples and sweeping lashes, had never looked more lovely, while there was something unpleasant about Essie's sly face. Nevertheless the girls resembled each other. "Well, they orter favor," Ivy thought to herself. "Ef what folks says is true, old Andy Weaver's the daddy of 'em both!" Her glance traveled across the room to their mothers, placidly paring apples, from Mrs. Philips's grim chalky face to the fair radiant countenance of Mrs. Byrd on the opposite side of the hearth. Both had been wild in their younger days. . . .

"Looks like women wasn't no big sight better in bygone days," Ivy thought, "an' what they are this day an' time!" But all this flashed through her mind almost instantaneously. She was intent on her guests' having a good time. To create more fun, she got out the love-letter she had received a few days before and handed it to Nova, asking her to read it aloud. Shouts of laughter greeted the words at its close: "Take all mistakes for Love."

"Hop Harlow—I've heern tell o' that feller, blessed ef I hain't!" one woman said; and another: "Hop Harlow, he useter live up Happy Creek!"

The women rocked back and forth on their splint-bottom chairs, spilling both apples and peelings from their laps, tears streaming down their cheeks.

"Law, Ivy, some feller's a-goin' to git ye yit!"

After the paring was done, the women still lingered. The night was far spent before the last one had gone. Enoch had thrown himself on the bed early in the evening and slept through all the noise. Ivy was giving the cabin a last hurried putting to rights before tumbling into bed herself. Her head felt heavy. So many had been breathing the air of the low-ceiled room, and it was permeated, too, by the strong, slightly fermented scent arising from the crocks that were standing about, full to the top of the cut apples, already stained a dark brown. She stepped out on to the porch to take a few breaths of the fresh night air. The air had a feeling of moisture in it, as if it were raining somewhere not far off. The trees were rustling loudly. She heard the rush of the wind through the pines above and below her, the dry leaves scurrying along the ground. The mountains were discernible only as a misty outline. Suddenly a gust of wind blew a spray of rain full into her face. As she stood on the porch, the rain began to come down in torrents, and the smell of freshly moistened earth rose to her nostrils.

But what was that—?

Her sharp vision had detected a shadowy figure drifting down from the corn-crib towards her gate. No one came this way, without warning, and she started to run back into the cabin for her ax when she heard her name called in a low voice.

"My goodness, Gid"—her knees were shaking— "I were skairt 'in two inches of my life! The water a-drappin', I never heered ye a-walkin', an' I never seen ye till—" But she stopped short as the faint light coming through the doorway showed her his face. "Lord, Gid, you look like you're sick! You're pale as a corpse! Come in an' have ye a cheer."

"No, thanks."

"I reckon you met up with some of 'em a-goin' home from the apple-parin'. I were sorry your mammy never come. Why, Gid, you're wet as ef you 'ud fell in the river! Where you been?"

"I've been up the river, up to Uncle Abel's, to git him to haul our things—"

Ivy stared incredulously.

"Me an' Mammy's a-fixin' to move to town."

"You hain't never speakin' truth!"

"What's the use, Ivy," he asked in a low trembling voice, "me a-stayin' around here an' grievin' my life away? Buck, he's turned Novy agin me. Buck, he's stole Novy's heart."

Tears rushed to Ivy's eyes. "Don't you reckon, Gid, she 'ull weary o' Buck? They 'ull be at outs, more 'an apt, afore long. Don't you reckon Novy 'ull want to come back to ye when her an' Buck falls out?"

Gid had taken off his dripping hat and stood with his face averted, his forehead bowed against the door-frame, his wet shabby clothes clinging to his long, lean figure, shaking with sobs. "Ef ever Novy wants to come back to me," he brought out brokenly at last, "I cain't deny her! I love her too good, an' things 'twixt me an' her has went too fur.—Buck," he added bitterly, after another pause in which his body was agitated with one deep sob after another, "Buck, he ain't never on earth a-goin' to marry Novy. Buck's got him a girl in town. He's a-foolin' around with one girl atter another—"

"Hit 'ull come home to Buck Byrd, a-partin' you-uns," Ivy murmured indignantly.

There was a long silence now, broken only by the sound of the rain, by the muffled roar of the river heard above the rain.

Gid at length mastered himself. "Ivy," he said mournfully, "Ivy, I've like to went crazy over my trouble. I've studied about it till I'm most gray-headed. I ain't done nothin' but study about it an' read the Scriptures. An' I cain't be satisfied with stayin' around here no longer. Novy, she's wrecked my life, an' I don't never agin want to see the river an' the old mountain an' these here hills an' hollows. I don't never, long as I live, want to see nothin' on earth where 'ull put me in mind o' Novy an' of all them happy days me an' her's had togither."

Ivy was crying.

"Ef it quits rainin', ef it fairs off, me an' Mammy 'ull move in the mornin'. I'm a-goin' to git me a job.—Ivy, Mammy said to tell ye she were sorry she couldn't come tomorrow to help ye with your apple butter."

"Law, hit don't matter," Ivy said sniffingly. "I 'ull git someone." But she had counted on Mag's help. With the all-day stirring, no one could manage apple butter alone. And her apples were ready to go into the kettle first thing in the morning. They would never keep—whom should she get in Mag's place? For a moment she was a little upset. But what was this trouble compared to Gid's and Mag's? In imagination, she saw Old Mag departing from the cabin where all her children had been born, from which some of them had been carried forth up the long trail to the burying ground. She saw Old Mag looking back sorrowfully on that cabin where she had lived, not the best life, perhaps, in her younger days, but where she had brought up her children without the aid of a father, brought them up roughly, and yet with passionate devotion. She saw the cabin down in its green cup in the knobs, saw the great weeping willow whose branches swept down over Mag's little log springhouse, fingering its mossy roof, saw it all as it would look when Mag was no longer there, no hens scratching and clucking about, no sign of life. . . .

Ivy laid her hand on Gid's arm, looking up into his long, handsome face, with its strongly marked features, a face ravaged by suffering and that all at once, for the first time, looked to her like Old Mag's.

"Gid, I don't reckon I 'ull never have the heart to pass down you-all's holler agin. I 'ull miss ye terrible, you and your mammy, both. But, Gid," she added in a low relieved voice, "I'm glad you're a-goin' away, fer you-all's sake. I 'ull tell ye what's a fact—I hain't knowed a minute's peace sence you an' Novy's trouble started, since I knowed you was a-carryin' weepons!"

Chapter Five

"THERE'S A GANG o' pa'tridges uses in our garden," Enoch remarked, as a bobwhite's whistle, clear and loud, came through the open window of the lean-to.

Ivy nodded. They were eating breakfast, the glow from the golden trees outside penetrating even the cabin, suffusing its usual dusk with a radiance like pale sunshine.

"I reckon there 'ull be plenty pa'tridges this year, I reckon there 'ull be several," Ivy said, a little absently. "Enoch, pass me them fried taters."

Enoch, complying, took occasion to remind his mother: "It ain't 'taters,' Mammy—it's 'pertaters.'"

"Law, yes," Ivy agreed, "I know 'pertaters' is right. I says 'taters' a heap o' times afore I thinks."

They went on eating. Enoch was full of Adam and Simon Peter's staying out of school, on the pretext of being sick, in order to help their daddy around the still. His eyes were shining. He had been at the still himself a day or so before. "The mash, Mammy, it were jest a-startin' to work."

Ivy set down the heavy coffee-cup she had started to lift to her lips. "Enoch, don't go mouthin' hit around what ye've saw at Mr. Philips's still. A still hain't no place fer no boy o' your age, nohow. First thing you know, the law 'ull be in, an' you 'ull git took up alongst with the balance of 'em. How would ye like hit to be sent to reform school?" But she had hardly uttered the last word when she heard a thin piercing scream. Jumping up, she ran to the door. Uncle Abel Dillard was standing in the road above, his bulky figure blocking her view of the bank in front of him, but his elbow crooked out and a switch in his uplifted hand. Ivy caught a glimpse of something pink.

"The Lord help my time," she exclaimed breathlessly, "ef hit hain't Uncle Abel an' Bertha Jane, an' him a-brushin' her!"

She could hear Uncle Abel talking in a low voice, and Bertha Jane crying. Suddenly Uncle Abel lashed the switch three or four times around the cowering little figure on the bank, Bertha Jane screaming each time.

The father drove the girl in front of him now, a few yards at a time, back in the direction from which they had come. All at once, however, Ivy became aware that Bertha Jane was flying back down the road. She had regained the point above Ivy's cabin when her father overtook her and, whirling her about, began to beat the girl savagely, whipping her this time until she fell face down in the road, then starting to kick her where she lay.

Ivy sped up the path to the road and, dropping down beside her, lifted Bertha Jane's head into her lap.

Bertha Jane's breath was coming flutteringly, a deathly pallor had settled on her small pinched face, her eyes were closed, and a bright-red stream issued from between her colorless lips. Ivy pulled up the skirt of her own dress, twisting the hem into a wad and holding it against the girl's lips to staunch the flow. "Honey, you orten't to run that-away, you with the tubercles! Bertha Jane, give in to your pappy!" she whispered now. "Don't be contrairy! Honey, you hain't hearty enough to stand no frailin'! Give in to your pappy! Don't let him beat ye no more!"

The red rivulet kept trickling down over Bertha Jane's chin, and Ivy kept wiping it off with the hem of her dress.

Uncle Abel came nearer. His broad unfurrowed face was still an angry purple, but he spoke in his usual bland purring voice: "I cain't spare her, me a widdy man. She were a-runnin' away from home. She were a-tryin' to git to town."

Ivy bent over the girl again. "Law, honey," she said, "you couldn't never on earth 'a made hit!" As she looked down, Bertha Jane lifted her swollen eyelids, heavily. The ghost of a smile flickered over her childish face, "I 'lowed I could ketch me a ride, ef I could git to the state highway. I were a-aimin'," she whispered, a word or two at a time, "to git me a job at the nickel and dime store." Her lids drooped again. A feverish spot had appeared on either cheek, and Ivy felt that her hands, icy a moment before, were burning now.

"Mr. Dillard," Ivy said stiffly, "Bertha Jane hain't a-goin' to be able to travel fer a right smart bit."

"Law, she 'ull be all right atter she sets a minute." Stooping down, he picked up the girl, her head hanging limp like the head of a flower whose stem has withered, and, placing her on the bank at the side of the road, seated himself beside her.

"Bertha Jane," he said, placidly, "coughs up a right smart o' blood of a mornin', but, law, her mammy, she were a-spittin' blood fer ten or fifteen year afore she went. Ivy, you have your health, I hope."

Ivy stood by in silence.

After some time Bertha Jane got to her feet. Her legs, thin as sticks, were shaking. When she had followed her father a short distance, she turned and, with a lingering gaze, called in a faint, husky voice: "Ivy, you come to see me!"

Ivy was standing in the middle of the road to watch them as far as she could see. "Law, honey, I 'ull come!" she called back. "I 'ull come to see ye soon!"

Ivy went slowly down the path to her gate. The river was smoking in the sun. The mists that had shrouded the mountains through the night were lifting slowly, leaving wisps of ragged white still clinging to their tufted, richly verdured sides, blended now of many soft warm tones. The grass, from which the frost was fast melting, shimmered like silver. Cobwebs hung on every bush and weed, their fine-spun threads each dripping with a row of brilliants, tiny points of dazzling rainbow light. "Looks like there's so much to delight a body," Ivy thought achingly, "but, oh, Lord, why does folks have to suffer so in this life?"

She had planned to wash her bedding while the fine fall weather lasted and, preparatory to doing so, had placed her tub and other receptacles under the eaves of her cabin during the recent rains. But this morning all the heart to do anything at all seemed to have been taken out of her.

She must go ahead, however, with what she had planned. Each day brought its work. She lifted the tick from her bed, carrying it into the garden, where she emptied it, setting fire to the straw, then placed her tub on a box under one of the apple-trees and proceeded to wash the coarse muslin tick-cover along with her quilts, hanging them on the garden palings to dry. Always before, since Aunt Jane's death, she and Old Mag had gone together each fall to get new straw for their ticks, going wherever they had heard it could be obtained. This year she would go with Mrs. Philips, up the river, to Uncle Mort Lowdy's.

It was early in the afternoon. Both women were bareheaded and each carried a sheet in which to bring home the new straw.

Doke was seated on the short flight of steps leading down from the door of his cabin. He was making a broom, they could see, binding the long splints of broom-corn into a circular sweep.

"Doke, he ties a good broom," Ivy said.

The older woman looked up with a twinkle in her eyes. "Doke, he's handy at 'most anything—anything where hain't work!"

"I've been a-layin' off," Ivy said, "to git Doke to tie a broom fer me—mine's 'most wore out."

"Had you-all heern about the killin'?" Doke shouted to them as they drew nearer. "Neff Withers an' Dexter Pickle—found the bodies up Grand-mam's soon this mornin'."

"Forevermore!"

Doke came to the fence. "Crum Taylor, he were possum huntin' last night, an' he were a-comin' home—hit were right atter sun-up—an' he seen two men a-layin' side an' side, clost to the road. He 'lowed they was jest drunk, an' he weren't a-aimin' to bother 'em, but then he seen some blood, an' he seen hit were Neff an' Dexter."

"Have the law been in?" Ivy asked.

Doke nodded. "But they hain't made no arrests.—Folks suspicions Bud Bullock an' Wallace Birthright."

"Why, I thought Bud an' Wallace," Ivy cried, "was sech good friends o' Neff an' Dexter!"

Doke laughed. "God, there hain't no good friends atter men's been a-layin' up drunk togither fer two or three days!—But looks like Bud an' Wallace," he added with another laugh, "was plenty sober to beat hit! I reckon they're yon side the mountain by this time."

"Wallace Birthright—he's my sister's son," Mrs. Philips remarked, her face impassive, as always, but her eyes moist and a strange gleam in them.

"Yep," Doke said "—Uncle Elijah Birthright's son." He gave some further particulars of the killing as he had gleaned them at the store.

After the two women had resumed their way up the river, they talked again, for a while, of the killing. A golden mist floated in the air. The sun glinted through the many colored leaves. The stately plumes of golden-rod, still erect, were faded now, but purple asters remained a froth of bloom and ladies' tresses, with their delicate twisted spikes, still nodded by the roadside. A great brown butterfly sailed through the misty golden air, crossing and recrossing in front of them. Occasionally a golden leaf fluttered to their feet. No birds were singing; even the grasshoppers were silent. But cow-bells tinkled somewhere, and the leaves overhead rustled a soft accompaniment to the ceaseless drone of the river. Now and again they heard the sharp rap of a chestnut as it fell to the ground. When they had passed the church, they saw a drove of young turkeys ahead of them in a grove of chestnut-trees that stood out, clear gold, against the brilliant blue of the October sky. They heard the turkeys peeping as they bobbed up and down, searching greedily for nuts that had spilled out of the burs, and the two women stopped and began hunting around through the leaves with the turkeys.

Shortly after they had left the chestnut grove behind, Ivy noticed the print of Bertha Jane's shoe in a low moist place in the road. Close beside it were marks left by Uncle Abel's heavy square-toed boots. A slight shudder ran through her, and she burst out now with an account of what had happened.

Hobbling along, her eyes bent on the ground, Mrs. Philips was trying to keep pace with Ivy's light easy swinging gait. "Uncle Abel has the name," she said, without looking up, "of bein' rough on his children."

Though the older woman was not talkative at any time, today she seemed even less inclined to talk than usual. Ivy fell silent herself for a while. A hundred times a day she rehearsed what she would say to Jim, heard his half-laughing answer: "Well, by God, Ivy, you ain't getttin' any worse-lookin', I'll say you ain't—So that's the boy! He's big to his age, ain't he? Well, Sonny, how are ye?"

When the two women reached the swinging bridge, they started across it single file, the bridge swaying with every step they took. In mid stream they paused on a common impulse and, leaning against the iron cable that served as hand-rail, looked up and down the shining curving river. No cabin was in sight. The mountains—everything was enveloped in the golden mist. There was something to Ivy that was faintly, indescribably, sad in the peaceful beautiful scene that lay before them, a reflection, perhaps, from the strain of sadness inseparable from human life; yet withal the scene seemed to her friendly, vaguely comforting.

Along the river-banks barberry bushes, with their delicate crimson-edged foliage, drooped under a weight of berries, which were mirrored, like drops of coral, in the clear water underneath. Trees that were pure amber in tone, others of a delicate-rose tint or a deep rich rose, stood out in contrast to the dark evergreen hemlocks towering above them. The golden leaves of the hickory-trees quivered and danced in a warm gentle breeze that was blowing, and all at once a shower of leaves took flight from a great beech that overhung the river and, fluttering down like a swarm of golden butterflies, settled upon the water and sailed daintily down-stream.

As the women stood gazing below them, both a little abstractedly, at the fish that were lying along on the shelving rocks of the river-bottom, Ivy suddenly remarked: "Gid's got him a job at the overall-factory, hain't he?"

"I reckon Marthy got hit fer him," the older woman muttered. She continued to gaze down at the fish lying with their silver-white bellies half-upturned and glistening in the sun. "Gid won't never make nothin' more 'an a possum hunter," she said at length, in a disgusted tone, and after another pause: "I 'lowed ef Novy loved him, I ortern't to put nothin' in the way of them a-marryin', but, law, the way he's been agoin' on here lately, bawlin, an' actin' the baby—I couldn't blame Novy ef she quit off a-lovin' him. Why, Lord have mercy, I wouldn't marry no man that carried on that-a-way—not to save him from torment!"

Ivy laughed, a little uneasily. Had Mrs. Philips's sharp eyes failed to discover what everyone else had seen—what everyone was talking about?

Mrs. Philips started to move on across the bridge. "Novy," she said, "wouldn't never see no peace ef she married Gid, him so jealous-hearted." A moment later she added, broodingly: "They was allays a-quarrelin'."

They walked on. "In town," Ivy remarked, "a body has to pay seventy-five cents a bale fer straw. Hit's a sight on earth what hit costs to fill a body's ticks, in town."

"Law, yes," Mrs. Philips agreed, but as though her thoughts were elsewhere.

They continued to follow the river. The fields were a little broader now than those they had left behind on their own side of the river. Cabins and log barns they came upon were somewhat larger and better. Occasionally a dwelling was of boards, painted white, and there were more cows and pigs to be seen. Here and there from a fence-corner glowed a pile of pumpkins, with a litter of pigs rooting around among them, or a cow crunching its full. In the fields they passed, men were pulling fodder, working unhurriedly, and Ivy and Mrs. Philips stopped as they passed to call out: "Have you-all heern about the killin'?"

As they reached their destination and started through the rail walk-around that served as a gate, a big black and white mongrel came bounding down from behind the old log house, an evil-looking beast with un-matched eyes, one gray-green, the other a bright China blue. Ivy shrank back. "Reckon hit's a bitin' dog?"

Mrs. Philips snapped her black eyes. "Law, yes—the bitin'est dog on the river.—Aunt Lily," she suddenly called at the top of her voice, "oh, Aunt Lily!"

"Hesh your fuss!" a voice rebuked the dog sharply, and at the same moment a tall emaciated slattern old woman came running out from the side of the house and down towards the walk-around as lightly as a girl. Grizzled reddish hair was streaming down around the old woman's shrewd long-nosed face, her feet were bare, and the dirty dark-gray Mother Hubbard she wore had fallen open in front, exposing a withered dirt-streaked bosom. "Hesh your fuss, you cock-eyed devil!" she screamed again at the dog. "Come right on in! I won't let him hurt ye! I wouldn't let him hurt ye fer nothin' on earth! You found me nasty, but I'm tickled to death to see ye both!" Seizing Ivy, who had emerged first from the walk-around, the old woman turned her round and round, looking her up and down with her faded bleary eyes, feeling of her dress with her long, claw-like fingers. "Why, bless the Lord, Ivy, you're a-lookin' like a queen!" Then turning to Mrs. Philips: "Law, hain't the fashions this day an' time the prettiest ever was on earth?"

The three women proceeded to the good-sized passageway which ran crosswise between the front and back room of the lopsided tumble-down house, and which, open at either side, was used as a porch. Dusty bunches of herbs and strings of red peppers hung from the roof, and on the floor, amidst crocks, baskets, rusty iron pots, and all sorts of rubbish, were a churn, a broken spinning-wheel, and separate piles of pumpkins, sweet potatoes, and onions. Through the open door into a front room an old man with a white beard could be seen sitting by the one small window.

The old woman set out chairs. "Don't let the old man see ye!" she warned, with a spirited nod in his direction, placing the chairs so that they should be out of his view. "He don't sleep no sounder 'an a cat, an' he 'ull be a-pokin' out here ef he sees ye. Wears a body out a-yellin' at him." Then drawing her own chair close to the visitors, she began talking with great animation, telling them of her chickens and ducks and turkeys and of her cow that had just had twin calves. "But, law, ladies, a body cain't git no milk—takes all fer them two." Several times she stopped what she was saying to point to the trees—"Why, I cain't hardly git nothin' done, fer lookin' at the trees, them yaller as sunshine!"

She was willing to listen, however, as well as talk, drinking in with lively interest every word that either Ivy or Mrs. Philips uttered. Once or twice she darted a look at the folded sheets they held in their laps.

Ivy and Mrs. Philips sat until they observed that the afternoon shadows were beginning to lengthen.

"Well, Ivy," Mrs. Philips said, "I reckon me an' you orter be a-goin'.— Aunt Lily, we 'lowed maybe Uncle Mort could spare us a little wheat straw, fer our ticks."

The old woman jumped up. "Why, yes, I reckon he 'ull let ye have some." She started towards the front room.

"Who did ye say hit were?" a quavering voice asked now, and Uncle Mort came out slowly, a genteel-looking old man, much cleaner than his wife. He walked without a staff, but his back was bent almost double.

The old man sat down feebly. Placing her lips close to his ear, Ivy undertook to tell him the news of the killing up Grandmam's. "Yes, yes, I hear!" He wagged his head impatiently, his beard brushing his chest. "I hain't as deef as some folks think. Neff Withers an' Dexter Pickle—well, hit hain't no big loss," he quavered with an air of some satisfaction—"wasn't neither one of 'em worth the ammunition hit took to kill 'em." Suddenly he opened his small malicious eyes a little wider. "Ivy, what's ever became o' that God-dang rascal where married ye?"

Ivy smiled, without answering. Her face had become a flame.

"Don't never hear nothin' from him, do ye?"

Ivy shook her head.

The old man leaned forward now, peering at her narrowly with a sly look on his sickly bluish face, with its sunken nostrils. "Your womanhood's a-wastin', Ivy—some man orter wife ye! Ef I could git shed o' that red-headed devil," nodding towards his wife, "I 'ud git ye to come an' live with me."

Aunt Lily's eyes had begun to dance. "Law, me, I 'ull be a-plantin' downhill-o'-life on the old man's grave," she said gayly, "afore ever he 'ull be a-plantin' ary vine on mine! I'm stout, ef I hain't got much meat on me." She came and laid her shaking claw-like hand on Ivy's shoulder. "Don't pay no 'tention, Ivy," she whispered, "to nothin' he says to ye! All men is childish atter they're sixty, an' the old man's nigh unto eighty-five." She went over to her husband now, screaming to him that the visitors had come to get some straw for their ticks.

"How much did ye want?" he asked a little suspiciously, looking from one to the other; but he led them slowly out to the barn, one hand behind him, resting on his back.

When the women had stuffed their sheets, tied the corners into a knot, and adjusted the big bundles to their backs, they still lingered, glancing back and forth at each other with irresolute looks. At last, after they had thanked him for the straw, Ivy inquired: "How much do we owe ye fer hit, Uncle Mort?"

"Well, I reckon I orter have a dollar. I reckon a dollar apiece is about right."

Ivy and Mrs. Philips exchanged a sudden look of dismay. "Uncle Mort, you 'ull have to trust us," Mrs. Philips shouted, half turning away from him as she said it, her back deeply bowed under its burden "—we hain't neither one of us brung a copper."

"Did ever you hear the like," Ivy exclaimed, when they had reached the road, "in all the days o' your life?"

"A man where 'ull charge fer straw fer ticks," Mrs. Philips mumbled, "he 'ud skin a flea fer hit's hide an' tallow!"

But they halted, hearing the patter of Aunt Lily's feet, as she came running after them, a small bright-yellow pumpkin in either arm.

"Here, I want ye both to have one o' my sugar-pumpkins—you kin pack 'em home in the straw—they're fine fer pies. An' you-uns come agin," she begged "—hit's meat an' drink to me! Come when ye kin stay all day, when ye kin spend the night."

Chapter Six

AT THE DOOR of the big dusky room at the right of the cabin Ivy was met by Mrs. Philips. On the bed facing the door she saw Mrs. Byrd lying back on the pillows, her eyes closed.

"A nice little girl!" Mrs. Philips said in an undertone, bringing a bundle for Ivy to inspect.

Ivy held her face against the new-born babe's round, silky, fiery-red cheek. "Law, hain't hit's little hide the softest!—Wasn't no trouble, was they?" she asked, in a whisper.

Mrs. Philips raised her eyebrows. "Hit were borned with the cord wropped around hit's little neck an' arm. That there's 'cause she's been a-climbin' under fences so much," with a slightly disapproving nod towards the bed "—the cord, hit gits tangled up that-a-way."

Mrs. Byrd opened her eyes. The bed looked clean, though it gave out a fetid odor. Ivy picked up a green branch that was lying near and began waving it back and forth gently, brushing the flies away.

"Law, hain't hit the sweetest?" the mother smiled. She closed her eyes again. "Ivy, I've got a heap to be thankful fer—thirteen children, an' all of 'em a-livin!" A big tear stole through her eyelashes, down over her fair plump cheek, with its look of having been polished, but a little pale at present. "Ivy, looks like I 'ud be the happiest woman on earth ef—ef hit wasn't fer Wash, him my first-born, an' him in the penitentiary!" Her eyes remained closed, but the tears had started to flow freely. "There hain't no tongue kin tell, Ivy, how hit's a-grievin' me, an' now Bill a-makin' liquor agin—I don't see a minute's peace! Ef the law gits Bill an' Buck, there won't be nary man-person left on the place, an' me with all these young uns—"

"I wouldn't grieve so, Mis' Byrd!" Ivy stroked the smooth damp forehead, pushing back the fair hair that was beginning to be a little thin about the temples. "You're out o' heart, Mis' Byrd, 'cause you're so weak."

Mrs. Philips came back from spitting out the door. "Betty, don't talk no more," she said in an authoritative voice, "or you 'ull start a-floodin' agin—"

"Well, I won't talk no more," the mother said meekly, but as Ivy laid down the green branch and started to leave, she opened her eyes again. "Ivy, looks like everything comes to oncet. I were in hopes I wouldn't be down till atter the molasses was made."

"Now, Mis' Byrd," Ivy chided good-naturedly, "there's plenty of us to make them molasses! I promise ye we 'ull make 'em good an' thick—I don't like no thin molasses myself. You jest lay here, Mis' Byrd, an' take ye a good rest. Don't weary yourself about nothin' on earth."

Ivy hurried to the field where the others were working. In the distance Big Bill and One-eye Buck were cutting down such canes as remained standing. Uncle Abel Dillard, driving one of his mules, was coming from their direction, bringing in another sled-load of canes, walking along beside the sled with the lines in his hand. At the end of the field nearest the cabin, the Byrds' mare was making the rounds of the treadmill, while Doke Odum, with two half-grown helpers, was stripping the cane as fast as a sledful arrived, and Short Dillard was feeding the stripped cane into the mill. Not far from the treadmill a rectangular pan, the size of a wagon-box, had been set up on stone piles so that it rested a foot or so above the ground. A fire was burning underneath. Children of all sizes were trudging back and forth, bringing buckets of the sap, which was issuing from the mill in a watery stream, and emptying them into the big pan, and Essie Byrd, her pert rodent face flaming with rouge, was walking around the pan, making a pretense of skimming its bright-green slimy contents, from which steam was beginning to rise in a pale thin cloud.

"Aye, God," Doke shouted as Ivy came near, "time you was gittin' here! We won't have no 'lasses fer nobody ef we leave 'em to Essie!"

Essie giggled, and Ivy, shouting back some laughing answer to Doke, took the young girl's place and started skimming in earnest.

Seeing so many children about—not only the Byrd children, but Doke Odum's swarm, the little Dillard boys, even Adam and Simon Peter—Ivy felt a slight pang. Enoch had cried bitterly when she refused to let him stay home from school for the afternoon. How could she blame the little boy? How good it was to be here, the air so soft and warm, yet not hot! The river, running along beside the field, so blue! The Byrds' geese, swimming along in the river, then coming back to the bank to stretch their wings and settle down sedately. Blue jays, with their clownish ways, keeping up a lively clatter, sounding their bell-like notes over and over. Cow-bells tinkling from the woods beyond. Cedar-trees, along the old rail-fence that separated the field from the river, blue with berries. Persimmon-trees, scattered among the cedars, hanging full of their purple-gold fruit, fruit that the frosts had made sweeter than honey. Plenty of talking, joking, laughing. Everyone—grown folks as well as children—going about with a piece of the succulent sorghum-cane, chewing on the cane. And now the contents of the big pan she was bending over changing gradually from a slimy green bubbling mass to a seething yellowish one, beginning to lose its crude raw smell and to send up the true rich fragrant fumes of molasses.

"Fall o' the year," Ivy thought "—hain't no time kin beat hit!"

Of course people had their troubles. She looked back up the river. One-eye Buck's battered Ford was standing in front of the Byrds' little log barn. "Yes, an' I reckon that 'ere old Ford," she thought, "hit were the cause o' partin' Gid an' Novy, Novy so crazy to git to ride in a Ford!" She thought of Mrs. Philips, stern and morose of late, eaten up with anxiety over Nova; thought of Mrs. Byrd, rejoicing over the baby born that morning, yet sick at heart over Wash and ridden with fears of the law, fears for Buck and her "man." She thought of Bertha Jane, as Uncle Abel's bulky stuffed-looking figure came into sight from time to time.

All these reflections passed through her mind, to be sure, fleetingly, obscurely, as she went on talking to different ones about her, shouting with laughter at the jests that were being tossed back and forth, and visiting with the various passers-by who stopped.

"By God, Molly Diggs has got her a man at last," Doke called out, as Luke was seen in the distance, approaching from down the river. Molly had been married the day before to Alf Bunts, hurt a few days earlier when the Ford he was in had plunged off a high bank into the river. "Molly, she's got Alf hog-tied now fer shore—he won't never walk agin, the doctors says.— Luke," he called, as Luke vaulted over the fence into the field where the others were at work, "I reckon you 'ull have to tie a apron round ye sence Molly's went—"

Luke flashed a smile in response. "I reckon me an' Mammy kin make hit." He came over quietly and took a stand near Ivy, who was squatting beside the pan, first on one side and then another, wiping off its inside edges with clean rags as fast as the froth settled on them in a line of scum.

Ivy stood up now and began walking around the pan, raking the long-handled skimmer back and forth steadily as the yellow foam mounted higher and higher. Essie had left. Teetering along self-consciously on her high heels, Essie had gone over to where Short Dillard, seated on the ground, his artificial leg thrust out stiffly in front of him, was feeding the mill with more and more canes. "Essie's got sech bold an' fistey ways," Ivy thought, as she watched the youthful couple laughing and fooling together. "Essie, she's so full o' nature, looks like she cain't keep her hands offen Short."

She changed to the opposite side of the pan, so that her back was towards Short and Essie. The bright clear-gold of the chestnut-trees was mingled with the warm bronze and copper of beeches and hickories, the rosy amber of maples, with the fire-red of sweet-gums flaming like torches here and there among the dark evergreen pines and hemlocks.

Only once a year, and only for a day or so, did the mountains shine with this particular misty jeweled light. Ivy kept glancing up at them from the boiling molasses. "Law, Luke, did ever you see the timber a-lookin' so pretty?"

But the molasses had reached a stage now where it needed her vigilant attention. Ivy plied the skimmer more steadily than ever, stopping only long enough to taste. "Here, Luke," as she dipped the spoon into the syrup again and handed it to him, "taste 'em yourself. They hain't bad, are they? Do you think they're a-gittin' done?"

"Luke," Ivy said, in a low voice, "have you got any idee how much hit costs to git to a place called Fort Omaha?"

"Why, no," Luke said, handing back the spoon and looking into the boiling molasses, starting to spurt up explosively into little hills at various points. "Why, no, I hain't no idee. Hit's a right fur piece. A hundred dollars, I reckon—right at hit." He continued looking intently at the boiling molasses. "You wasn't aimin' to go to no sech place, was ye, Ivy?"

"Law, no!" Ivy laughed. "I were jest a-studyin' about how much hit 'ud cost a feller to git there. I knowed you'd been to a heap o' far-off places, what time you was in the war."

When the first boiling was done, Ivy dipped out the molasses, pouring it into the waiting tin buckets and glass jars. There was a little lull in the work now, while everyone stopped to eat. The older ones took turns with the spoon, blowing on it to cool it, while the children, ranged along on some logs that were lying near and each provided with a stick or thin piece of board, slowly, blissfully, licked off every drop of sweetness that adhered to their sticks, then ran and dipped them again into a bucket that had been set aside for their use.

Presently, however, everyone was back at work again.

The evening star had appeared in a tender azure stretch in the west before the last boiling was finished and the molasses had all been measured up.

Enoch had come after school, and Ivy had sent the little boy home with the two half-gallon bucketfuls she had received as pay. She was going home herself by the long way, past Old Mag's. Some of the children had told her of a kitten that Mag had left behind.

As she was getting ready to start, she saw Mrs. Philips coming and waited for her. The days were getting so short; it would be good to have company. It was a lonely road past Old Mag's.

When they reached Mag's cabin, the older woman remained in the road while Ivy ran down and searched for the kitten.

"I don't see how no person on earth kin go away an' leave their cats," Ivy panted, as she ran back up the path from the cabin with a small black kitten in her arms. "They ortern't to leave no black cat, nohow. A black cat 'ull cure the shingles—a body with shingles to rub agin 'em."

"A black cat 'ull keep the witches away, I've heern say," she added in a little lower voice, a few moments later, as they left the hollow and began climbing higher and higher. Suddenly Ivy glanced back over her shoulder, believing she had heard a slight rustling sound in the tall thick bushes beside the road, and even a sound of breathing. She half expected to see that someone was creeping up behind them. . . . But it was nothing—only the leaves rustling. The wind always began to blow down from the mountains at nightfall. There was no one, nothing. . . . She hugged the kitten closer to her.

When the two women had reached the top of the ridge, the full moon had risen. Their way lay past the old Minton place, and Ivy's eyes traveled stealthily in the direction of the deserted Minton cabin, with its staring front window half-curtained with wild grape-vines.

"I looked fer Novy to be down to the Byrds' today, Mis' Philips," Ivy said, her voice shaking a little "—there's allays so much fun an' carryin'-on where folks is a-makin' molasses—"

Mrs. Philips darted a sideways glance at Ivy, then dropped her eyes to the ground again. "Novy hain't well," she muttered "—her ankles has been a-swellin'.—Looks like she's a-takin' the rheumatiz."

"Mis' Philips," Ivy said, almost inaudibly "—hit haint none o' my business, an' you know I wouldn't never on earth say no harm word agin you or Novy, but had ye saw anything different—in the way Novy's a-lookin'—here lately?"

Mrs. Philips hobbled on down the hill. She made no answer.

When they reached the foot of the slope, Ivy touched the older woman's arm. "Mis' Philips, you hain't miffed, are ye?"

The older woman halted. There were no tears in her eyes, but a stricken look, and Ivy could see that her mouth was twitching. "Law, no, child," she said, "I hain't miffed!" She shook her head, the smooth bands of black hair, black as a crow's wing, that enclosed her chalky face gleaming faintly in the moonlight. "I hain't miffed!"

CHAPTER SEVEN

IVY HAD PUT off gathering walnuts until later than usual. When at last, the day after she had been at the Byrds, she started her search, she found only a pile of hulls under each tree she visited. The afternoon was already advanced, the sky beginning to be overcast, but she remembered a certain tall old walnut on the Minton land less likely to have been visited than those by the roadside or in the open fields.

Crawling through the fence in front of the deserted cabin, she followed a trail along one side of the deep bowl dropping below the cabin, hurrying on down to a ravine that lay beyond it, walled in steeply on both sides by virgin forest. Reaching a little hollow up one side of the ravine that for a width of six or seven feet was almost bare of trees clear to the summit, Ivy scrambled half-way up it to where the walnut stood. Gathering the nuts she found there into a good-sized pile, she secured two stones, squatted beside them, and began pounding the nuts between the stones to remove their hulls.

What large fine ones they were! Her feet were sunk in deep layers of leaves. Near her, where it had fallen obliquely across the little draw, was a huge log completely covered with shaggy emerald moss. How green everything was here in the perpetual twilight of the deep woods! She caught the gleam of a jack-in-the-pulpit's scarlet cluster down below her among the ferns. Partridge-vine trailed daintily over the ground all around her, its dark shining little evergreen leaves sprinkled over with coral-red berries. Small glossy plants of mountain tea hung full of bright red berries. The holly-trees above her glowed with berries.

And what good smells! Ivy breathed in the aromatic vitalizing scents of the forest with conscious pleasure, though better than all she liked the smell of the soft green walnut-hulls she was crushing between the stones. Holding a hull to her nose, she sniffed it strongly.

Her hands were already a deep ugly brown, her fingernails stained yellow, but she was glad to have found some nuts at last. After a little while, however, she began to feel lonely here in the woods by herself. She missed Old Mag. Mag had always been ready on a moment's notice to venture forth with her, to roam the fields and woods. . . .

A gust of cold wind blew down the draw. Scanning the patch of dull-gray sky above her, Ivy saw that dark ragged-looking clouds were moving swiftly across it. A few drops of cold rain fell on her upturned face. It was going to storm. Winter was not far off—

Suddenly she spied someone below her, coming along by the little stream that tumbled down through the ravine, approaching in the opposite direction from which she had herself. It was Gid! He was picking his steps stealthily. All at once he caught Ivy's gaze bent upon him.

"Law, Gid," she called down, "what on earth you doin' up this holler? Why, I thought you was in town!"

"Jest wanderin' around."

He climbed up the slope rather weakly, catching at the bushes, and threw himself on the ground, his long, slim body stretched out on the moss and leaves, his feet in their worn-out tan shoes extending down the slope. His bony shoulder protruded through a rent in his soiled and rumpled shirt, unbuttoned at the throat and lacking a tie. He needed a shave, smelled sweaty, unclean, and slightly of liquor. His handsome young face, with its dominant high-bridged nose, was extraordinarily pale and he looked as though he had been through some wasting illness.

"He's been a-layin' out!" Ivy thought. "When did ye come in?" she asked in a frightened tone.

"Oh, awhile back," he answered indifferently, some time after she had asked the question, as though it had just reached him. His face was towards her, but he had pulled his cap over his eyes.

Ivy went back to pounding the nuts. Her hands were shaking a little. All at once she thought of something. "Gid," she glanced at him uneasily, "Gid, hit wasn't you, were hit, I heern in the brush last night, soon after sundown, when me an' Mis' Philips was a-comin' home— a-comin' up the ridge over yon—?"

His lip curled. "Might 'a been."

Ivy's heart had begun to beat uncomfortably. "Gid, you hain't had no dinner, have ye?" She paused for his answer, and when he gave none: "You hain't had nary bite, have ye, sence, sence—"

His lip curled again. "Well, I ain't been foundered—"

Reaching over, he took a nut from her pile and, his hands trembling violently, cracked it open with the stone she had been using, proceeding to pick out the moist green kernel with a nail he had found in the pocket of his ragged khaki breeches. He had pulled himself up so that he was in a sitting posture, with his knees elevated. Cracking several more nuts for himself, he nibbled at them absently.

"Gid, did ye quit off your job at the overall-factory?" Ivy asked, after some time. There was something about his face that made her dread to look at him; yet when he failed to reply, she glanced in his direction again. He was looking into space, elbows on his knees, face clasped in his hands.

Suddenly he turned on Ivy almost fiercely: "How the hell kin a feller work when he's in *my* fix?"

"Heap o' times," Ivy murmured soothingly, after another pause, "work 'ull take a feller's mind offen his troubles—"

"Not off o' *my* troubles! Novy's wrecked my life!" He dropped his face in his hands and sat that way, with his face hidden.

Ivy went on with her work. "Walnut-kernels is a-bringin' forty cents a pound," she said, when some time had passed. "Useter be we didn't git on'y fifteen. But a body to pick 'em out in idle time, they could make a right smart even at that. I mind one winter in time agone, me an' Aunt Jane a-gittin' two dollars an' a half fer ourn. Law, me, hit were a sight, all the muslin an' sech stuff we got a-tradin' 'em in—"

Gid dropped his hands from his face. "Ivy," he startled her, "Ivy"—he was staring at her fixedly, though his big hollow eyes had a strained far-away look— "Ivy, I told ye I didn't want never agin to see nothin' where 'ud put me in mind o' Novy. But, Ivy, I had obliged to come back! I cain't stay in no town! Ivy, I kin see them two afore me day an' night, day an' night, day an' night," he went on wildly, his voice weak and breaking, yet defiant, his face working until it was terrible to look upon. "Ivy, I cain't eat, I cain't sleep, I cain't do nothin'! I kin see 'em afore me day an' night, day an' night, day an' night, them two togither, an' him—"

He stopped short, clapping his hand to his head, holding it in a vise-like grip, pressing his hands against his temples. "God, I'm a-goin' crazy!"

Ivy crept across the few feet between them and took hold of his arm. "Gid, you're light-headed, 'cause you hain't had no victuals," she said in a hoarse terrified voice.

He dropped his hands and stared at her again, his big dark eyes glowing with fire, wide open, his whole face quivering. "Ivy," he said huskily, "I love her enough to kill her—"

"Gid—!"

"—cain't no man love a woman more 'an that."

"Gid," she begged, placing her two hands on his shoulders, and looking straight into his wild eyes, full of anguish, "don't say sech as that! You've had a heap to contend with—Novy hain't give ye justice! She's ruint herself with everybody—the way she's done ye. There's no fairness in hit. But don't make things no worse! Don't bring no more trouble on your pore old mammy, you her baby, you her heart's blood!—Come, Gid, go home with me. I 'ull make ye a cup o' coffee. I 'ull git ye somethin' to eat. I won't hull no more nuts today—"

Gid sat looking doggedly at the moss and dead leaves at his feet.

Ivy began filling the gunny-sack she had brought for the purpose with the nuts that were ready to take. "I reckon, anyhow, hit 'ull be all I kin pack." Lifting the sack to her back, she started working her way carefully, with trembling limbs, down the slope. At the bottom, she turned, to go back up the ravine, the way she had come.

"Ivy," Gid detained her, "let's go round t'other way. You know them two big old walnuts top o' the ridge. Let's go by 'em. You kin see, an' ef no feller ain't been afore ye, you kin git all ye want from them there trees tomorrow—" The strange far-away withdrawn look had gone from his eyes, Ivy saw.

"Well—well, I don't know," she hesitated. "Hit's clost to sundown, an' I'm a-shakin' all over. I'm mighty nigh froze, Gid, hit a-turnin' so cold, an' hit's a right smart furder—"

"Oh, it ain't much furder, Ivy. We kin travel fast. I 'ull spell ye with your load."

"Well, I don't know—"

She still hesitated, but, reluctant to hold out against him, at last yielded to his suggestion, climbing the ridge behind him.

But how cold it was! In her thin summer dress, she shivered as one gust of wind after another struck her. The sky was completely overcast, dark threatening clouds were scudding across it, the mountains were wrapped in a gray veil, and there was a different feel to the air from before. "I heerd the crows this mornin'," she shouted, as they followed the trail along the top of the ridge, Gid striding ahead of her, the sackful of nuts on his back. "The old folks says when you hears crows of a mornin', hit's a-goin' to weather, hit's a-goin' to be rough."—Gid was nice to carry her load for her. "Gid, he's got a heap o' manners." Everything was all right. Nothing could happen—

She could not help observing, however, that as they neared the deserted cabin, Gid had slowed down. The trail led to its back door, to a weather-beaten shed used as a kitchen in the Mintons' day. She could tell from certain slight, almost imperceptible movements of his head that Gid was listening. . . .

Some old overgrown apple-trees, a wild-plum thicket, and a tangle of other wild growths hid the cabin from view until they were almost upon it. Ivy's heart began to pound as she became aware that Gid, a rod or so ahead of her, was standing still. Letting the sack of nuts down from his back, he flew ahead noiselessly, straight towards a dark opening where the shed door had once swung.

She heard Gid's hoarse yell: "By Jesus, I've got ye!"—saw Buck's form in the light checked suit start up in the doorway, Buck staring, with white lips; saw Gid whip out his revolver and raise it, heard his shaking voice, deliberate, almost cold: "'Lowed I 'ud find you an' her, her with my child in her belly, where I bigged her! Ruttin'-time is over, Buck, fer varmints— but, by God, not fer you-all"—Heard Buck's panting: "You old long, hungry hound, go to hell!" Gid's flippant, sneering: "I 'ull meet ye there—meet ye tonight!" Then Buck's husky, faltering: "You son of a brush-whore!" and Gid's roar: "Say that agin! Say that agin!"

Frozen with horror, her eyes starting from her head, her ears pounding with blood, her head going round and round, she saw Nova, in a new dress, of a violet color, with a fuller skirt than Nova was wont to wear, cowering behind Buck, shrinking farther back into the blackness of the shed, her beautiful young face, with its brightly rouged cheeks, working hideously, her eyes rolled up, mouth wide open, hands uplifted, clutching at the air; she heard her cry: "*Ivy!*" piteously, saw her turn and run back into the corner like a trapped rat; saw Buck reel, heard her own tortured scream—

And all had happened, as she remembered it afterwards, in one mad blinding instant. All this had been in a space of time no longer than the twinkling of an eye, no longer than while the heart ticks once—no longer, and yet, somehow, it had lasted for years and years.

But all at once the haze that had gathered over things was dispersed. She saw Nova's coat stretched out on the moldy polluted earth of the shed floor. Minute items of the scene before her, in the dim interior she stood gazing into, rooted to the spot, suddenly became enlarged—horribly, unforgettably magnified. She saw cow droppings on the dirt floor, cobwebs, a toadstool, beetles running about—she saw Buck's head, which had been jerked back convulsively, resting on the floor, his one eye staring up at the rafters, lips stretched back so that his gums were exposed, teeth parted, his knees drawn up, and two streams flowing from his left side, the lower one from his bowels, into which his fingers were still digging spasmodically, as he had clutched himself in his moment of agony. His outstretched elbows appeared to have stiffened, she perceived. The blood already had wet the whole leg of his light breeches, was gathering into a little pool at his side, a pool that was slowly, visibly, enlarging. She saw Nova, who had fallen in a heap, her back towards the door—

And she smelled something sweetish, the smell when folks killed a cow, a cow no longer good for milk, to have the meat—

Gid had sunk down beside the shed outside.

Ivy grasped his shoulder. "Git up!" she whispered.

Gid continued to stare at a clump of dead golden-rod stalks a few feet ahead of him in the sedge-grass, gray ghostly plumes that waved back and forth in a wind that was blowing down from the mountains.

Ivy shook him. "Make haste!" she whispered frenziedly. "You cain't stay here—"

Gid looked up. An expression almost of peace had settled on his pale ravaged face. "She learnt me to read!"

"Law, yes, but git up! Make haste!"

"Ivy"—a strange wan smile played around his mouth—"Ivy, I never fouled her face. I aimed low."

Ivy peered at him helplessly for an instant, her brows knit. "What kin I do? What kin I do?" she cried aloud, in a hushed voice, wringing her hands. She was breathing heavily, her whole body soaked with sweat.

"Ivy, I wisht I could bring 'em back—"

Ivy was suddenly filled with fury. "Ay, Lord," she almost hissed into his ear, "too late to be a-studyin' about sech as that!" She started tugging at him again, whispering frantically: "You cain't stay here, but ye must tech 'em afore ye go—"

A tremor passed over the youth's scarecrow figure, and now he began shaking from head to foot, like one with the palsy.

Ivy pulled him towards the shed by main force.

At the door-sill he sank on his knees, groveling at Ivy's feet, clinging to her skirts.

"You must lay your hand," she commanded, "upon their corpses."

His breath was coming in gasps, his lips moving, though no sound was issuing from them.

Suddenly Ivy was filled with fury again. "This hain't no place fer no chicken-heart!" she whispered, casting a scornful glance at him. "Ye don't want 'em to hant ye, do ye? There—watch out! Watch out! Don't step in no blood!" She placed his hand on the dead girl's shoulder, where she had pitched forward, then touched it lightly, still gripped in her own, to Buck's still figure.

"What did ye do with your gun?" she asked in a wild whisper, when they were outside again.

He indicated he had thrown it into the thicket behind them.

"You must git hit! Hit 'ud be evidence agin ye!" she whispered. "You must drap hit in the river! There won't be no moon eff hit storms," she panted, "an' you kin travel fast—you kin be yon side the mountain afore day." She glanced up at his white ghastly face, where he loomed above her, weaving back and forth like a drunken man. "Pray God to forgive ye, Gid, fer what ye done!" She clung to him, imploringly, for an instant, then specks came before her eyes. Her strength left her. She felt weak as water. When she opened her eyes, Gid was no longer in sight. She started towards the road, but, thinking of the nuts, ran back to get them.

In the road she darted a glance around her, but no one was in sight— no one as far as her eye could reach. Ahead of her, when she came to the top of the long, curving slope that led down towards the Philips' cabin, she saw the Philips' cow, in the middle of the road, pacing home slowly, its bag bulging, the bag swaying from side to side.

She saw smoke rising from the Philips' chimney. "Mis' Philips is a-cookin' her supper," she thought. She turned aside, bent under her load, taking a hidden and roundabout path, one that wound in and out of the knobs, one she seldom used. If she passed the Philips', Mrs. Philips might come to the door and call to her—

But, after all, it could not have happened. A cricket chirped close beside her in the long grass. "Oh, no—" she thought, dreamily. A sort of numbness was creeping over her, where a few moment before her faculties had all been so alive.

Chapter Eight

IVY SUDDENLY SAT up in bed, holding the bed-clothes tightly around her. The two mothers were standing close beside the bed in the thick blackness, yet plain as day.

"Oh, God, how kin I stand 'em a-lookin' at me that-a-way?" Ivy moaned, burying her face in the quilts.

"Oh, Mis' Philips, Mis' Philips!" she cried to one of the figures by the bed, to the one with the stooped back, in the clean gray calico dress, with the snuff-stained lips. "Oh, Mis' Philips, an' ye loved Novy best o' all your children!—I wisht I had never been borned into this world!" Gradually the two women beside the bed gazed at her less steadfastly, their forms grew more indistinct. Ivy fell asleep again, dreaming now that she was looking down into a new-dug grave, and that a man she had never seen before lay there in the clay, staring up at her. His eyes had popped open, and his jaw had dropped, as sometimes happened to the dead, jolted over the long rough road to the burying-ground. One of his wide-open eyes was moving in a sinister way. The dead man's hair and beard—if he were really dead—were bright red. As she looked down at him, a little skink, with a slimy vicious striped tail, blue and black—one of those "scorpions" of which she lived in dread—ran across the dead man's face, disappearing horridly into his gaping mouth, and she woke with a stifled scream to find it was day.

The trees were still tossing. Overnight they had been swept almost leafless. The sky was a dense dull gray, the mountains hidden from view; the river looked cold and lifeless and the ground was sprinkled with snow.

Crows were barking, quarreling hoarsely, louder than usual. The Byrds' geese were screaming. Bobwhites were calling back and forth with loud affrighted cries. Every thing seemed to be agitated. . . .

Who would find the bodies? How long would it be?

For a moment she thought of keeping Enoch out of school, of telling him she felt sick and needed him with her. But, no, that would be foolish. . . .

She must find something to do, something that would keep her from watching the road, from stealing glances down at the Byrds' every other minute, keep her from listening for the terrible screams that would burst forth presently. . . .

Suppose it should be, not hours, not days, but weeks she must go on this way, listening, watching, her heart hammering!

But such thoughts were crazy. A search had started already, no doubt. Someone would find them soon. Though not many folks had reason to pass that way, yet it was not so out of the way either. . . .

She set water to heating in the fire-place, filled her buckets again at the spring, and carried her wash-tub in from under the apple-tree. She seldom washed indoors, even in winter; it was only Wednesday; and on a day like this clothes would never dry. But she had washed her dishes, made the bed, swept the cabin. She must do something, and she could never in the world sit still this morning and sew on patchwork squares or pick out walnut kernels—

She had started to rub another piece on the wash-board when Spot barked and she grew dizzy. A woman in a black sweater, with a man's black felt hat on her head, was coming down the path towards the little square of porch that adjoined the lean-to. It was Mrs. Philips. Ivy held to the rim of the wash-tub. She longed sickeningly to disappear before she was seen, but she forced herself to walk to the door, wiping the suds from her arms with her apron.

Mrs. Philips was smiling, she saw with astonishment, her eyes crinkling, as she had not seen her smile since the day of the birthday dinner for Old Mag—since that day when they had all been so happy together.

"Ivy, you're a-washin' soon in the week—"

"Yes, I didn't have nothin' else to do this mornin'—I were afeared somethin' 'ud happen—I were afeared I wouldn't git no other chancet," Ivy kept on confusedly, hardly knowing what she was saying, her face averted. "Come in, Mis' Philips—"

Mrs. Philips stopped to spit off the porch. "Ivy, don't let me hinder ye—"

"Law, no, you won't hinder me. I've got plenty time—law, yes! Have ye a cheer, Mis' Philips." They sat down before the fire in the front of the cabin. Ivy picked up the kitten from the hearth, where it was curled, almost in the ashes. "Hit's a pettish cat," she said, stroking the kitten, her hand shaking. *She must say something!* "Hit don't never git enough pettin'." Her voice was coming to her from what seemed a great distance. She wondered if it sounded queer to Mrs. Philips.

But the older woman was looking into the fire composedly. She spat into the fire several times before she turned, with a pleased, though slightly embarrassed, look, clearing her throat. "Ivy, I reckon Novy an' Buck is married."

Ivy started, almost dropping the kitten. "Novy an' Buck!—Do ye reckon?" she asked hoarsely after a brief pause. *Oh, if her teeth would only stop chattering!*

"Novy never come home last night. I reckon her an' Buck went to the magistrate over at Poplar Tree. I reckon they was 'shamed to come home, them jest married, an' then hit a-stormin', too. They stayed all night with some of the kin over there, more 'an apt.—Novy named hit to me, night afore last, that her an' Buck was a-aimin' to marry."

"Her an' Buck-!" Ivy murmured, her eyes shifting about in every direction.

"I reckon Buck 'ull make her a good man," Mrs. Philips said hopefully, looking into the fire again. "But ef he makes her a good man or a bad un," she said, after a pause, lowering her voice and leaning forward now, her hard black eyes softer than Ivy had ever beheld them, "hit were best, Ivy, fer Novy to marry—"

"Law, yes," Ivy breathed. She must tell her now! She must scream it out at the top of her voice: *"Mis' Philips, Novy hain' t married—Novy's dead!"* She must tell her that the back of Nova's new dress was all dark and sticky—yes, no matter what happened, she must shout it into the ears of the woman bending towards her trustfully from across the hearth: *"Novy hain' t married—Gid kilt her!"*

"I 'ull be a-goin' along, Ivy." Mrs. Philips got up stiffly, moving towards the lean-to. "I jest stopped by to tell ye—"

"Won't ye set awhile?"

"No, I 'ull be a-goin' along—"

"Won't ye stay fer dinner?"

"No, I 'lowed I 'ud go on down to the Byrds' an' see what *they* knowed. Might be Novy jest stayed all night with Linsey an' Essie." She paused in the doorway, smiling again, but raising her eyebrows. "Maybe her an' Buck hain't married atter all—not yit! Don't say nothin', Ivy, to nobody, till we knows fer certain, an' come git ye some buttermilk, or send Enoch. I'm a-churnin' now of a Tuesday an' of a Friday. I kin spare ye plenty to make your bread an' to drink, too."

Ivy covered her eyes. A dry sob rent her body. "Law, Mis' Philips, you've allays been so good to me—"

The older woman patted her shoulder. "What's come over ye, child? I hain't no better to ye 'an ye deserve!—An' ef ye want some cabbages, to make ye some kraut, come fer 'em afore the old man turns the hogs into the patch. Won't cost ye no more 'an jest to come an' git 'em."

CHAPTER NINE

IVY SIGHED DEEPLY as she sat beside the open door of her cabin, a box of patchwork in her lap. Enoch had not yet come from school. She must finish this quilt; she had started it more than a year before. From time to time she looked off the calico squares she was sewing together, her eyes resting idly on the river, on the mountains barely visible through the smoky November atmosphere. A hen had suddenly flown up and was pecking at the cracks in the porch floor. The kitten was curled up at her feet, and inside the gate Enoch's little dog was stretched out, snapping at flies which the warmth of mid afternoon had brought forth. Chickadees in the leafless apple-trees kept up their ceaseless chatter. Ivy's thoughts kept going back to one thing over and over. . . .

Doke, looking for his cow, had come upon the bodies on the third day after Buck and Nova were killed.

A sort of deadness on her, Ivy had helped Mrs. Dodd and Aunt Sally Lowdy prepare the bodies for burial. She had toiled along beside the two half-crazed mothers, following the wagon to the burying-ground as it jolted over the hummocky ground, the two coffins always before her eyes. She had stood amidst the silent throng, tense with suppressed excitement, that the double burial had called forth—folks from all up and down the river, from in and out all the hollows. She had heard Mrs. Byrd's and Mrs. Philips's wild screams ringing out through the silence when the old people first, then women with babes at their breasts and children clinging to their skirts, lastly young men and maidens, filed past the open coffins, bending over, each to take a last swift shuddering glance at Buck's and Nova's dis-colored decomposing faces. . . .

Two weeks had gone by since that day. Life had resumed its usual tenor—folks making sauerkraut, shucking corn, talking already of other things. . . .

"Did ye put out your hand—?" a voice kept asking Ivy. "Did ye risk your hide to save 'em, same as you would 'a ay, Lord!—to save your own young un, to save Enoch?"

She looked up now to see Doke coming down the ridge road. Doke's lively chaffing talk would be welcome.

Doke tossed the sack he was carrying on his shoulder at Ivy's feet and threw himself on the porch step. "There, don't say I hain't no friend o' yourn! I brung ye a mess o' mustard greens. They was growin' in Old Mag's garden—no need fer 'em to go to waste an' I knowed you liked 'em." He stretched himself lazily and lighted a cigarette. "Well, Ivy, have you heern the news?"

Ivy started. "*What* news?"

"*What* news!" he mocked, turning his head and looking at her boldly for a moment. "Why, no news—on'y Short Dillard and Essie Byrd is married."

Ivy breathed more easily. "Law, me! When was they married? Yester-day—? You say they was—?" She had put down the square she was sewing on and looked off, above Doke's head, her gaze focused absently on the sycamores that grew along the river, gleaming faintly through the whit-ish haze that lay over things, their bare bleached branches thrust up like gigantic ghostly fingers among the dark evergreen hemlocks and cedars. "Well," she sighed at last, picking up her sewing again, "I'm glad fer Bertha Jane. She 'ull have Essie to help her now. I laid off to go see Bertha Jane agin tomorrow. I didn't know I 'ud find no bride an' groom—"

"I say bride an' groom," Doke broke in with a guffaw "—a whole gang o' fellers was a-serenadin' 'em last night, with tin cans an' sech as that, an' Uncle Abel, he come out, when the fellers was a-raisin' hell, a-callin' fer Short to come out to the road an' to bring the bride out fer 'em to see—Uncle Abel he cussed 'em out proper. Said, by God, he didn't want no shivararees round his place, nohow. He wasn't a-goin' to have no sons o' bitches a-ridin' no boy o' hisn straddle a plank, like they done Jack Feathers. Jack, he hain't been no 'count sence his weddin' night," and Doke added a few coarse words to make his meaning perfectly clear.

"Hesh your mouth!" Ivy rebuked him unsmilingly.

"Lord, Ivy, you hain't got no fun in ye here lately! Why, I hain't saw ye laugh—God knows when!"

"How kin a body laugh with all the sad things that's a-happenin'?"

Doke threw a sharp sideways glance at her. Ivy's eyes were bent on her sewing. "Well," he said, "you won't find nobody where don't say Novy got what were comin' to her." He blew out a column of smoke. "Buck, too, I reckon.—Anyway, Ivy—why, good God A'mighty, ef a feller was to set down an' study about all the folks where's a-layin' up in the buryin'-ground, an' about them where folks is a-lookin' fer 'em to die, an' them where's got kilt, an' all like o' that—why, *hell*! he wouldn't never laugh agin, long as blood warmed his body!"

"Law, I reckon," Ivy agreed, after a pause, threading her needle again. After all, there was something in what Doke said. She listened with slightly more interest as he began to recount some of the other news he had gleaned at the store. . . . A warrant had been issued for Gid's arrest. Gid had quit his job before the killing, and not hide or hair had been seen of him since.

Doke got up to leave. He stepped back on the porch now, drawing a small object from the pocket of his tattered coat and holding it out. "Ivy, did ever ye see this here afore?"

"Law, yes—Shirley give me a box of 'em." It was an ordinary bone hair-pin of medium size. Ivy thrust it into the coil of hair at the nape of her neck. "Where did ye find hit—in the road?"

Doke came a step closer, pulling off his battered hat and running his fingers through his great mop of hair. "I 'lowed hit were yourn." He looked down at her with an expression all at once quizzical and slightly torment-ing. "Beats me, Ivy, what in the devil you was doin' there—but I found hit—a-layin' on the ground—fornenst Buck. Hit were fouled a mite—"

Ivy had risen from her chair, dropping the box of patchwork from her lap. "You—you hain't a-tryin' to pin hit on *me*, are ye, that I—?"

"You wouldn't have no cause, Ivy—none I knows on. But yet an' still—"

Ivy covered her face. "Lord, God!" Everything had begun to go round and round.

"Don't be skairt!" Doke was saying softly. "Don't be in no ways oneasy! I hain't a-goin' to cheep!"

Chapter Ten

ALMOST EVERY DAY now Ivy traveled up the road to give Bertha Jane a lift with her work. Under Essie's persuasions— there was too much work, Essie said, at the Dillards'—Short had secured a job in town and taken his bride with him. Once more, after a brief reprieve, all the cooking and washing of heavy overalls and scouring of muddy floors had fallen upon Bertha Jane. But one day when Ivy arrived, she found Bertha Jane no longer able even to move around feebly, as she had been doing for some time past. Covered with a quilt, the girl was lying on the big upholstered couch belonging to the parlor-set.

Ivy bent over her anxiously. "Law, Bertha Jane, you hain't no worse, are ye?"

Bertha Jane smiled faintly: "Looks like I hain't able to go no longer," adding with another flickering smile: "Looks like hit hain't so lonesome a-layin' in the couch as a-layin' in the bed."

Next day when Ivy came, she brought a soft warm wrapper, one that Shirley had sent her.

"Here, Bertha Jane," she said, as she unwrapped it, "I brung ye a present. I were a-aimin' to give hit to ye fer Christmas, but a-gittin' so cold like hit is, I 'lowed maybe hit 'ud be best fer ye to have hit now."

Ivy took off the girl's cotton dress, replacing it with the wrapper. The exertion of changing had brought on a coughing-spell, and Bertha Jane lay for some time without speaking. When at last she opened her eyes, her eyelashes were heavy with moisture.

"I'm glad, Ivy," she smiled through her tears, "that you brung hit, ef you kin spare hit, 'cause I don't reckon I 'ull be here when Christmas comes."

Everyone by this time had become aware that Bertha Jane's end was not far off. Folks were bringing squirrel soup, and when Ivy reached the cabin, often now she would find a solemn circle already assembled around the couch, women who would sit for hours without speaking and only rise to spit into the fire or out the open door.

Even Uncle Abel could no longer deny the seriousness of Bertha Jane's condition. He had gone to town and brought her back a bottle of medicine and a loaf of "light bread."

"Law, yes, I'm a-lookin' fer her to die," he would sigh to those that asked him of her, bemoaning the extra work that had been put upon him. "Me a widdy man, an' Short, he's left me, too, him an' Essie. Hain't nobody but me an' the little boys to do things—things no man a-livin' orter be called on to do—cookin' an' washin' dishes an' sech as that."

One day Ivy had been sitting beside the girl for an hour or so, fanning her with a cedar branch that lay at hand, bringing her fresh rags to cough into, easing the girl's tired and aching body in such ways as she knew. No one else, it happened, besides herself, was in the cabin when she heard an unusual noise and, going to the door, saw a heavy truck making its way lumberingly up the washed-out river-road.

Ivy met the driver at the gate. He proved to be a young man she knew, a tall broad-shouldered good-looking youth, a young giant with fair hair and dark eyes, one of the Grubbs from up Josiah Creek. He had been in town for a year or so and now had a regular job driving a van for a furniture company that sold on the installment plan. "Sorry, Ivy, but them's our orders. We met up with Uncle Abel back yonder a piece, an' he says he hain't got no money to pay on hit. Short is three payments behind, an' one of the company, they seen him; an' Short, he said he didn't reckon he 'ud git to pay no more on the set, him jest married, an' fer 'em jest to come an' git hit—"

"Law, yes, Sylvester, but I cain't never on earth ask that pore little thing to git outen the couch, her a-lovin' hit so! Bertha Jane, she hain't no time to live. Don't you reckon," Ivy pleaded, "you-all could leave hit fer that little bit o' time, ef you was to tell 'em how things was—?"

"Good Lord, Ivy, they wouldn't listen to nothin' like that! Town hain't country." Sylvester lighted a cigarette, lounging against the fence to smoke it. "They hain't in business fer love—that's what they 'ud say. We 'ud jest git cussed out an' liable to lose our jobs, too. We had orders to git the thirty dollars that was owin' on hit, or fer us to haul the hull set back to town."

"Thirty dollars," Ivy repeated reflectively. She looked across at the little forge on the river-bank, opposite the cabin, but without seeing it. After a moment or so she asked: "Ef you-uns was to git the thirty dollars, you'ud leave hit here, wouldn't ye?"

"Well, Short, he told 'em straight out he wasn't a-goin' to pay no more on hit. But—Why, yes, I reckon, Ivy, ef we was to git—"

"I 'ull pay ye," Ivy broke in.

"*You!*— You say you will—?"

"Law, yes! You-all kin jest ride me back to my place. I 'ull give ye the thirty dollars. But don't ye come a-botherin' round here no more, not whilst Bertha Jane—" She stopped, the lump in her throat catching her.

"You needn't to weary yourself about that," the young man laughed. "Gosh, we stuck four times—"

On Thanksgiving Day, Ivy came to the Dillards early. There was little to mark Thanksgiving out from other days in the year, though a few families celebrated the day with young coons or possums for dinner, and at the Dillards, quite unexpectedly, there was turkey, one of Uncle Abel's flock he was saving to sell at Christmas-time having thrust its head into the pigsty the day before and had its head snapped off. Ivy cooked the dinner, coaxing the sick girl to eat a small portion of the turkey: "Here, honey, turkey is dry eatin', but yet an' still hit's right good. Try an' see ef ye cain't swaller a few bites." After dinner she washed the dishes, then took her place again beside the couch.

Outside, it was snowing, the snow falling in big thick flakes, the ground already white. The doors were closed and the room lighted only by the glow given off by a half-consumed green log burning slowly in the fire-place. Uncle Abel was in the kitchen, dozing beside the step-stove. The room was very quiet. There was only the faint hiss and crackle of the burning log, the river's soft ceaseless murmur, and the sound of Bertha Jane's quick breathing.

Bertha Jane opened her eyes. "I named hit to Pappy to git me a night-gown when he went to town a Tuesday"— Bertha Jane's breath was coming in pants, and her lip trembling a little— "but Pappy, his money give out—"

Ivy stroked the girl's thin, dry hand. She sat looking across the room, into the fire. After a while she leaned over the couch again. "Bertha Jane, hain't ye never had no night-gown—?"

Bertha Jane shook her head gently.

"Me, neither," Ivy said, "but a heap of 'em is a-wearin' 'em this day an' time.—I hain't never had none," she added a moment later, musingly, "on'y some Shirley sent me, an' looks like them's too fine fer a body to wear!" She laughed, though a little uneasily. . . . How could she possibly give up those two night-gowns Shirley had given her? They were too thin, anyway, for the sick girl, and with their short sleeves—

In the morning, after she had done her own work, she started as usual for the Dillards'. She had passed Doke Odum's cabin, almost reached the church, when, suddenly whirling about, she started back down the road over which she had just come. "Hain't no need," she said to herself, "me a-bein' so mean!"

She took the night-gowns from the drawer where she kept them, gazing on them fondly for a moment or so. "I don't reckon I 'ull never need 'em, nohow," she thought, a few big tears falling. She had broken into her fund. The prospect of being reunited to Jim was growing dimmer. . . .

To her great disappointment, Bertha Jane took no interest at first in what she had brought her. But in another moment Ivy realized that the girl was deathly sick and unable to fix her attention upon anything but the torturing suffering that had come upon her.

The spasm passed. Though exhausted, Bertha Jane seemed fairly comfortable now, and Ivy showed her the night-gowns again. Bertha Jane could scarcely believe that Ivy was giving them to her. "Ivy, looks like I'm a-havin' a better time a-dyin'," she said, her face quivering, "an ever I had a-livin'."

When the girl had lain quiet for a while, Ivy asked: "Bertha Jane, would ye like me to put one of 'em on ye? The room's warm—I don't reckon you 'ud take ye no chill."

Bertha Jane nodded, smiling weakly; and, sitting on the edge of the couch, Ivy held her up in her strong arms, removing the undershirt from the girl's slight and emaciated, yet badly swollen body and slipping the soft silken night-gown over her head. "Law, Bertha Jane, I wants folks all to come an' see ye! There hain't nothin' becomes ye so well as pink!"

Ivy laid her back gently against the pillow, pulling the night-gown down neatly all around her, and smoothing out the wrinkles. But as her hand passed over Bertha Jane's distended stomach, she was electrified from head to foot by feeling something suddenly move—by a lump that pushed out strongly against her fingers. Ivy jumped back, reeling on her feet and staring down with dilated eyes at the partially exposed figure on the couch.

"Law, Bertha Jane, someone's bigged ye!" she cried in a low, hoarse, horror-stricken voice.

She dropped down beside the couch, hurriedly covering the girl with a quilt. "Who bigged ye, Bertha Jane?" she asked in a whisper.

Bertha Jane made no answer. She had begun to sob.

"Why, honey, I didn't know you 'ud been a'talkin' to no boy on earth; I ain't never heern o' you a-keepin' company with no one!—Who were hit bigged ye?" Ivy repeated, bending over the girl and struggling to keep her own sobs down.

Bertha Jane's eyelids lifted, an appealing yet anguished look in her childish eyes. "I'm afeared to tell!" she whispered, another terrible paroxysm of pain suddenly seizing her.

"Hit hain't labor a-comin' on ye, do you reckon?" Ivy asked in a strained whisper, as she watched the girl writhing on the couch. What should she do? How could she keep from Uncle Abel what was about to happen? She kept wondering frantically what she should do, as she held tight to Bertha Jane's cold little hands, Bertha Jane clinging to her convulsively. "Oh, Ivy, help me, cain't ye? I'm a-sufferin' death!"

"Yes, yes, honey, hit 'ull be better atter a little." . . . No, she couldn't keep it from Uncle Abel! There was no earthly way.

A lull came. Ivy released herself and stole out the back door. Uncle Abel was sitting on the back porch, bent over a basket on the floor into which he was shelling corn.

"Mr. Dillard," Ivy said, dropping her eyes, and in a low hurried voice, "I don't know how come her that-a-way, but Bertha Jane's in need of a granny-woman. There hain't no time to lose."

Uncle Abel kept on rubbing one ear of corn against another, his eyes fixed on the big basket between his legs. Some deep wrinkles had appeared on his low brow, crosswise. "Hain't no need fer no granny-woman," he said quietly; "me an' you kin do fer her."

"Law, no! Law, no!" Ivy cried in a low voice, excitedly. "I hain't never been with no woman where's down, not by myself, an' I don't know how to do fer her, not rightly! I hain't never tied no cord! Mr. Dillard," she begged, "won't ye go fer Mis' Philips? Mis' Philips, she won't mouth nothin' to no one—"

"I kin tie the cord," Uncle Abel said, still not looking up, the kernels of corn raining down from his fingers into the half-filled basket underneath, "an' there hain't much o' nothin' else—"

"Oh, yes, sir! Oh, yes, sir! Hit might not come right! Heap o' times the

feet comes first. I wouldn't know what to do, an' Bertha Jane, her bad off
with the tubercles afore this here—"

Uncle Abel continued to look down stolidly at the corn he was shelling, going on with his work.

Ivy watched him for a minute or so; then, suddenly turning on her heel,
she went back to the room where Bertha Jane lay. Without even stopping
to wrap her scarf around her head, she slipped into the old coat she had
worn when she came. Luke lived hardly more than a mile away. Luke could
be trusted. Shutting the front door of the cabin behind her noiselessly, she
ran up the road, turning a short distance beyond the Dillard cabin into the
hollow where Luke lived, alone with his widowed mother since Molly had
married. She was badly frightened at taking into her own hands affairs
that might properly be considered Uncle Abel's. She could feel the blood
beating in her arteries, pounding in her ears. Yet she kept on.

Half-way up the hollow she heard a sound of sawing and presently
saw Luke on a wooded slope ahead of her, at one side of the hollow, some
distance up it, sawing a tree down, with one of his neighbors at the other
end of the saw.

"*Timber!*" Luke yelled, the old logging cry, in warning, as the tree
started to fall, but it had hardly measured its length down the snowy side
of the ridge before Ivy had reached the place where it lay.

"Luke!" she called up sharply. "Come down here, won't ye? Quick!"

"Get me the shears, Ivy!" Mrs. Philips said, raising her eyebrows.

She pared her nails, then went into the kitchen to wash her hands, returning with some lard, with which she greased her hands and forearms.

Bertha Jane was lying on the bed. A few moments before the older
woman arrived, she had asked Ivy to help her move from the couch. "I'm
afeared I 'ull nasty hit," she had whispered. "I'm afeared I 'ull foul hit, an'
hit so new an' nice!"

Mrs. Philips took charge now, examining, while Bertha Jane emitted
smothered cries, to see what progress was being made, and confiding to
Ivy in an undertone: "Hit 'ull be a right smart time yit."

All day long the agony recurred, at shortened intervals, with frequent
exhausting coughing-spells in between, an occasional hemorrhage, and
times when Bertha Jane lay motionless save for her short panting breaths
and for the gentle constant movement from side to side of her small childish head with its square-cropped brown hair. Each time when the torturing pain started afresh, she would look up at Ivy and Mrs. Philips, her
bloodshot eyes beseeching them to help her. But more than anything else

she seemed conscious of the trouble she was putting them to. She kept thanking them for the efforts they were making in her behalf.

Towards nightfall the torture increased.

"Give down to your misery, honey!" Mrs. Philips would say, over and over. "Don't scringe, honey! Don't scringe!" as Bertha Jane recoiled tensely before each fresh onset of agony that tore through her poor wasted little body.

Drops of sweat oozed from the girl's face, a ghastly blue. Again and again her aching limbs were convulsed, but without result.

Mrs. Philips lighted the lamp with its smoked and cracked chimney, placing it on the chimney-self. She brought a fresh log and put it in the fire.

After a time the boys one by one crept through the room silently and climbed the ladder to the loft where they slept.

Sometimes Bertha Jane screamed outright, sobbing out afterwards: "Looks like I cain't help hit!"

"Won't hit never be over?" she whispered once or twice faintly to Mrs. Philips through her dry swollen lips.

Some time during the night Uncle Abel, in his stocking feet, passed through the room, almost unnoticed, following the boys to the loft.

In the dim chamber below, the agony went on.

But a little before day, with a last horrible shriek, Bertha Jane gave birth to a living child, a boy.

Mrs. Philips handed the tiny form to Ivy. "Seven months, looks like—" She turned back to Bertha Jane, who had fainted with the final convulsion of her racked spent frame.

A half an hour later Ivy approached the bed again, a bundle in her arm. Bertha Jane had recovered consciousness, and Mrs. Philips was urging her in a low earnest voice: "Blow on your hands, honey! Blow on 'em a right smart harder—that 'ull bring the afterbirth."

Ivy plucked the older woman by the sleeve. "Look ahere a minute, Mis' Philips," she whispered in a frightened voice, drawing Mrs. Philips with her across the room. On the hearthstones sat the basin of water in which Ivy had washed the baby, a little wizened creature, like a very old man.

"I were a-takin' that 'ere slime—you know—that phlegm—outen hit's little mouth," she whispered, "an' all to oncet I felt hit limp as a rag!"

Mrs. Philips took the baby from her, thumping it on its back, forcing its lips open, and blowing her breath into its tiny mouth, then immersing it in hot water. "Hit's plumb dead," she said at last, just loud enough for Ivy to hear.

Ivy took the baby back into her arms. She sank down into a low chair beside the hearth, laying the doll-like figure, wrapped in a bit of old quilt, across her knees. "Oh, Mis' Philips, I'm afeard—"

The older woman patted her on the shoulder. "Don't cry, Ivy! You hain't got nothin' to blame yourself fer! The pore little feller didn't have on'y a spark o' life in him."

Late in the afternoon of the next day Ivy and Mrs. Philips were on their way to the burying-ground, Ivy carrying a white paper shoe-box with the dead baby inside. Uncle Abel had dug the grave, secretly, in the moonlight, the night before.

Most of the snow had disappeared, though a storm of some kind was brewing again. Dark threatening clouds were moving swiftly across the sky, with patches of bright blue in some places and in others bands of azure shining out in odd contrast to the black banks of clouds about them. The mountains were a rich indigo-blue.

The women, their heads bound in woolen scarfs, had been on their way for almost two hours. They had passed a few cabins, but there were no more cabins now. They were nearing the end of their journey, following an old path across a bare billowy stretch of knobs, climbing gradually towards a high ridge ahead of them on whose summit they could see from afar the little fenced-in inclosure of the burying-ground with its huddle of trees.

The two women walked on silently, Ivy a step ahead.

Through the clear sharp air the deep depressions on the mountain sides appeared to be great black gashes. Leafless trees stood out plainly in distant forests in one direction and another. Every weed-stalk seemed to stand up separately for observation. Colors were all distinct and vivid. The pale feathery plumes of dead golden-rod nodded and tossed above the tremulous orange-brown sedge-grass waving around them.

Only a little while before, the two women had followed this selfsame path, a wagon jolting ahead of them, that wagon with its dread double burden.

Ivy stole a pitying glance at the white face, the deeply bowed figure of her companion. "Law, she's aged fast sence Novy went! A body wouldn't think—"

As they reached the gate, Ivy paused, facing around squarely, and tapping the pasteboard box in her hands. "Mis' Philips, looks like I cain't study about nothin' else who—were hit, have you got any idee, where bigged Bertha Jane?"

The older woman returned her direct gaze, standing in silence for a moment, her eyes narrowed. Then a slight disdainful smile gathered around her lips and she tapped the box in Ivy's hands with her own fingers. "Hain't ye guessed, Ivy? Hain't ye guessed yit who were hits daddy?"

Ivy stared. A glimmering of the truth, faint and far off as yet, had begun to dawn on her. "Why, no! Why, no!" she gasped.

The older woman dropped her eyes. "There's more things happens in this world 'an some folks knows on," she muttered, stepping ahead to unfasten the gate.

CHAPTER ELEVEN

THREE DAYS LATER BERTHA JANE was carried over the same rough trail. It was a day of bright sunshine, but of bitter cold. As the small procession, folks afoot in single file, wound its way over the knobs behind the wagon bearing Bertha Jane's body, more than one remarked in an undertone: "Law, hit 'ud be a fine day fer killin' hogs." But there was no intention of disrespect to Bertha Jane.

Everyone expressed satisfaction at the handsome provision Uncle Abel had made for a girl who, if she had left no particular mark on those she had come in contact with in the course of her brief existence, at any rate had done no harm. "Law, her pap is a-puttin' her away nice, hain't he? A body wouldn't want no finer coffin 'an that 'ere."

The real mountain winter had begun now. Along the river, up and down the creeks, traps were set for minks and musk-rats, and at the store Andy was doing a brisk business in buying up pelts from whoever brought them and shipping them to the furriers in New York. Doke would stop at Ivy's gate almost every day: "Dog-gone, that number-one mush-rat pelt I were a-showin' ye day afore yesterday—what do ye think?—hit brung a dollar an' a half!" As Christmas approached, while the hunting and trapping still went on, while the nights continued to be in an uproar with the baying of hounds and the outcries of men and boys scouring the knobs for whatever little wild creatures remained, yet ardor in these pursuits was cooling to some extent, interest beginning to center more and more in killing hogs.

All the talk now was of how much the hogs of different ones would weigh and of the presents of fresh meat that were being circulated by those who already had butchered. Even those who had only one small hog to kill sent around messes of spareribs and backbone and sausage.

Ivy rejoiced each time freezing cold followed a spell of milder weather. "Snow on the mountain—hit's good on folks' meat! Ef hit had stayed the way hit were, the meat would 'a started at the bone—"

Ivy was getting her share of the general good cheer. She had helped at several places with rendering the lard and making sausage, bringing home pay in the form of lard or some of the "offal"—the hog's liver and feet, or its head. Besides this, different ones to whom she had rendered no aid at all had sent her gifts of a similar character.

Ivy felt exhilarated and even joyous as she stood with the others on these sharp glistening winter mornings watching to see a hog dispatched with a bold thrust of the knife or a sharp blow behind the ears. The big black kettles, with fires burning brightly underneath, the dry snow that cried under her heels, the women in sweaters, their heads bundled up and their hands purple-red with the cold, the freshly sharpened knives, the blood-stains all around in the snow—the whole scene, associated in her mind as it was with the idea of plenty, of holiday good will, affected her pleasurably.

At times, however, she still wondered how she could feel any happiness. How full life was of sorrow and shame and sin! Yet how sweet life was, too! As she came and went in these days when the mountains were a glowing purple at sunset and the stars cut the sky at night, when everywhere was a sort of leisurely bustle and the feel of Christmas in the air, if outwardly she was cheerful and lively, underneath was often a vein of sober reflection. Life, she thought, was something like the river. Sometimes the river was muddy and swollen from rain; sometimes frozen over; sometimes polluted by the factories up in Virginia, transformed to a strange oily stream that was streaked with harsh and ugly colors; but again so clear that you could see the fish lying along on the rocks at the bottom, clear and sparkling, dimpling in the wind, laughing in the summer sun.

Life, like the river, might be disturbed, changed, but some time again, sooner or later, it would be shining and lovely. Like the river, it flowed on and on, whatever the disturbances, the changes, on and on—

And now Ivy thought again of Jim's coming. Good and evil in life. Good and evil in Jim. Good and evil in herself—ay, Lord! The old aching longing for Jim rose once more. It was almost a year now since Jim had written Old Mag those few lines on a postcard. "Some sweet day. . . ." Spring of the year, nor yet fall, had brought him. Well, of all times, Christmas was the most fitting and likely for Jim to surprise her.

Climbing down the slope to the Byrds' as soon as it was light enough for her to see her way, Ivy wished that they might have killed their hogs sooner. It was the day before Christmas. She had washed her clothes, to have everything clean and fresh, but she had not yet finished making her Christmas cakes. She had been waiting for her hens to lay more eggs. It would not be a good day, either, she thought. The air was too soft. Steam was rising from the river, and the mountains were half hidden by a dingy grayish-white veil. "Most folks wouldn't never on earth kill hogs on sech a day as this."

Doke and Uncle Abel were already on hand when Ivy arrived at the barn-yard. The hogs would weigh around five hundred pounds apiece and be too heavy for Big Bill to handle by himself. Doke had been up all night, hunting. He was somewhat tipsy, gleeful and full of talk in spite of the dismal morning.

Mrs. Byrd in one of her husband's old coats and Ivy in a sweater stood around with the children watching through the gray uncertain light while the men stuck and bled the hogs, plunged them, one end and then the other, into the barrel of scalding water, then dragged the two huge carcasses over to the waiting platform, laying them out side by side, and began plucking out the hair from their hides by handfuls, rapidly.

"Law, hain't these two the grandest hogs ever was!" Ivy exclaimed, as she and Mrs. Byrd fell to work themselves, scraping the hair from the hogs' heads and ears where it resisted plucking. "I reckon," Ivy said, "hit's because Mr. Byrd is so hairy."

Mrs. Byrd nodded without lifting her eyes from the knife she was using. "A man where's right hairy allays has good luck a-raisin' hogs."

The hogs were hoisted up now, suspended on gambrels, and Doke began gutting them, letting the entrails pour down into the tubs underneath. Tipsy though he was, Doke had been working at every stage of the proceedings with greater dispatch and precision than the other two men. He was cutting now with swift sure strokes, and keeping up a running fire of bragging, jovial talk. "Abe Pippin, he kilt Uncle Mort Lowdy's hogs fer him an' cut 'em up, an', good God, you orter saw the meat! Looked like hit 'ud been chawed off by a dog."

"Dog-gone, I 'ull have me a coon an' a goose an' plenty good hog meat fer my Christmas dinner," Doke was saying as Mrs. Byrd and Ivy returned from the river, a bucket of water in each hand, dashing the water into the insides of the hogs to cleanse them.

"Goose!" Mrs. Byrd exclaimed to Ivy in an undertone, as they started back to the river for more water. "I 'ud like to know where he got hit, without hit's one o' ourn! Well, he won't git no hog liver, nohow," and she squeezed Ivy's arm "—me an' you's a-goin' to have the hogs' livers, one fer each of us."

"Taters an' hog liver fried togither," Ivy said "—hain't hit the best thing ever was?"

It was good to have Mrs. Byrd more like her old self. Since Buck's death she had smiled only with an effort, but now she was lively again and full of fun.

Towards noon the men, through with their part of the work, all disappeared, but Mrs. Byrd and Ivy went on working, melting the great sheets of flaky leaf-fat in one of the big kettles they had carried inside and set in the fire place, as it had begun to drizzle, then pouring the lard off into buckets and crocks, but while they waited for the lard to melt, running back and forth to the kitchen, where they were making sausage, mashing the meat with a hammer.

Even with the doors open the day was so dark that the two women could hardly see what they were doing.

As nightfall approached, it suddenly rushed over Ivy with fresh force that next day would be Christmas. She had been so busy since early morning that she had dwelt very little on the fact, but now, tired out, she began to tremble slightly.

So strong was her conviction that Jim would come at Christmas-time that when Big Bill, a little before it was completely dark, appeared at the door and beckoned her with a motion of his head to the back porch, Ivy was scarcely even surprised, though she had started shaking all over.

Big Bill was smelling of Christmas liquor. He lowered his voice. "Ivy, I seen someone at the store I hain't saw fer a time."

"Hit hain't Jim—Jim Ingoldsby—I don't reckon—?"

"Why, yes, hit were Jim! You wasn't a-lookin' fer him in, was ye?"

"Law, yes, I knowed in reason he 'ud be a-comin' in some sweet day!" Ivy tossed her head, laughing a little. Her teeth had begun to chatter and her cheeks were burning almost unbearably.

But her whole thought now was to get home and clean herself up—she was splattered with grease from head to foot.

"Well, I reckon, Mis' Byrd, we're about done. I 'ull be a-goin' along. . . .
Yes, the same to you-all—Merry Christmas to ye all. . . ."

How would Jim look? How would he seem? Above all, how would she
seem to him? All her self-assurance had deserted her. Her heart throbbed
with uneasiness. She had to tell Enoch, too, that his father had come.
How would he take it? When she told him, in a word or two, the little
boy, scrambling up the slope a few feet ahead of her, turned his head, then
jerked it back again, but through the gathering dusk she had caught sight
of the frown with which Enoch met the announcement, seen the wave of
crimson that flooded his face.

"Law, Enoch," she called ahead to him, palliatingly, almost apologetically, "I reckon your daddy's brung ye somethin' nice—maybe a pair o' new
shoes!"

It was sleeting now. There had been a rapid drop of temperature. The
icy sleet stung her uncovered head, but Ivy was barely conscious of the
fact. When she reached her gate, she saw Doke's form, mistily outlined,
advancing down the road. Doke held up his hand. He had been to the store.
He had seen Jim. All at once Ivy felt full of dread, but she sent Enoch on
into the cabin with the bucket of lard and the package of liver and waited
at the gate.

Doke was weaving as he came down the path past her corn-crib. Before
he reached her, Ivy caught the fumes of fresh drink, and it was clearly in
her mind not to let him arouse her, "him so aggravatin' when he's sober, an'
worse still when he's a-drinkin'." She had no time now for quarreling with
Doke. She was fuming inside at this delay in getting off her soiled clothes.

"Well, Ivy, I jest seen Jim."

"Jim Ingoldsby? Law, yes, I knowed he were in."

"You say you did?—Some person's been afore me then, seems like, with
the big news."

"Go 'long, Doke! I hain't got no time to waste—"

"No time— Why the devil hain't ye got no time? You've got all the time
there is, hain't ye? But what ye a-tremblin' fer, Ivy? You're a-tremblin' like
a leaf, an' your voice is jest a-shakin'—"

"Doke, I cain't stand here all night—"

"You cain't, cain't ye? An' hit Christmas-eve! Ivy, you orter give me a
Christmas gift. You know—But what your cheeks a-gittin' so red fer? Why,
they're red as a rose!"

"Doke, I cain't stand here an' listen to your meanness, me a-gittin' wet
to the bone—"

"Is your house too good to ask a body in? I hain't a-honin' to stand at no gate. Well, Ivy, Jim had a roll o' green-backs on him—by God, hit were big enough to choke a calf."

"Law, I reckon."

"But he's took his money an' went back to town, I reckon, afore this."

"To town! Why—why he jest come in," Ivy faltered.

Doke nodded. "He heern a plenty, what time he were here, not to want to stay no longer." Doke brought his face nearer, laughing roguishly into hers. "I fixed him fer ye, Ivy!"

"*You—!*"

"He won't bother ye!"

Ivy backed away, staring. "What did ye tell him?"

"Ca'm yourself!" He tried to place his hand on her arm, but Ivy held herself away.

"Ef you mean—what ye found o' mine," she cried out breakingly "—tell hit to whomsoever ye will! Truth 'ull stand when this old world's afire. I didn't have no more to do with killin' Buck an' Novy 'an you had yourself. Is hit that 'ere," she cried out now, in a louder voice, "ye named to Jim?"

Doke shook his head.

"What were hit, then, ye told him, you old long-tongued thing, you—you—"

"In the name o' God, Ivy, what ye rarin' on me for? Didn't ye name hit to me awhile back that you never wanted to lay eyes on Jim Ingoldsby agin long as—"

"What were hit? What were hit ye told him?"

"So hit were a lie, out an' out, were hit? God, I 'lowed you was speakin' truth—"

"Tell me, you low-down—Tell me what ye told Jim!"

They looked at each other fixedly for an instant.

"I told him I wisht, by God, he 'ud kep' hisself away a right smart longer—we was all enjoyin' ye."

"Cain't no man livin' pin whore on me!" Ivy shrieked, springing at his throat. Lost in delirium, clutching, clawing, she began giving blow for blow, without a word, without a tear, without heed to Enoch's wild screams, without hearing anything, without seeing anything—anything save a creature before her that had destroyed all she had striven for through years and years, all she had dreamed of, that had robbed her of Jim, her man, robbed her just when she had found him after all the longing, the hunger—

She was down now, battered to the ground, rolling in the dirt like a dumb beast, her dress soaked with rain and mud, half torn off her, her hair streaming around her face, one eye swollen shut, the blood pouring down from a cut above the other and blinding her.

Enoch was standing over her. He had brought the ax. "Here, Mammy," he was sobbing to her, "kill him, same as he was a rattlesnake, same as he was a copperhead! Bust his skull!"

But everything had become black. Everything was over—over for her and Enoch. The end of the world had come.

She struggled to her knees again. Her swollen broken lips opened and closed, but no sound issued from them. Her head felt queer. Where was she? What was it all about, anyway? Everything was foggy, floating away from her. She sank back to the ground.

Chapter Twelve

IT WAS LATE in the afternoon. Ivy sat by the fire, her head in her hand, her eyes resting broodingly in her lap or sometimes on the slowly burning green log in the fire-place. Thus she had sat since early morning, except when she had roused herself to bring out the little gifts for Enoch that she had hidden—a fancy box of pencils, a toy pistol, and the Christmas treat of two oranges and a bag of candy.

She had kept the doors locked all day, stationing Enoch outside to say that she was away, should anyone call. Through her dull aching thoughts, from time to time she heard the snap of his toy pistol, heard the chickadees chattering in the snowy apple-trees.

She was no better now than old Teresa Boardwine, who spat tobacco juice into the men's faces at the store when they enraged her. No better than Pernie Botts. . . .

"What's hit gained me," she thought bitterly, "me a-tryin' to git above my raisin'? I hain't nothin' but jest a old mountain woman where 'ull fight same as a man ef she flies mad, same as ary old drunken sot."

By this time the country would be ringing with it. She could hear the snickers: "Law, Ivy allays a-holdin' her head so high—"

"I reckon me an' Enoch 'ud best go away," she thought. How could she face folks, after this? Maybe she had best get a job in the factory again. "The dam 'ull come, anyway," she thought. There had been another piece in the paper about it. "The dam's a-comin', an' we won't none of us be here no time, nohow. The dam, hit 'ull flood us all out. . . . I reckon I could make hit at piece-work ef I was to try agin, ef I was to try a right smart harder 'an I done afore. There's a heap of 'em where hain't no smarter 'an me a-makin' hit at piece-work this day and time."

She was roused by Enoch's tapping at the door. "Mammy, let me in! I'm a-perishin' with the cold! My feet's about to freeze! I don't reckon no person else 'ull come nohow, it's a-gittin' so late."

Ivy mended the fire and sat down again close to the hearth, holding her hand to her brow as she had before, keeping her bruised swollen face and her blackened eye partly in shadow. Enoch took the chair opposite, holding his feet against the hot ashes to warm them.

"The moon's a-shinin' an' it still day," Enoch said.

"Law, yes, hit's full moon," Ivy said.

"The moon, Mammy, it looks pretty, a-shinin' on the river."

Ivy sat with her head bowed.

"Mammy, I wouldn't grieve so—I reckon me an' you is better off without him. He ain't no 'count, or he wouldn't 'a let no man blackguard ye that-a-way, like Doke done—"

"Hit hain't that," Ivy said, after some time, immovable in her chair "—hit hain't on'y that. Hit's what I've laid afore ye!"

"Law, Mammy, that ain't nothin'!" The little boy got up impulsively and crossed the hearth, laying his hand bashfully on her hair. "That 'ere ain't nothin' fer ye to weary yourself about. Why, there ain't no person a-livin' where 'ull blame ye fer fightin' with Doke Odum, him mighty nigh the lowest-down man on earth ef he takes a notion—"

A shudder ran through Ivy. "But I wanted ye to have respect to your mammy!" She covered her face completely.

"Ef all the women in these here mountains, Mammy, was good as you are"—the little boy pulled her fingers apart, kissing her on her swollen lips— "there wouldn't be no need to build no church-house, an' fer no preacher."

Ivy shook her head, covering her face again. Enoch went on stroking her hair, awkwardly.

"Mammy, I've got somethin' to tell ye—somethin' good! You had a Christmas gift you don't know nothin' about. Old man Stringfellow—you know, them Stringfellows where lives 'way up yon, in the nineteenth district—he brung ye a load o' wood, it all sawed up."

Ivy lifted her head.

"He said he knowed you had a hard time a-gittin' your wood in winter, an' he 'lowed you 'ud appreciate a load o' wood fer a Christmas gift much as ary thing he could give ye."

"Why, I don't hardly know them Stringfellows," Ivy said. She gazed up at the little boy bending over her solicitously, her face beginning to work. "Law, Enoch, people is so good, hain't they?"